C000164076

About the Author

The author was born in Kenya and grew up there in the critical formative years as the country transitioned from colonialism to independence. He first lived in England when he attended university. Since then, he has spent almost equal amounts of time in England and the Caribbean. He now lives in Norfolk with his wife and in close proximity to his two daughters and five grandchildren.

Displacement

Robert Catt

Displacement

Olympia Publishers
London

www.olympiapublishers.com
OLYMPIA PAPERBACK EDITION

Copyright © Robert Catt 2021

The right of Robert Catt to be identified as author of
this work has been asserted in accordance with sections 77 and 78 of
the Copyright, Designs and Patents Act 1988.

All Rights Reserved

No reproduction, copy or transmission of this publication
may be made without written permission.
No paragraph of this publication may be reproduced,
copied or transmitted save with the written permission of the publisher,
or in accordance with the provisions
of the Copyright Act 1956 (as amended).

Any person who commits any unauthorised act in relation to
this publication may be liable to criminal
prosecution and civil claims for damage.

A CIP catalogue record for this title is
available from the British Library.

ISBN: 978-1-78830-852-6

This is a work of fiction.
Except in the case of historical facts, names, characters, places and
incidents originate from the writer's imagination. Any resemblance to
actual persons, living or dead, is purely coincidental.

First Published in 2021

Olympia Publishers
Tallis House
2 Tallis Street
London
EC4Y 0AB

Printed in Great Britain

Dedication

Dedicated to my family, past and present, here and there, who mean everything to me.

And to those people of Laikipia, and elsewhere in Kenya, who have worked so tirelessly trying to save the rhino.

Acknowledgements

The quotations and extracts from UNDER MILK WOOD, by Dylan Thomas, published by Weidenfeld & Nicolson, copyright ©The Dylan Thomas Trust, are reproduced by permission of David Higham Associates, Administrators of the estate of Dylan Thomas, for publication in the United Kingdom and elsewhere worldwide, with the exception of the United States of America, its territories and Canada.

The same material by Dylan Thomas from UNDER MILK WOOD, copyright ©1952 by Dylan Thomas, is reprinted by permission of New Directions Publishing Corp. for sales in the United States of America, its territories and Canada.

The author is most grateful for these permissions kindly granted.

He also expresses his gratitude to Kristina Smith, the commissioning editor at Olympia Publishers, and all the staff there who have assisted in so many ways in the publication of this book. Their dedicated work and expertise on editing, proof-reading and design are gratefully acknowledged.

Also to be thanked is Charles Tucker for arranging initial feedback on the first draft of the book and Julia Forsyth for her subsequent independent review of the manuscript and her most helpful suggestions.

Finally, the author acknowledges with loving thanks the assistance of Penny, his wife, for her help in producing the maps and contributing towards the cover design, as well as for her patience, forbearance and support over many long months of writing, while his mind was firmly fixed on other times and places elsewhere, sometimes almost as far as five thousand miles away.

Contents

AWAKENING OCTOBER 1969

a stranger in a strange land

Exodus 2.22

Drifting in and out of the realm of subconsciousness, between sleeping and waking, the luminous light of an African morning beckoned him towards the dawn of a new day. The early morning dew on the high Laikipia plain still lingered on a myriad of spiders' webs, the iridescence gradually fading into rays of sunlight, tinging the snow on Mount Kenya a delicate pink and shafting through small, scattered rising plumes of smoke and dust. He sensed sounds, of cattle perhaps, but further off the noise of wild animals, gazelle, zebra, giraffe and, in the distance, the unmistakeable commotion of elephants crashing through the trees. But the noises began to morph into different sounds, the banging of doors, unfamiliar muffled voices, and the light faded to being greyer and colder. He opened his eyes to an overcast English autumn morning.

It was time for Ben to get up for his first day at Bristol University. He pulled on a thick cotton checked shirt, bought for him the previous day at Marks & Spencer by his anxious mother, who had travelled to England with him for a visit to friends and who was concerned that he should keep warm in an unfamiliar climate. His trousers were distinctly cavalry twill. Sitting down he slid his feet into light fawn suede boots, *safari* boots recently acquired from the Bata store in Government Road, Nairobi. A tanned face reflected in the mirror as he carefully parted and combed across short blond hair.

Having made his way from his room and around the quadrangle of Churchill Hall he entered the central block and headed in the direction of the clatter of the canteen. There the general sense of unfamiliarity he had felt as he encountered people on the short walk over became focused into a sharp realisation of difference. Most of the young men looked what his grandmother would call 'distinctly shabby', or in his father's old army terminology 'shit order'; his eyes took in faded jeans, cords, bell-bottom trousers puddling round Chelsea boots, loose-fitting shirts, leather jackets and even camouflage jackets of the sort he used to wear in the cadet force at school. But what struck him most were the pale white faces, many adorned with varying degrees of stubble, moustaches and beards, crowned with long hair flowing down necks and in some cases shoulders. There were a few glances in his direction, some curious, some he felt amused. Perhaps, he said to himself, he was being oversensitive, but, by God, he had never before felt such a misfit; a stranger in a strange land.

As he helped himself at the counter to an array of long since cooked breakfasts, one of the kitchen staff, a small middle-aged Welsh woman, with an accent he could barely understand, offered him something which he took to be "black pudding". She was surprised that he did not know what it was, but her patient explanation did nothing to persuade him to have one. Still he thanked her kindly, keeping to himself the thought that it sounded like something they gave to the dogs on the farm.

He found his way to a table across the room where there was space at one end. Some fellow students were getting up as he sat down, but two remained. One was wearing a faded patchwork jacket. He had long blond hair encircling a smiling face. The

14

other had on something which Ben later discovered was called an 'Afghan coat'. He had somewhat shorter, dark curly hair and a wispy beard and moustache which somewhat reminded Ben of a picture of King Charles I in a history book back at school. They were mildly curious to see him and friendly enough in a faintly interested way. He gathered that they were both from Yorkshire and had been discussing the recent success of the football team they supported, Leeds United. It was not a conversation that Ben could really contribute to. But one of them then asked him "where are you from?"

"Kenya," he replied.

"Ah, that's in South Africa," was the response.

"No, East Africa," said Ben.

"Oh yes, of course, one of the British colonies."

"No longer," said Ben, a note of slight irritation creeping into his voice, "it's been independent since 1963."

"Is that so?" said the other student getting up to go, not being a question which required an answer.

With that they left him, one of them saying somewhat half-heartedly "See you around." Well, thought Ben, trying to be positive, it's a start at least.

Half an hour later Ben pulled on a roll-neck jersey knitted for him by his grandmother and grabbed a plastic mac. He set off walking resolutely across the Downs towards the top of Whiteladies Road and the descent down the hill to his first lecture. As he did so it began to rain and the wind gusted enveloping him in an unfamiliar swirl of autumn leaves. While struggling into his mac a bus went by, the faces of its passengers framed in warmth and light. Two of the faces were those of his breakfast companions. Their look, he thought, was of slight concern for him, at least not indifference. Cheered by this he put his head down and quickened his pace.

BEGINNINGS

Whatever you do or dream you can begin it. Boldness has
genius and power and magic in it.

Johann Wolfgang von Goethe

Slightly breathless, and with water dripping from his plastic mac, Ben stood outside the Wills Memorial Building looking up at the imposing stone tower. His mind briefly drifted back to the considerably smaller tower at his old school in Kenya, the Duke of York which he had left just before Christmas the previous year. He walked into the central hall, extracted himself from his mac, firmly gripped his newly acquired briefcase, and turned right into the Law Faculty. He made his way down the corridor towards the sound of voices seeping out from a door on the left leading into a lecture theatre. On entering he saw that the room was about half full, but filling up with others coming in behind him. Glancing at his watch he noted that it was shortly before nine o'clock when the lecture was scheduled to begin.

He was rather surprised to notice that at least half the students were women. He had perhaps, almost subconsciously, expected there to be mainly men doing law. This was maybe conditioning from always having been at school with boys. And he had never heard of any women lawyers in Kenya. Momentarily he felt the discomfort of being out of step. But his attention quickly turned to surveying the landscape of the room and its occupants. Most were casually dressed in a wide range of styles and colours; there were a lot of floppy coats, some hats and berets, and necklaces dangling symbols, stones and the odd wooden crucifix. Some, but not all, of the men had longer hair than the women; one in particular caught his eye, sporting an impressive afro crowning a round pale face; he had never before seen such hair on a white man.

But where to sit? Some students were sitting in pairs or small groups and were chatting together. Others sat alone, examining their new textbooks, fumbling in bags for notepads or furtively glancing around. One in particular looked up and caught Ben's eye. He was about his age, tallish and well built, with rather handsome features, brown eyes and dark hair swept back to his collar. But what Ben immediately noticed most of all about him was that he was wearing a roll-top sweater rather like his own. Without any particular thought process, he heard himself saying, "May I sit here?"

"By all means," was the reply. "I'm Edward; please resist the temptation to call me Ed, or worse still Eddie."

"Clear enough. I'm just plain Ben, so there are no rules for my name."

Edward looked at him carefully, slightly curiously, and with an expression hinting at friendly amusement said, "I suspect there's nothing very plain about you."

There was no time for further conversation. At that moment a rather serious and scholarly-looking man swept in, took his place on the dais and glanced around the room as the general hub-hub subsided. With a slightly pained expression he then began his lecture on an introduction to the English legal system.

As the lecture finished Edward turned to Ben, who was carefully putting his notes back in his briefcase, and said, "How about a coffee? There's a machine in the common room across the corridor; pretty disgusting, the coffee that is, and actually maybe the common room as well, but it's convenient."

"That sounds good," replied Ben getting up and following Edward out.

Some of the other students were heading in the same direction and there was a queue for the machine. As they waited Ben's eyes were drawn to a striking-looking young woman standing over by one of the windows talking intently to a couple of other students. He had half noticed her previously in the lecture theatre. The sun had come out in a reluctant sort of way, but the shafts of light coming through the window were just strong enough to light up her glossy, shoulder-length light brown hair. Her long grey skirt and loose-fitting blue velvet jacket only partly concealed an attractive figure. She seemed to become aware of his gaze and partly turned towards him, her blue eyes beneath slightly furrowed dark eyebrows fixing him with a look which combined fleeting interest and slight irritation. Oh God, he thought, how embarrassing, I've been caught ogling. Edward, picking up on what had happened, chuckled and, lowering his voice, said, "I see that you have noticed Charlotte, Charlotte Jenkinson; bloody attractive girl, but don't even think about it."

"So you know her," said Ben.

"Oh yes, she went to school with my sister and our families are old friends."

"So why the warning?"

Edward gave a low laugh, "Because she has become a trendy leftie and looking at you, no offence meant, you look anything but. Where in fact do you spring from?"

"Kenya."

"Fucking hell," said Edward, trying to suppress louder laughter, "you're an old colonial. You would be well and truly savaged."

Ben was taken aback. Edward, realising that he had gone a bit over the top, quickly added, "Anyway she's spoken for. Her long-standing boyfriend is in his last year at Oxford and there's a general understanding that they'll get married when the time is right."

There was a stirring in the common room as people began to gather up their things and move towards the door. It was time for first meetings with tutors. Ben found it hard to resist watching Charlotte as she headed out. As he did so she momentarily caught his eye, but then abruptly turned away into the corridor.

Edward, grinning broadly, put a forefinger up to Ben's face and shook it from side to side. As they were parting to go their separate ways he asked, "Which hall are you in?"

"Churchill," replied Ben.

"OK, that's just over the road from where I am, in Wills. Come over to my room this evening if you like, meet some kindred spirits, and we could go to the pub for a drink."

"That would be good," said a slightly surprised but pleased Ben. "Any particular time?"

"Well you will probably want to eat first in hall, so come over any time after."

"Great, see you then." It was with a comfortable feeling and a confident air that he went off to find his tutor.

Before going to meet Edward that evening Ben popped his head into the common room at Churchill Hall. It was filled with students watching a programme on television, plainly something popular and amusing judging by the numbers there and the amount of laughter. He asked someone standing by the door what was on. With a surprised look the answer came back, "*Rowan &*

Martin's Laugh In, of course. Look there's Goldie Hawn."

None of this meant anything to Ben, so he found himself just saying "Oh", but obviously with a puzzled look on his face.

"Don't you watch it at home?" he was asked.

"No, ah no, we don't have TV."

This provoked an even more surprised look, even bordering on incredulity. But Ben didn't feel like embarking on a wearisome explanation about Kenya and how VOK (Voice of Kenya) television had only come there in recent years. He had seen it occasionally at friends' houses in Nairobi, but it was not the norm, there had been no TV at school, and certainly not where he lived. So he contented himself with a brief farewell and hurried away to find Edward.

Wills Hall looked very different from Churchill Hall, much older, although in fact it had only been built about thirty years before, in the nineteen twenties. Its name (as with the Wills Building housing the Law faculty) reflected the University's connection with Wills family. The fortune made by their famous tobacco empire funded the University's foundation in 1908 and financed many of its finest buildings. The Hall was constructed on the pattern of an Oxford college with a quadrangle of accommodation blocks and rooms arranged on staircases (called 'houses', A to N). The initial quadrangle had sufficed until rising student numbers made necessary the building of a further accommodation block, New Court, an L-shaped configuration of three linked houses; the original quadrangle then becoming known as Old Court.

Over the main entrance Ben noticed a shield emblazoned with the Wills family crest and their motto *Pro Aris et Focis*. One of Ben's subjects for his Cambridge Overseas Higher School Certificate had been Latin and he had no difficulty in working out a literal translation "for our altars and our hearths", although he found it more difficult trying to fathom out what this was meant to convey. With this perhaps rather unimportant thought drifting into the recesses of his mind he went in search of a porter to direct him to Edward's room.

Finding his way from one of the staircases in Old Court Ben knocked tentatively on a door. Almost immediately it swung open to reveal Edward smiling in welcome. "Great you found your way, without too much difficulty I hope? And with good timing because we're getting thirsty."

Stepping into a room rather more homely looking and less stark than his at Churchill Hall, Ben's eyes briefly took in a comforting clutter of books and games kit strewn about and some framed photographs, before resting on two other occupants, both about his age. "This is Nick," said Edward gesturing towards a tall, fair-haired man wearing faded cord trousers and a baggy sweater. "And this is Hugh, although I call him Hughie if I want to annoy him."

Hugh, shorter and darker, wearing jeans and a collarless shirt with a striped scarf draped over his shoulders, laughed and said, "I can always retaliate by calling him Ed."

"And here we have Ben," said Edward turning towards him. "He's the one I told you about, our new resident bushman, all the way from Kenya, but I think that he has the makings to be one of us."

It wasn't quite the introduction that Ben would have wished for, but he clung to the thought that it had reassuring overtones as he responded, "And you must be the kindred spirits I've heard about, although I can't say I'm sure what the hell that's all about."

Edward laughed and said, "My dear boy, just look at us and

Wills Hall. This is a pretend Oxford College and a refuge for ex-public schoolboys like us; tailor-made."

Seeing Ben looking a bit nonplussed Edward added, "I applied to Oxford, as did Nick, Hugh tried for Cambridge, but here we all are. Was Bristol your first choice?"

"No actually, I applied to Oxford, Oriel College; rejected, I've tried to kid myself because I wasn't available for interview, but probably not good enough or, I'm beginning to think, not the right fit."

Edward looking delighted and laughing again, louder still, said, "Well you're the right fit here, welcome to the repository of Oxbridge rejects."

"Come on," said Nick, "cut the crap, I'm getting thirsty, we can further educate the boy over a few pints."

Gathering up coats and scarves they headed into the dank, dark autumn night and made their way towards the beckoning lights of a nearby pub. As they went in Ben noticed from the sign that it was called 'The Swan', although he was sure that Hugh had mentioned that they were going to 'The Dirty Duck'. He was still working this out in his mind, and thinking again what a lot he had to learn about this complicated country in which he found himself, as they made their way to a table in a corner away from the bar and plonked themselves down.

"Right," said Edward, "this was my idea, so I'll get in the first round. Pints all round I assume?"

Ben found himself nodding in agreement and was soon confronted with a pint mug containing a dark brown liquid topped with creamy white foam. To the sound of "Cheers lads" he took a sip and did his best to conceal his surprise at the warm and rather bitter taste; very unlike the ice-cold Tusker lager he enjoyed at home.

Edward noticed this immediately and said, "A bit different from what you are used to?" and, clapping him on the back added, "You'll come to appreciate that good old English ale is one of the great pleasures in life. But, on a more serious note, I suppose that we must do as we said we would and fill you in on the ball-aching subject of kindred spirits, without, I hope, getting too heavy and boring about it."

"Ben, how well do you know England?" interjected Nick.

"Well's that's just the bloody thing I am rather wrestling with." replied Ben. "I was brought up to believe that it's the mother country, and even home as many people there refer to it, including my dad."

"You must at least have visited from time to time and got to know it to some extent?" remarked Hugh, by way of a statement rather than a question.

"Only once," said Ben, "when I was nine. My dad had three months' home leave, as he called it. We flew to England, spent a month or so visiting some relatives of my dad and then went back to Kenya by sea; six weeks round the Cape, and the best part of the holiday as far as my sister and I were concerned."

"But what about your mother?" asked Hugh. "Doesn't she have any family ties here?"

"Nope, none at all. She was born in Kenya and has lived there all her life. My grandfather was one of the early settlers who went out there from Ireland after the First World War to farm. There he met my grandmother, who had been born and brought up in India, and who was visiting a brother who had also settled there. They married and never left."

"Well," said a rather more serious-looking and thoughtful Edward, "if you don't actually know much about your mother country, you will have to learn to grasp that it is divided on class lines." Clapping one hand on Nick's shoulder and the other on Hugh's he added, "The thing is we all come from similar upper middle-class backgrounds and we all went to public schools. I was at Charterhouse, Hugh was at Oundle, and, remind me, where were you Nick?"

"Winchester."

"Christ you must be bloody brainy or you wouldn't have made it there," interjected Hugh.

"But it still didn't get him into Oxford," said Edward in a tone of bitter amusement.

Feeling there was a danger of straying off the subject Ben quickly asked, "So what difference does any of this make?"

Leaning slightly towards him, lowering his voice Edward hissed, "It means that we have almost fuck all in common with a large proportion of our fellow students who come from different backgrounds and went to state schools."

Looking slightly uncomfortable Nick quickly interjected, "But that doesn't always apply, not at least to some of the middle classes and even working classes who were bright enough to go to grammar schools."

"Maybe," added Hugh rather glumly, "but we start off having bugger all in common with the working classes from the comprehensives."

"That may be a starting point, but," insisted Nick, "this is our opportunity, which we may not have really had before, to mix with other classes and break down these bloody barriers." There was a distinct fervour in the rising tone of his voice. "This is what's needed in this country of ours."

"Oh God, this is getting far too heavy," said Edward looking at Ben. "Anyway, I reckon that you're beginning to get the picture and you'll pick it up as you go along. But just a final word

24

of warning, don't be surprised if you are regarded by some, not just as an object of curiosity, but one of suspicion."

Ben looked puzzled.

"Well come on, get real, I bet you went to one of those old colonial schools, run on public school lines."

"Yes, I did," said Ben, still looking a bit doubtful.

"There you are," said Edward with the triumphant note of having made his point, "you may well be suspected of being an imperialist reactionary." He clapped him on the back, adding with a laugh, "Guilty until proved innocent."

The conversation lightened and moved on to other things, shared interests, sport.

"Do you play rugby?" Edward asked Ben.

"Yes, I do."

"Any good?

"Well, I was in the first fifteen at school."

"Sounds promising, position?"

"Fly half."

"Don't tell me you were the highest point scorer."

Not sure whether Edward was beginning to take the piss, Ben answered slightly stiffly, "Well I was actually, thanks to taking most of the kicks."

"Excellent," said Edward. "You must join the university rugby club. I played at school and I think that Hugh did too; not sure about Nick."

Hugh nodded in agreement, but Nick said, "No, I play racket games."

"Typical bloody swot bag Wykehamist," grinned Edward, then adding, "Anyway Ben, do give it a go."

"Will do," said Ben.

"Great, you will meet yet more of us lot, although with a few of the Welsh contingent thrown in, and bloody good players they tend to be; we'll probably need them," said Edward.

Seeing Ben once more looking a bit puzzled, he quickly added, "They don't play rugby at most of the English state schools."

Ben felt his head swimming slightly. There was a lot to take in, but by this stage Nick and Hugh had also got in rounds. He was on to his third pint and getting a taste for the stuff.

As that week unfolded Ben pondered what had really been something of a shock to his system. He had expected his arrival in England to go to university to be a new experience, something very different from what he had been used to and, indeed, an adventure in his life to be looked forward to with eager anticipation. However, what he had not anticipated was to feel like a traveller in a foreign land. But the swirling tide of these thoughts gradually began to turn and ebb with the increasing realisation that he was in an interesting and stimulating environment. He began to get to know fellow students in Hall and in tutor groups, not all of whom were quite as different from him after all. They extended over a wide range of backgrounds with differing outlooks and views which were not without interest to him. Such interest was often reciprocated on their part, in wanting to know about him and his background. Friendly overtures were at times offset by what he felt to be a lack of understanding at least, although at the same time what for him had been rather subliminal issues started to come more into focus. Was there perhaps scope for a common bond after all?

His thoughts on such matters were interrupted by Edward seeking him out in the common room on the Friday afternoon and saying, "End of the first week, we've survived and, more to the point, you've survived; let's celebrate by skipping Hall supper and going out for a bite to eat and, importantly, a few drinks. I'll try to get Nick and Hugh to join us and maybe even, if they can be persuaded to be with such reprobates, a couple of girls."

"That sounds great," replied Ben. "Where do you have in mind going?"

"Well, we should probably eat first, line the stomach and all that, so how about pizza, in the pizzeria down Park Street?"

Ben felt the confidence that had been building up in him start to drain somewhat as he stammered in response, "Sorry, what's a pizza?"

"Stop arsing about," said Edward but as realisation dawned he grinned broadly and added with a note of incredulity, "You really don't know do you? By God, we're going to have to take this bushman in hand!"

That evening Ben found his way to the pizzeria. Edward was already there at a table with Nick and Hugh. Exchanging greetings he sat down with them, noticing that there were still two spare places at the table.

"Who else is coming he asked?"

"You'll see," smirked Edward.

At that moment Charlotte appeared with another girl Ben had not seen before. Ben was surprised, but he had to admit to himself rather pleased. Charlotte also looked somewhat surprised to see him and gave him what he interpreted to be a wary but not wholly disinterested look. It was the best at least that he could hope for.

"Sorry, I didn't know you were coming," said Charlotte feeling that the exchange of glances was rather awkward.

"No fine, I didn't know you were coming either. This was all fixed by Edward," replied Ben.

Grinning, Edward interjected, "I thought that you should get to know each other."

Ben felt uncertain what was implied by this or whether, indeed, Edward was having a bit of fun stirring the pot.

Charlotte's friend was then introduced as Jennie, who was doing history of art, and they all sat down together. Preliminary chat was interrupted by Edward announcing with a mischievous grin, "This is a very special occasion because it is Ben's first ever pizza."

Seeing blank faces round the table, somewhat defensively Ben quickly said, "Yes, true actually, as far as I'm aware pizza restaurants haven't yet made it to Kenya, certainly nowhere near where I live up country, and I think not even to Nairobi."

"How interesting," said Jennie kindly.

But Nick wanted to know more, asking, "Well, do you have any what may be termed ethnic restaurants with food from other parts of the world?"

Feeling rather challenged, Ben replied, "Well, yes, some, there's a rather good Chinese restaurant in Nairobi, the Pagoda, where I went for my birthday last year, a French bistro, Indian restaurants of course, and some other places." Seeing Edward smiling rather indulgently he shot him a look and found himself adding, "Oh, and recently Colonel Sanders has arrived on the scene."

"What on earth do you mean by that?" immediately asked Charlotte.

"Kentucky Fried Chicken, of course, 'it's finger licking good', so says the cut-out of the figure of the Colonel standing outside the place at Westlands in Nairobi." Ben immediately regretted having added the last bit, but went on to say, as if by way of justification, "Anyway, the Africans, in particular, love it;

fried chicken is right up their street."

"Doesn't something about that strike you as somewhat ironic?" challenged Charlotte.

Startled and somewhat uncertain Ben responded, "It hasn't occurred to me, no."

"Well think about it," said Charlotte. "Africans are being drawn to a place with echoes of the American deep south which has a history of slavery."

"Christ, that's going a bit far. I think it's the taste of the chicken, rather than anything else," retorted Ben rather hotly.

"For God's sake, let's lighten this up," interjected Edward, thinking perhaps that this get-together may not have been quite such an amusing idea after all. "It's Friday night; time to wash away the week and enjoy ourselves."

The mood lightened. Conversation flowed with the wine. Ben's first pizza was tasted, accompanied by good-humoured ribbing, and pronounced by him to be "not at all bad" which was taken to mean really rather good.

Ben was sitting opposite Charlotte and every now and then he caught her eye. There was something in those brief exchanged glances, he felt, a kind of spark, but of what? Interest perhaps, but also wariness on both their parts. He couldn't help but be attracted by her looks, despite having been warned off. She was obviously very bright and sparky and there was an undoubted element of fascination on his part, although tempered by a feeling of being challenged to some extent. Well again he had been warned and maybe she was discomforted by not knowing what to make of him. That would not be surprising, thought Ben somewhat ruefully.

Edward and the others seemed genuinely interested to know more about Kenya and Ben's life there. While telling them about the school he had gone to, Charlotte asked, "Was it for white boys only?"

"Yes originally," responded Ben, "but by the time I went there things had changed and they had started to admit Africans and Asians."

"OK, so how many Africans were there when you joined?" enquired Charlotte.

"Only two actually."

"Big deal, so it was still in effect a colonial school run on racial lines."

"No, no," quickly interjected Ben feeling himself becoming rather crossly defensive, particularly when he didn't think that he had anything to justify, still less to apologise about. "You have to understand that things were changing, independence was coming and actually happened at the end of that year."

"And I suppose that change really did then come?" interjected Hugh helpfully trying to lower the temperature a few degrees.

"Certainly," said Ben.

But Charlotte hadn't quite finished. Looking very directly at Ben she asked, "So did in fact many Africans come to the school while you were there?"

"Many, many; they became a majority, certainly in the lower levels of the school. It evolved really into an African school." And he added slightly sarcastically, "I was surrounded by Africans."

He immediately regretted the last remark as it provoked Charlotte to say, with matching sarcasm, "God, I suppose next you will be saying that some of your best friends are Africans."

If this was a question at all, it was probably only rhetorical and Edward quickly intervened saying, "For fuck sake, as I've said before, lighten up," and shooting a look at Charlotte "it's Friday night, we're meant to be enjoying ourselves; no more needs to be said on this subject."

But Ben felt stung into the need to respond. He looked directly back at Charlotte, caught her eye and said firmly, "Actually, I wasn't going to say that, but, in point of fact, the person I regard as my very best friend happens to be an African."

NEW BUGS JANUARY 1963

Suave rosam suave rosam
Floreat per hanc domum
Concinamus Eboraci
Nihil Praeter Optimum

Duke of York School, Kenya
School song, verse 1
Words by Tom Evans

The suburbs of Nairobi had thinned out by the time the car reached Dagoretti Corner and headed down the Ngong Road towards those *Out of Africa* hills of Karen Blixen fame. In the area which bore her name stood proud the Duke of York School. It had been formed in 1949 by the British Governor, Philip Mitchell, as an additional school to cater for the increasing white population of the colony. The first students were briefly housed in Government House itself, but over the next few years the school became fully developed in its own extensive grounds covering several hundred acres. A wide range of buildings was complemented by extensive games pitches, a swimming pool, tennis and squash courts, a rifle range, an assault course for training the cadet force, and even a nine-hole golf course was in the process of being established. And with all this there still remained large areas of bush and undergrowth, the *bundu* as it was called by its Swahili name, a refuge for adventure and escape from school rules, for illicit smoking and drinking, and occasional thuggery. In its short history the school had already developed a proud tradition, based supposedly upon the principles underlying an English public school, many of which in fact had long since become outdated in England itself. It had become a bastion of the white establishment, instilling British principles into young men of the colony. But the forecast winds of change had already started blowing, billowing down from the Great Rift Valley escarpment into colonial corridors; windows were beginning to rattle, perhaps even tremble.

As the car turned right into the long drive a thirteen-year-old boy looked keenly out of the window. In truth he was tired. It had been an early start that day from the farm to Nanyuki and the long drive on to Nairobi. But he had been re-fuelled by traditional Kenya Sunday lunch at the Norfolk Hotel, chicken curry with all the bits and pieces. And he was energised by excitement and nervous anticipation. He was going to be boarding at big school, some six hundred strong, a far cry from what he was used to and a long way from home. The new boys were 'new bugs', the lowest of the low in the rigid hierarchy of the school, except perhaps for the new day boys, very much in the minority, who would suffer the double branding of also being looked down upon as 'day bugs', boys who went home to Mummy every night. The car passed under the railway bridge proudly bearing the school shield, the white rose of York with the motto demanding *Nihil Praeter Optimum*, nothing but the best, and swept into the heart of the school. Ben sat forward and braced himself.

They found their way to the boarding house to which Ben had been allocated and his father pulled up the car nearby. "Come on," he said breezily getting out of the driving seat, "I'll give you a hand in with your trunk."

"Yeah OK, let me just say good bye to Mum." Ben levered

himself out of the back and went round to the front passenger window which was being wound down by a smiling, slightly anxious-looking woman, with bright blue eyes set in what might have been a fair complexion had it not been for years of weathering by the African sun. Bending slightly, he leant towards her, sensing she wanted to kiss him. He wanted to give her at least a quick hug, but in the general melee of other boys arriving, bigger boys, slamming car doors and waving cheery goodbyes with hardly a backward glance, a pervading sense of potential embarrassment resulted in merely a quick squeeze of an outstretched hand.

"You'll be fine, fine, I know you will, you always are. Off you go, good luck and remember to write."

"OK, thanks, bye Mum," replied Ben turning away quickly towards his father standing by the open boot of the car. They each took a handle of the black tin trunk, its lid newly stencilled in white paint with the name 'B L Hooper', and headed for the House. There they were met by a cheerful commotion, a throng of boys, some about his age or a bit older, some a lot bigger, and even a few looked like grown-ups was the thought which struck Ben as they were directed to the junior dormitory. By the door stood a tall, dark-haired boy, very much the same height and build as Ben's father. His blazer, Ben noticed immediately, had an extra stripe round the lower sleeve and was edged with braid. Below the breast pocket were proudly displayed school colours, strips sown one below the other bearing the names of several of the major sports. This was someone to be reckoned with, admired, perhaps even feared. But there was barely time to contemplate any of this. "I'm the prefect in charge of this dorm," he announced in a deliberately authoritative tone. "He'll be shown the ropes," he said to Ben's father somewhat dismissively. The hint was taken; prolonged farewells were probably not a good idea anyway.

"All the best, Ben," said his father hurriedly, firmly grasping his shoulder by way of encouragement. "We'll be down to see you in a few weeks for your first exeat Sunday and take you out for some proper grub." With that the trunk was put down near the lockers at one end of the dormitory and his father turned away, one hand raised in farewell above his retreating back.

Ben also looked away quickly and surveyed the scene. But his attention was distracted by some senior boys who were peering through the door. They looked rather conspiratorial and were talking quietly, but not so quietly that he did not hear one of them say "look man, we've got a *kaffir* in the House." He followed their gaze past a first day of term whirlpool of boys and half unpacked trunks, things everywhere, newly acquired uniform and games kit (as per the extensive school clothing list) with name tapes duly sewn in place, through the noisy throng to a lone figure standing rather forlornly by a bed at the far end of the dormitory.

Slightly hesitantly Ben walked in, glancing around him. He took in mostly new faces, but then two he recognised, Ian and Mike, friends from his previous school upcountry. He knew that they were going to be there because they had asked to be in the same house, but nevertheless the familiarity brought a momentary sense of relief. "Hi," he greeted them. "Can I bag a bed next to yours?"

"Sorry, all taken," replied Ian.

"That one's free though," added Mike jerking his thumb in the direction of a bed next to the boy at the end. "But I expect you don't want to be right beside a black." The word 'black' bore the trace of a South African accent, quite common among sections of the white farming community with that particular ancestry.

"No way do I want to be there," Ben blurted out.

"Well, tough luck man," said Mike unhelpfully "it's the only bed left. You should have got here earlier."

"Yeah, I was told you need to be early to bag a good bed," added Ian equally unhelpfully.

Somewhat disconsolately Ben made his way towards the vacant bed. As he did so the African boy half turned towards him. He only looked briefly at Ben but with a certain intensity which Ben found disconcerting. He had obviously heard what had been said and Ben began to feel uneasy about what had been an instant and even instinctive reaction on his part. Not surprising perhaps. He had lived all his life in Africa but had never lived with Africans. He began unpacking in silence, aware that he was being watched warily. After a few minutes, for some barely conscious reason, he felt that it was up to him to break that silence. He stood up from where he had been putting things in his bedside locker and glancing towards the boy said, "I'm Ben."

There was no immediate answer and so Ben then asked, "What's your name?"

"Kariuki," was the softly spoken reply.

"Ah, so you're a Kikuyu," said Ben instantly recognising a well-known tribal name. "But what's your first name?"

"Joseph," and he added shyly, but smiling slightly for the first time, "you can tell from this that I went to a mission school and it's the name which was given to me when I was baptised by the fathers; but I like to be called Joe."

"Was it good to go to a mission school?" asked Ben.

"Well, it got me a bursary to come here."

Seeing Ben looking uncomprehending, Ian, who out of

36

curiosity had come over to listen in, interjected, "Yeah, a bursary; my dad told me, it's something to do with the Government, I think, paying school fees for," (he paused momentarily in carefully selecting the next word) "Africans coming here."

"So that was good?" said Ben trying to sound positive.

"Yes, my father is pleased—" and he added slightly defiantly "—because freedom, we call *uhuru*, is coming." His face took on an expression, partly thoughtful and partly confused as he went on, "But my father didn't always like me being at mission school."

"Why?" asked Ben.

"Because, he said, they wanted to teach away some of our tribal traditions and beliefs, to be a good Christian you see." The last words were added with a nervous grin. But rescue was at hand from a conversation descending into uncomfortable depths.

There was a sudden bellow from the older boy Ben had seen on the way in.

"Right, you rabble, shut up and listen. My name is Dawson and I'm your dorm prefect, worse luck for you and me. You new bugs, in the first year, are all rabble and so are the second form guys in the next dorm, although they are slightly more senior rabble and will give you some shit in trying to order you around. But you blokes better get into your thick skulls that my orders and the orders of the other prefects and head of house are the ones that count. If one of us shouts RABBLE you stop whatever you are doing and come running as fast as you can; the last one to get there will be given whatever the job is. Understood?"

There was no immediate response from the sea of numb and blank faces.

"I repeat," he said, raising his voice even louder, "do you bloody understand?"

And this was met by a hurried chorus of subdued acknowledgment.

"One more thing," he said. "After supper I shall choose two of you lucky bastards to be my personal rabble, to make my bed every morning, to polish my shoes and cadet boots, to look after my games kit, to put out my laundry and to carry my books to school." With that he turned and swept out of the dormitory, looking ever more important.

Shortly afterwards the bell for supper came as something of a relief and boys from every direction filed towards the separate dining block. Ben found himself sitting with some other junior boys at the end of one of the long tables. Joe Kariuki was at a neighbouring table and they exchanged nervous glances. The second years were on initial table duty, collecting food from a serving hatch and depositing it in front of the senior at the head of each table. "Don't worry, your turn will come," one of them hissed in passing by where Ben was sitting. He began to wonder whether there was going to be any end to the duties to be heaped upon him. At that moment he received a plate upon which was a dollop of cheese potato, but nothing much else. He was glad that he had had a good lunch earlier.

Back in the dormitory later the formidable Dawson strode in and made his presence known in no uncertain terms. "Right, stand by your beds. Time to choose two of you to be my rabble. Who will be the lucky ones?" There was more than a hint of sarcasm in the question, but it required no answer. The selection process simply began.

Dawson walked slowly down the centre of the dormitory between the two lines of beds looking each boy up and down. Turning at the end he paused by Joe Kariuki and looked at him long and hard before saying, "You look like a shoe-shine boy; the job is yours."

Ben had to admit he felt relieved that he hadn't been chosen, but such thought had barely settled in his mind before Dawson wheeled round and said to him, "And don't think you've got away with it; you'll make my bed every morning. The other duties you will take it in turns for."

As Dawson walked back down the dormitory two boys were unwise enough to smile smugly at what they thought had been their lucky escape. But there was no escaping the eagle-eyed attention of Dawson. He rounded on them at once. "And you two will start house duties tomorrow morning with some second formers who will show you the ropes. It means you will get up early, turn off security lights, tidy up the common room and generally get the House shipshape." No one then dared move a muscle until Dawson had departed and was safely out of sight.

A more cheerful atmosphere then began to settle on the dormitory. There was a bit of ragging about, flicking of ties, boasting and banter. Old acquaintances were renewed, new ones tentatively formed. Ben chatted happily enough to his friends Ian and Mike. Joe was making himself busy, rearranging his bedside locker for the umpteenth time. He was clearly being left out.

And suddenly it was all change again. A bellow of "RABBLE" was heard echoing around the corridors of the House. It induced a mad scramble for the door of the dormitory, things being dropped and discarded into a wake of running feet. Other boys emerged from elsewhere into the bumping, jostling throng that surged towards the call. Ben and Joe had started with the disadvantage of being at the far end of the dormitory. But they weren't quite the last to arrive. A second former stumbled along just behind them from the direction of the lavatories, frantically fumbling at doing up his shorts.

The call was from no lesser person than the head of house, Andrew Harris, mature for his eighteen years, tall, slim but wiry, glasses below a high forehead, clever looking, definitely superior. He surveyed the panting mass before him. His eyes alighted on the stark difference of the one black face.

"What's your name?" he asked.

"Joseph," was the soft reply.

"This is not a bloody kindergarten; what's your surname?'"

"Kariuki," he said hastily.

"Right, well you weren't quite last, I know, but I think it would be good training for you to make coffee for the prefects' common room. The job's yours."

If there was any sense of unfairness, nobody dared say a thing. The boy who had been struggling with his shorts smirked and shambled off.

Back in the dormitory, just before lights off, Joe came back looking weary and confused. Ben said nothing, but nodded to him as he went past. Joe slid into bed and pulled the sheet up nearly over his head. It had been a long day.

The first week of term progressed with firmly established routines of lessons and games and, for the rabble, seemingly endless rounds of duties. Ben had never felt so tired as he did at the end of each day. But, as he slipped into the rhythm of the school, he began to appreciate how much there was to offer; it was stimulating, at times frightening, though also exhilarating. He tiptoed towards enjoyment.

For all its toughness, its strict discipline and rigid hierarchy, the School was a thriving and paradoxically cheerful place, for most at least. The teaching was to a high standard, the staff being mainly British, many Oxbridge educated. Some had been there since inception. Others had come in later, including a few old boys whose affection for the place was such that they had returned from their further education to their *alma mater*. The resources were superb, by any standard, particularly for sport by which great store was set, although music, drama and the arts quietly flourished on a different level. There was a real spirit in the School, comradeship, fierce loyalty, pride in being Yorkists. Life lessons could be hard but also well learned. The end product, for the most part, was of strong, resourceful and, for those with capability for learning, well-educated young men. And perhaps the most telling measure of the place was that lifelong memories and friendships were forged. But now there were new challenges beyond the scope of any previous experience. Time had begun to catch up.

Towards the end of the week, one evening before supper, Ben, Mike and a few other boys were having a kick-around with a football on one of the pitches behind the House. Standing alone at the side of the pitch, watching rather forlornly, was Joe. Ben suddenly noticed him, almost in the same instant as he found himself with the ball at his feet. Without any clear thought process he kicked the ball towards Joe and it rolled invitingly to his feet. Joe quickly overcame his initial surprise and aimed a firm kick to return the pass to Ben. But he was wearing his new, unfamiliar and unyielding, black leather shoes. The ball skewed off to one side, away from the action. Ben looked startled. Mike and a couple of the other boys did nothing to hide their amusement. There was fleeting embarrassment on Joe's face, but then some inner reserve of true character reasserted itself. On a rising tide of determination Joe pulled off his shoes and socks and ran barefoot in pursuit of the ball. Reaching it he turned quickly and dribbled it at speed back towards the waiting boys.

Recovering from his initial surprise, Mike moved to tackle, but Joe deftly accelerated past him and neatly flicked the ball through the legs of the boy standing behind him. Running on to it, he struck firmly with his right foot and the ball curved past the boy keeping goal into the top right-hand corner. Joe turned, panting slightly and looked directly at Ben who appeared frozen in the position from which he had passed the ball to Joe. No one else moved until, a few seconds later, the tableau dissolved with the sound of the dining hall bell.

Later that evening, just before time for bed, Ben and Joe, already in their pyjamas, happened to be padding back to the dormitory from the bathrooms at the same time. As they reached their beds there was a call of "lights out". In that instant Ben grinned at Joe and spontaneously threw a fake punch towards him with his left hand, while at precisely the same time hitting his own chest with his right fist to make the sound of a blow being struck. Joe happily responded in the same way. Instantly a thunderous voice rang out "ragging in the dorm after lights out." There at the door, half lit from the landing, loomed the formidable figure of Dawson.

"We weren't ragging, I swear," blurted our Ben. "It was just pretend fighting. We never even touched each other."

Even if Joe had been minded to say anything, there would have been absolutely no point in doing so.

"You're both going in the book," said Dawson as he wheeled round and strode out. There was a complete stillness in the dormitory. Not even an eyelid flickered.

Anxious hours passed towards the inescapable outcome of the following day. Prep ended in the common room and the house master emerged from his study to take evening prayers. As they concluded the head of house stepped forward and handed the house master the dreaded book containing the two most recent names listed for punishment. Beating required his sanction, but only a quick glance sufficed for his signature. He trusted Harris and the prefects to do what he unquestionably believed was required to maintain that all-important discipline.

Ben and Joe returned to their dormitory but found it hard to participate in the usual jollity and horseplay before lights out. As the time approached, they undressed in silence and put on their pyjamas. Ben sat on his bed clasping his knees to his chest. Joe lay completely motionless, eyes staring but unseeing. Minutes seemed to linger rather than pass, but the nightly call duly came.

"Lights out!" shouted Dawson from the door. "Everybody into bed and if I hear the slightest sound there will be hell to pay. Hooper and Kariuki follow me."

Ben and Joe trudged after him in the direction of the prefects' common room.

"Right, wait here," they were told as Dawson went in and shut the door behind him. Sounds and smells seeped out of the room; muffled voices and laughter; burning toast; the Beatles.

The door opened to reveal Harris holding a slip-on leather sandal. His eyes swivelled from one to the other of the dejected figures standing before him.

"Right," he said, "turn round; I hope there's been no smart-arse padding applied here." And with that he tweaked back the waistband of each boy's pyjama trousers. No protective layers were to be seen; just clenched buttocks, white and black respectively.

"OK, let's go, I'll limber up with you," he said to Ben directing him into the room and pushing the door shut behind him with his foot.

Ben blinked hard. He bloody well wasn't going to blub, but his eyes were moist and it was almost as if he were looking through the shimmering haze of a hot, dusty afternoon. He blinked again to see before him Dawson and the other prefects lounging on a battered sofa and chairs in a comfortably untidy room. There were things strewn about; piles of books and files; mugs of coffee; plates of half-eaten toast on a low table; a bag of golf clubs propped up in a corner. Assorted LPs and singles, some out of their sleeves, were piled beside a small battery-operated record player. The words of *Love Me Do* permeated the surrounding sounds. He was momentarily distracted by posters on the walls; pop groups, sports cars; and women; one in particular caught his eye, long blonde hair flowing over a wet T-shirt.

"Over in that corner, bend over and grab your knees," came the command.

Ben did his best to brace himself in position as Harris stood a few paces away flexing the leather sandal. But nothing could have prepared him for the shock of his beating. Harris took a few rapid steps towards him to gain momentum as his long, sinewy arm brought the sandal cracking down. The searing force of the blow almost knocked him over, but he somehow found reserves of grim determination to hold his ground as he was struck painfully for the second time. The third also hurt like hell, but the fourth, fifth and sixth were of diminishing effect as thankfully numbness of body and mind set in.

"Right, bugger off and send in Kariuki."

Stooping slightly he walked stiffly out of the room, past watching eyes. He didn't dare look at Joe, but just nodded in his direction. As the door closed he hurried down the corridor, but not quickly enough to avoid hearing the first crack, then the second, slightly more muffled. He put his hands over his ears and picked up his pace back towards the dormitory. As he reached the door some instinct deep within him made him stop and wait. Moments later Joe appeared walking with an awkward gait. However, that was not what Ben noticed. He saw only, glowing through a single tear, a bright light of defiance, anger rather than hatred, above all determination. Feeling humbled, but also fortified in some strange way, he reached out both hands and clasped Joe's shoulders. "Man, I'm sorry," he said, "it's my fault that this has happened."

Joe glanced down and his brow furrowed for a moment. He then looked up, very directly at Ben and softly said, "It's OK, because I know that you are my friend."

Within a few days they were able to smile again with the realisation that they had something particular in common. Their backsides were much the same colour.

HEROICS

The time you won your town the race
We chaired you through the market-place;
Man and boy stood cheering by,
And home we brought you shoulder-high.

A.E. Housman
A Shropshire Lad XIX

Ben had begun to look different, so more alike those around him. His sleek, sun-bleached hair was growing longer. Blue denim shirts made his eyes look bluer still. Levi cords puddled round now battered Bata safari boots. On the firm advice of Edward, an ex-army camouflage jacket had replaced the plastic mac.

So too did other differences diminish and seem less stark. His circle of friends widened as he realised that he was fortunate enough to be surrounded by many bright, interesting and amusing young people from a wide variety of backgrounds. He enjoyed being with them. For their part they often actively sought him out. They wanted to be with him, to do things together, and to learn more about him. The comforting and reassuring realisation for him was that he was becoming an object of real interest, not mere curiosity.

And there were so many girls, girls, girls. Coming from a very cloistered, all male school society, it was a wholly new experience to be surrounded by girls on such a scale. This was not to say that he knew nothing of girls of his own age. Some of his friends had sisters he saw from time to time. There were also the daughters of farming community neighbours in Laikipia and Nanyuki, some of whom he had been virtually brought up with, more like sisters than girlfriends. Then there had been the school dances for the senior boys; potentially exciting, but often fraught affairs. Each boy was entitled to invite a partner from one of the girls' schools. There were two main ones, The Kenya High School, known as "the *Boma*" (short for heifer *boma*) and Limuru School for girls, particularly popular with the upcountry families; also there was the Catholic Loreto Convent, but its strictness proved rather more challenging territory for these purposes. It was then a matter of nervous anticipation whether one would be invited back to one or more of the dances at the girls' schools. The invitations brought either considerable kudos or embarrassed disappointment. Staff supervision at the dances precluded anything too adventurous. There was a certain amount of snogging, but close embraces for any length of time were usually interrupted. One headmistress was known to patrol the dance floor armed with a golf club which was inserted between torsos judged not to be keeping an appropriate distance. Inevitably some bragged of more adventurous encounters behind the bike shed; in truth bravado in most, but not quite all, cases. And yet with all the girls around him now, the one Ben had noticed first was still of most interest.

Charlotte, strikingly good looking, intelligent, but also challenging, even at times intimidating, and strictly unavailable. Why couldn't he get her out of his head, for God's sake? Since the night of the pizza, they had been somewhat wary of each other. But there was certainly no question of avoidance; far from it. Often, they found themselves sitting near each other in lectures, usually with Edward and a friend of Charlotte's, Liz,

47

together with a few others in what had developed into their immediate circle. They drank coffee in the common room, ate lunch in the café opposite the Wills Building and spent some evenings drinking at the long bar in the Students' Union. And, of course, they talked. Ben found Charlotte continuing to be challenging at times, but he hoped that he was right in detecting also some genuine interest on her part. He became more confident in their sometimes lively exchanges, even finding them stimulating. The realisation dawned on him that she was making him question and re-think things that he had taken for granted. But he also began to believe, he fervently hoped correctly, that there were glimmers of understanding on her part of him, of what he was all about. Things were about to be taken to a new level.

It was a grey, windy, almost end of autumn afternoon at Coombe Dingle. Only a few withered leaves clung precariously to the trees. But the chill in the air did nothing to diminish the heat of the contest on the rugby pitch. Bristol University first fifteen were at home to arch-rivals Exeter. Ben's maroon and white shirt was streaked with mud, he had taken a few painful knocks and he was panting hard as the half-time whistle blew. But he was also exhilarated; the adrenalin was pumping; he had scored and converted the only try for Bristol; he had also just made up for an earlier miss by kicking a penalty to bring the score level on points.

As they broke from their half-time huddle, Edward clapped Ben on the shoulder and said, "We can do it; we can bloody well win this game." Ben only half heard him. He had just noticed two figures coming into view and joining a group of spectators. One was Liz, the other was Charlotte. There was barely time to register any thought about this. The whistle went. The ball was kicked high towards the Bristol team. It was game on.

And hard fought it was. Exeter kicked a penalty. Ben brought the score back level with a penalty from a distant but at least fairly central position. The play surged up and down the pitch. There was drama to be had in the finish. Despite determined defence just short of the line, Exeter bundled the ball over for a try; although, fortunately for Bristol, a gust of wind took the conversion kick just wide. Five minutes to go. "Come on!" was the rallying cry as Ben drop kicked the ball deep into Exeter territory. The Bristol forwards pressed hard; knock-on by Exeter; scrum. As Edward went down into his wing forward position, he shot a look back to where Ben was standing at a slight angle behind the scrum half. Ben nodded back at him. No words were needed to stress that this was their last chance. The ball came cleanly out of the scrum and was whipped back to Ben. Sensing an opportunity, he accelerated towards the corner, made as if to pass outside him, and then swerved to the left drawing the defence towards him. As the crunching tackles went in he was just able to offload, flicking the ball behind him to the right, into the arms of one of the props whom he had seen out of the corner of his eye, lumbering up in support. The big man had gained momentum and crossed the try line dragging two defenders with him. The vital score, but in the right-hand corner. It was not going to be an easy kick for a right footer. Ben took the ball some way out and positioned it carefully. He hit it well and it rose high and higher still towards the goal. The charging Exeter forwards turned and looked back just as the ball struck and bounced off the right-hand post. A draw; relief in some quarters, disappointment in others. Ben sat forlornly from where he had taken the kick, his hands clasping muddy knees. Edward pulled him to his feet.

"Come on, no need to take it to heart," he said, putting an

arm round Ben's shoulder. "No shame in missing a bloody difficult kick after you'd had a blinder of a game. And a draw was probably a fair result."

Ben looked doubtful and his mood was still tinged with disappointment as they trooped off the pitch.

"We must just go and have a word with Charlotte," said Edward, "as she's been good enough to turn out on a chilly afternoon."

"I didn't know she was coming," replied Ben.

"I asked her."

"Does she often come to watch you play?"

"Oh no, you, silly arse," laughed Edward, clasping Ben again round the shoulder, even harder. "She didn't come to watch me."

They went over to the girls. Ben felt that Charlotte was looking at him rather intently, or was he imagining it, he wondered? It was Liz who spoke first.

"That was quite a finish."

"Could have been better," said Ben, still feeling rather despondent.

"Do you feel you should have got that last kick over?" asked Charlotte.

"It was kickable, but it would have been easier if had been on the other side."

Seeing the girls looking rather uncertain Edward interjected, "That's because Ben is a right footer; he could have swung the ball in from the left side, but on the other side he had to kick straight and there is always a risk of hitting the near post. But hell, enough of the post mortem which I'm sure is really boring. Let's meet up later and treat ourselves to a meal out; it's Saturday evening after all."

"Any suggestions?" asked Charlotte.

"How about the Llandoger Trow?" said Liz. "I went there with my parents at the beginning of term and clocked it for a return visit. It's a bit off our usual track, but really good."

"Oh yes, I think I know the place you mean," said Edward. "It's an old timber-frame building down in the city centre."

"That's the one," said Liz. "I was told when I was there that it dates back to the seventeenth century and it's meant to be terribly famous because it's connected in some way with *Treasure Island*, and I think also *Robinson Crusoe*."

"Ah," said Edward with a grin, "so it will be something of an English education for the bushman."

Ben glared at him, but cheered up visibly when Charlotte said, "I'm up for it and I might try to bring Jennie too."

"Good, good," said Edward rubbing his hands together "and I'll mob up Nick and Hugh. So we're on. Let's aim to meet there at about eight."

Eyes turned to Ben who had knelt down to re-tie a bootlace. "Great," he said quickly looking up, "but where do I find this place?"

"It's between Welsh Back and Queen Charlotte Street, near the old city centre docks," replied Liz.

Ben looked a bit doubtful. "I haven't really been down there yet. But I'm sure I'll find it," he added quickly, not wanting to appear wet, particularly in present company.

"Well, we shall all meet up later then," said Edward as the girls turned to go. He and Ben made their way to the dressing room to shower and change. "We can go together if you like and I'll show you the way to the pub," said Edward.

"No, no really, I'll be fine," quickly responded Ben, feeling for some not really clearly formulated reason that he had a point to prove.

"OK then, you can always ask for directions if necessary; it's a pretty well-known place."

Later that evening, in his room in Hall, Ben went to particular trouble to look his best, although he also felt slightly irritated with himself, even rather embarrassed that he was doing so. He chose to put on his favourite blue shirt and toyed with the idea of also wearing a silk neck scarf, recently acquired copying a trend he had noticed with other students. On, off, on, off again. He stuffed the scarf into his jacket pocket for possible future use. For the umpteenth time he looked in the mirror and combed back freshly shampooed, glossy fair hair. Long enough had been spent; rather too long; it was getting late and he had to find his way.

He set off and took the bus he had become familiar with as far as his usual stop near the Wills Memorial Building. Not knowing quite what route the bus continued on, he had decided to walk from there down to the city centre. At the bottom of Park Street he struck out in what he hoped was the right direction, following some other students, a couple of whom he recognised. Lights illuminated the Saturday evening bustle. People and traffic swirled around in gusts of late autumn wind. Cutting across to a quieter, darker street, on the edge of a square, Ben suddenly became aware of a different kind of commotion. Peering through the gloom Ben saw five youths surrounding a young black man. Drawing closer he could see one was about his age, three slightly younger, and one younger still. What they all had in common was almost a complete absence of hair; barely visible stubble on closely shaved heads. Their tight-fitting clothes were also similar, as were heavy boots. The black man was being pushed around and taunted. Ben looked around. The other students he had been following had melted away into the mistiness of the old harbour. It was just him and them.

At that moment the black man was knocked to the ground. The youths circled around him, making monkey noises and shouting abuse.

"Go home you black bastard."

"We don't want niggers in this country."

"Go back to the trees where you belong."

"And have a banana."

The last remark induced much laughter. Sensing that they might be distracted by their own perceived wit, the black man began to struggle to his feet. But his ordeal was not over. Immediately he was pushed to the ground and, as he rolled over, kicks thudded into his body from a variety of angles.

Was it bravery? Was it some deeply ingrained instinct? Ben had no real time to think. But he did not run. He found himself shouting out.

"Hey, guys, he's had enough. Leave him alone now."

Attention rapidly switched in his direction.

"Fuck off; this has nothing to do with you."

"But what's it got to do with you either? I can't believe he's done anything to you."

It was not a debate the youths were prepared to enter into. The one about Ben's age strode towards him menacingly. As his face came up close Ben noticed that he had a cross, or was it perhaps a dagger, tattooed on his forehead? There was no time for further speculation.

"I thought I told you to fuck off. This is none of your bloody business."

"Actually, I have reason to think that it is," Ben found himself saying.

"Are you trying to be a clever dick?"

Ben didn't answer but stood his ground. The kicking of the black man stopped and the other youths now gathered in front of Ben.

"What the fucking hell are you waiting for? Get the hell out of here." As the words spat out of the tattooed face, Ben was shoved backwards. It could have been the moment for flight. But a red mist of anger and indignation eclipsed fear. Ben stepped firmly forward. As he did so a fist with a skull and crossbones ring on one finger came swinging towards his face. But it was wild, rather than well-aimed, and Ben was just able to tilt his head backwards. He saw a momentary look of surprise on his attacker's face as he failed to make contact. In that instant Ben struck back, driving his right fist hard against the man's unguarded nose.

"You fucking bastard, you've broken my nose; I'm going to kill you!" he screamed with pain and fury as he staggered back and with blood beginning to spurt from his face he then lunged forward again. This time Ben was able to fend off the wild uncoordinated attack by bringing a knee up hard into the man's crutch, causing him to double up and sink to his knees. But as he did so the other youths joined the fray. Blows rained onto his face and head. He did his best to protect himself and stay on his feet. However, weight of numbers dragged him down, wrestling and knocking him to the ground. Kicks then came in to his body as he tried to roll away. In a moment of adrenalin-fuelled self-preservation, he somehow just found the strength to grab hold of a boot aimed at his face and pulled it up as far as he could. The kicker lost his balance and fell heavily backwards. The thud of his head hitting a kerb coincided with the approaching sound of a siren. Immediate disengagement; the youths stumbled off, one bent double, one pulled to his feet and dragged away. Ben levered himself up on to his elbows. One eye was closing but the other took in the black man, a few yards away, groaning as he tried to sit up.

"Are you OK?" he called out.

"I shall survive, thanks to you. I'm sorry for your trouble. And how is it with you?"

Ben cracked a smile through cracked lips. "I'm going to survive too," he said, dragging himself to his feet and making his way over to the other man now sitting up, shoulders slumped forward. "Where are you from?"

"Ghana."

"Ah, I'm from Kenya."

The man looked up at him curiously. "Not English?"

Ben hesitated for a moment. "No, not really."

"But when did you go to Kenya."

"I was born there. It's my home. I've only just come to England to go to university."

There was a pause as he was looked at closely. "Yes, there is something different about you."

The siren grew louder with the approaching police car. Two officers emerged, one calling out, "What's going on here?"

"God, I'm glad to see you," said Ben. "You're just in the nick of time, but how come?"

"A 999 call," said the other officer. "Someone saw what appeared to be an attack or some kind of fight. There's also an ambulance on the way. Are there others involved?"

"They've scarpered," said Ben.

"Can you describe them?"

"I'll do my best. But I can start by telling you that one has a broken nose and another a cracked head."

"I see you've got blood on your shirt."

"Some mine," said Ben looking down, "but I think mainly from the broken nose."

"We're going to need full statements, but it looks as if first you better go to Casualty; and the man over there," he said, taking in the rest of the scene. Moments later an ambulance pulled up. One paramedic came over to Ben and after some preliminary checks pronounced that he did indeed require some patching up and X-rays. His colleague was bending over the other man, still sitting on the ground, talking in reassuring tones.

"You've been well and truly roughed up, but we'll take care of you; you're in good safe hands now."

"It would have been much worse if that other man had not come along."

The paramedic glanced over his shoulder in the direction of Ben. "A good Samaritan," adding reflectively, "and a good Englishman."

The black man winced as he struggled to his feet. After a moment's thought he said, "In fact, he is an African, like me."

Much later that evening Ben stretched out on his bed back in Hall, moving very carefully, having just been dropped off by an ambulance car. At the hospital he had been stitched up above one eye and one hand was bandaged. He had also been treated for some other more minor cuts and bruises. X-rays had revealed two cracked ribs. He had a split lip. His mind swirled with big things and little things. Had he been brave or stupid? Should he have gone for help? Might he have made things worse? How long was he going to be off rugby? When could he next wash his hair?

The train of unanswered, perhaps unanswerable, questions stopped abruptly with a gentle but insistent knocking on his door.

It opened partly and a face peered round into the room; Edward's very concerned face.

"Christ, so it was you."

Ben looked up questioningly, levering himself into a slightly more upright position.

"We were worried when you didn't show up; thought initially that perhaps you'd just got lost. But then more time went by and we heard from other people in the pub that there had been some kind of incident nearby and that they had seen a police car and ambulance. We still didn't twig immediately that this was anything to do with you; couldn't imagine how it could possibly have been. Doubts though then crept in and we thought that we'd better come and find you."

Edward had edged into the room and Ben became aware that there was someone behind him.

"Please come in, do."

Edward stepped forward followed by Charlotte.

"I'm sorry," said Ben. "I should have tried to get word to you, but by the time I thought of it I wasn't sure how to do so."

"No need to apologise," said Edward quickly. "You've had quite enough to deal with by the sound of it. Word has got round what happened and we've heard some pretty colourful accounts; although looking at you I can see that there may not have been too much exaggeration."

Ben caught Charlotte's look, intense and serious.

"I know girls are not supposed to be here at this time of night," she said. "But to hell with that. I wanted to see if you're OK and if we can do anything for you."

Nothing in that moment could have lifted Ben's spirits higher. Sitting up a bit more, happy, but in a way humbled, he felt strangely shy as he replied. "That's really good of you; much appreciated. But I'm not sure that there's anything you can really do, for now at least. I've been sorted out as best as possible at the hospital and I've just got to get on with it."

Charlotte was still looking at him carefully.

"Have you got a sponge?" she asked.

"Yes," was the slightly surprised answer, "in the top drawer over there with my wash bag."

"And where can I get some water?"

"In the bathroom down the passage."

Charlotte left the room carrying the sponge. Edward said nothing but gave Ben a quizzical look. A moment later she was back.

"Can you shift over just a bit? Carefully does it." Sitting down beside Ben she said, "There's quite a bump coming up on your forehead, the other side from the stitches. I think it might help if I sponge it with some cold water."

Ben murmured approval and he felt his hair being gently stroked back and a soothing coolness seeping into his brow. It was the first time that she had touched him.

Edward had pulled up a chair and was glancing round the room. A small watercolour painting caught his eye. An African scene; a few thatched huts and a thorn tree at the foot of a range of four distinct hills. "Kenya, presumably?"

"Yes," said Ben turning his head slightly. "The Ngong Hills." He paused reflectively and then intoned, "*I had a farm in Africa, at the foot of the Ngong Hills ... at an altitude of over six thousand feet. In the day time you felt that you had got high up, near to the sun, but the early mornings and evenings were limpid and restful, and the nights were cold.*"

Seeing uncomprehending looks he quickly added, "The opening words from *Out of Africa* by Karen Blixen. I've missed out a few, I think, but that's the main gist of it. Beautiful and evocative, which, I suppose, is why they have stuck in my mind for the most part."

"I don't know the book," said Charlotte.

"Well," said Ben, "if you want some relief from wading through legal textbooks, you might consider reading it." He studied her face carefully. "I think actually it might interest you."

Seeing her looking a bit doubtful he added, "It's not one of those rather tedious 'my adventures and daring deeds in the African bush' sort of books. It's far more of a literary work, beautifully written. She had a real feeling for the place, and, most importantly, for its people."

"Well," she said, "that's quite a hard sell. You've made me feel that I ought to give it a go sometime."

God, he thought, I'm being a bit heavy perhaps, so doing his best to sound jocular he went on to say, "But most importantly I went to school in Karen, the place named after her, at the foot of those self-same hills. On Sundays we would sometimes be allowed to roam about up there; taking packed lunches and going off with friends for the day; freedom."

Pausing he looked at the picture, long and hard, or perhaps longingly.

"My grandmother painted it for me, as a kind of reminder I suppose; not that I shall ever forget."

Edward's attention had drifted off. Looking round the room he noticed a few records, LPs in their covers. Beatles, Kinks, Mamas and Papas, Simon and Garfunkel's new release *Bridge Over Troubled Water*; fairly predictable. But he did nothing to hide his surprise in picking up *Under Milk Wood*, the BBC's recording of the Dylan Thomas play for voices with a distinguished all Welsh cast led by Richard Burton.

"Do you really listen to this stuff?" he asked.

Ben's split lip didn't prevent a smile. "I do actually; something I've been introduced to recently. There's a bit of a story attached to it."

"A lot of words," said Edward rather doubtfully.

"Yes, but they make up a kind of symphony of words. I find they sound better and better every time I hear them; and best of all with a few drinks inside you. We must give it a go some time."

"You really are a bit of a dark horse, you know."

Something else had caught Charlotte's eye; a set of small leather-bound books on a shelf by the desk. "May I?" she asked getting up and looking at them more closely.

"Certainly," said Ben, "they're rather special."

"Latin," remarked Charlotte opening one and then inspecting the others. "The works of Cicero; beautifully bound, and old I see, published in 1827." It was her turn to be surprised. "Extraordinary thing for you to have," she said, turning back towards Ben.

"Ah, a talisman. Another legacy of Samburu."

She looked at him searchingly. But his head had sunk deep into his pillow and his eyes were shut. Suffused with memory his mind was drawing him away. Further and further and further away; nearly five thousand miles away. He had already started dreaming. Now he needed to sleep.

SAMBURU NORTHERN FRONTIER PROVINCE

In addition to the rugged splendour of its landscape the very name "Northern Frontier Province" conjures up an atmosphere of mystery and adventure. It is indeed a vast and little visited region, where travelling, even nowadays, is tough and where the nomadic tribes have changed little over the centuries.

Samburu—Isiolo Game Reserves
A Field Guide to the National Parks of East Africa
(1967 edition) by John G. Williams

"I'll drive you to Isiolo tomorrow."

"So I'm on," said Ben. "Thanks Dad, I feel really up for it."

And so he was. He had enjoyed the freedom of being at home on the ranch in Laikipia since leaving school at the beginning of December. He had got over (for now at least) the crushing disappointment of the letter, which had arrived on his nineteenth birthday of all days, informing him that he had been rejected by Oxford. Christmas and New Year had been a whirlwind of festivity; parties at home and visits to friends in Nanyuki and Nara Moru; drinking and eating far too much; barbecues (even the turkey had been barbecued) and then more barbecues. His sister had returned to her teaching job in Nairobi. Dad was busy. The last of the mince pies had been eaten and Mum had said firmly that she was not making any more. He had nearly nine months to fill before travelling to England to start university.

There was the opportunity for fun, excitement, new experience.

Dad had a friend who worked for Wild Life Lodges, based in Nairobi, but with places in prime wildlife locations; the famous Treetops near Nyeri, Keekorok in the Maasai Mara, and Samburu Game Lodge in the Samburu-Buffalo Springs Game Reserve, to the north and west of Laikipia. It was Samburu where Ben was destined for. Dad's friend had sent word that there was a relief manager at the Lodge who could do with some extra help. Ben had jumped at the chance. The newly appointed assistant manager (is that really me, he thought?) was on his way.

The road from Nanyuki took them round the north of Mount Kenya, its snow seemingly shyly concealed by the gathering cloud of a highland morning, on to Timau, then dropping down steeply to the great plains beyond. By the time they reached Isiolo they were in hot, arid country, strikingly different from the high farm land not many miles to the south. Isiolo had all the appearance of a frontier town and indeed it was, although a long way from the frontier. The gateway to the wild country of the Northern Frontier Province, or Northern Frontier District, NFD, as it was popularly called, provided a gathering place for hardy inhabitants of the region, Boran, Samburu, Turkana and particularly Somalis who to some extent had made it a place of their own. A market was in full swing with women from outlying irrigated *shambas* selling vegetables and nomadic traders haggling noisily. The talk was of cattle and camels, interspersed with news from Marsabit and beyond to Moyale, on the frontier itself. Goats scrabbled about in the dust and disgruntled donkeys jostled for the sparse shade of a tree. Ben's father pulled up the car outside the district administrative offices.

"Right, this is where we've arranged to meet," he said,

getting out and stretching. Ben followed, enveloped by heat and dust.

"You must be the Hoopers," a voice called out. Beside a nearby Land Rover stood a stocky, powerfully built man of about thirty. A packet of Sportsman cigarettes stuck out of a pocket of his bush jacket. Pushing sunglasses up into sun-bleached hair, he extended a hand, the wrist encircled by a jumble of elephant-hair bracelets.

"Hi, I'm Rob West."

"Hallo, Mr West," said Ben in the grip of a muscular handshake.

"Well, I appreciate the respect, but there's no need for the formality. We're not at school now," he added smilingly, but rather unnecessarily. "So just Rob will do fine. And you're Ben I gather?"

"Yes, that's right," Ben nodded, feeling rather foolish.

"OK," intervened his Dad brightly. "So I'll leave you to get going. Keep him busy."

"There will be no problem there," was the quick response.

"And Ben, have fun too. I'm sure you will. If you need to get in touch, you can radio through." With a wave of his hand he headed back to his car. Starting up he swung the wheel and turned across the dusty road, scattering some bedraggled chickens led by a bright-eyed cockerel.

Ben followed Rob to the Land Rover. He slung his zip bag containing a few spare clothes and bits and pieces into the back and then levered himself into the front passenger seat.

"OK, all set; let's hit the road," said Rob. Weaving their way between tribesmen and free-roaming domestic animals, they slowly cleared the end of the dusty main street with its line of *dukas* selling blankets, rice, *posho*, cheap tin pans, paraffin and charcoal, *pangas* and other necessities of hard-lived life. They started to pick up speed, trailing an increasing cloud of dust. Ben glanced back, but there was nothing now to be seen. His eyes turned resolutely forward to the road ahead. He was heading north.

The corrugations in the road vibrated through the Land Rover. Anything which could move rattled and shook making the vehicle a kind of instrument of percussion. Dust permeated onto every surface, including foreheads and even eyelids. The sun relentlessly maintained the heat of a dry season afternoon. Rob swerved sharply to avoid a particularly large pothole.

"These bloody potholes," he complained loudly. "They fill partly with sand and you just don't know what lies beneath. Only last week, on this journey, some razor-sharp stones ripped a tyre to shreds. And let me tell you, man, the last thing you want to do is to have to change a wheel with the sun on your back, particularly when some bugger then drives past and covers you in dust just for good measure."

Ben nodded in agreement, not knowing quite what to say, and coming out only with a rather lame "Sure."

Rob gave him a quick sideways look before fixing his eyes on the road ahead, steering a course over the least bad corrugations and searching for the next potholes requiring avoiding action.

"I understand you've just left school. Where were you?"

"Duke of York."

"Good old, Duko. That's where I was, man, back in the fifties. It was great in those days, but I hear that now it's full of *kaffirs* and *bunyanis*."

Ben felt uncomfortable. He didn't want to sound too heavy or self-righteous, but he was instinctively defensive.

64

"Yeah, well of course it has changed, it had to, with the coming of independence, and particularly since then a lot of Africans and Indians have come in. But it's still a good school; it's done me well."

But Rob had not done yet. "And I hear that the name is changing to *Lenana* or some such crap."

"Yes, to be named after a famous Maasai chief; I think that he might have signed a treaty, or something, with the British."

Rob risked taking his eyes off the road for just long enough to give Ben a pitying look. "Well, I don't know about that, but it will probably be known more as 'banana' and the blokes who go there will be 'the banana bunch'." He laughed loudly at his own joke.

Ben stared straight ahead, saying nothing.

"So," he was asked after a reflective pause, "what's the plan for you?"

"I'm off later in the year to go to university in England, Bristol."

"To do what?"

"Study Law."

"Christ man, you must be some kind of brainbox. So you've done Highers."

Ben felt like saying "of course" but he restricted himself to "That's right." And then for some reason, which he immediately regretted, he found himself adding, "I did English, History and Latin."

There was an explosive noise from Rob. "Latin, fucking hell, I could barely pass my English for school cert; and then I was out of there, man; time to move on in the real world."

Ben hoped fervently that he would not be asked how he had done in Latin. Although proud of his A grade, it was distinctly not an occasion for any such revelation.

But Rob had not quite finished with the subject. "Anyway, what's the point of bloody Latin? It's a dead language. Far better do something practical. I trained as a mechanic." And he added proudly, "There's not much I can't do with a diesel engine, which is just as well for keeping a generator going in a game lodge."

Ben felt annoyed that he was being made to feel defensive again, but at the risk of being inflammatory he felt compelled to say more. "It taught me to think clearly," he said firmly. "A training of the mind, if you like. And I don't think that I really understood elements of English grammar until I did Latin, things like present and past participles, relatives and subjunctives."

Rob shot him a look of complete incomprehension. "I don't know what the hell you're really talking about, man."

The heavy heat in the Land Rover felt heavier still for a moment. Ben stared out of his window with apparent interest, but saw nothing. Rob sensed the need to try to get them off to a better start.

"What about sport at Duko?" he asked brightly.

"Yeah, it was great."

Not enough information. Rob wanted more.

"Did you make any of the teams?"

"Yup, firsts in rugby, hockey and cricket. And I also represented the school in athletics, sprinting and javelin."

Initial surprise was replaced by something akin to relief as Rob responded enthusiastically, "Good man, I'm glad you found time for all that too. I made the first fifteen in the fourth form, my last year. I was pretty chuffed about that and I got my colours too."

"Good on you. I was in for two years, but not until lower sixth and then upper sixth when I got my colours as well."

Rob risked taking one hand off the wheel. He slapped Ben's right shoulder, shouting with delight, "So you're a proper Kenya boy after all; you had me worried there for a while."

Well meant, but not well thought. Confused and frustrated Ben's mind reeled and railed. What is it with these Kenya cowboy types? No wonder the saying 'Kenya born, Kenya bred, strong in the arm and thick in the head'. Not regarded as an insult, but a badge of honour for God's sake. And yet beneath the surface of all that there are some really good blokes. Rob is probably one of them, he thought, by way of hopeful reassurance. At that moment the voice of the very man in question penetrated his consciousness.

"Just coming into Archer's Post."

A left turn took them on to a narrower, even rougher and dustier road, little more than a track. They were heading for the gate leading into the rugged, wild landscape of the Samburu Game Reserve, awe-inspiring in its magnificence.

"Do you know the Park?" asked Rob.

"Yes, a bit. I've been with my family on a couple of trips when we've camped in Buffalo Springs. And we've crossed the river into Samburu."

"Well, that's a good start. You're going to get to know it even better in the coming weeks."

They had passed through the gate and were heading into the heart of the forty square miles or so of the Reserve. Off to the left Ben saw lines of giant acacias and doum palms along the north bank of the Uaso Nyiro River, flowing lazily round great flat-topped rocks and through torpid dry season pools. Ahead and to the right odd hills of various shapes and sizes rose above the plains. One high humpback in particular, dominating the foreground, attracted his attention.

"That's Koitogor," said Rob. "It has an altitude, at its highest point, of something over four thousand feet. So that means it rises about a thousand feet above the surrounding plains. It's a useful landmark when you're out in the Park and there's a good track round it for game drives; we call it the Seven Mile Circuit."

Ben nodded. There was so much to see and take in. More and more animals and birds were coming into view. A flock of vulturine guinea fowl scattered before the advancing vehicle. Not far off, to the right, was a small herd of the tallest and most beautiful of the zebras; Grévy's zebra, so smart in their very narrow and close-set black stripes on a white ground above round, creamy bellies.

"Pretty natty," laughed Rob, following the direction of Ben's eyes. "Looks as if they're wearing pinstripe suits."

"A lot smarter than the common zebra," agreed Ben.

"There's the airstrip," pointed out Rob. "You may be asked to drive out here from time to time to pick up people who have flown in."

Beyond where he was indicating stood three giraffe, looking watchfully in their direction. Handsomely different from giraffe found elsewhere in Kenya, these were reticulated giraffe, liver-red in colour marked with a network of white lines.

"Good to see some of the less common animals," remarked Ben.

"You're too right man; welcome to the NFD. All these beauties and beisa oryx, blue-necked Somali ostrich, gerenuk, two species of hyena, crocodile in the river, more birds than I can count; I could go on and on."

"And big game as well," said Ben confidently, wanting to make it clear that he was no Nairobi city boy; he had been brought up not far to the south.

"Yup, lion, cheetah, some leopard, though you'll be lucky to see them, buffalo, elephant in numbers, particularly near the river, and some black rhino."

"And how's the rhino doing?" asked Ben showing his knowledge that this was becoming an issue.

Rob sighed and furrowed his brows. "I'm afraid that poaching is an increasing problem. The Game Department can barely keep up with it. They need more rangers who are better prepared and better armed, more patrols, more resources, more everything; but, of course, no prizes for guessing, this all needs more bloody money, man." Slapping his hands on the steering wheel, he added, his voice getting louder, "They're sending out men armed with clapped-out old Lee-Enfields to take on blokes with AK-47s for God's sake."

"Where the hell do the poachers get AK-47s?"

"Well, I can tell you that the Somali *Shifta* seem to have a ready supply of them and others coming into poaching are now getting them too. There's big money behind this, make no mistake."

"So the poachers are getting rich?"

"Christ no, they're paid what seems a lot to them, particularly when times are hard and they need to feed their families; but very little really. The people who are creaming it are the fat bastards behind it all and fucking Arabs and Chinks for their dagger handles and medicine, or some such bullshit."

"Ground-up horn is used as an aphrodisiac, isn't it?"

"So they think. It's just keratin, the same stuff that makes up hair and fingernails for fuck's sake. So why don't they just bite their bloody nails, if that's what's needed to turn them on? I tell you, they're going to do for the poor old rhino."

Ben was shocked into silence for a moment before asking

"How bad do you think it's going to get?"

"Put it this way, I reckon that in the not too distant future there will be no rhino in Samburu, or perhaps anywhere much else for that matter."

They were getting closer to the river.

"Anyway," said Rob, his voice changing to sound determinedly more cheerful, "this is still a fantastic place; really, really special, man. I always feel lucky to be here and I reckon it will be the same for you."

A left turn took them down a little spur road and the entrance to the Lodge came into view. Ben leant forward, looking ahead intently.

"There's the office and manager's house," said Rob pointing to the left. In front of them stood the Lodge itself, on a thickly wooded broad bend of the river. Stretching away from the main building the rooms in thatched chalets fronted onto the river itself; no fences, just uninterrupted views.

"Great location," said Ben approvingly.

"Sure is; built on the campsite of one of the most famous of the old time elephant hunters, Arthur Newmann. Not hard to see why he chose it."

Ben had been allocated one of the end rooms. He grabbed his bag and made ready to find his way there.

"Should be nice and quiet," said Rob, adding with a grin, "except for the sounds of animals of course."

"Suits me."

"Just as well. Go and dump your things, settle in, have a look round and then we can meet up for a cold beer before dinner. I'm shacked up in the manager's house while he's away."

As the sun at last began to relinquish its grip on the day, leaving its legacy of warm, balmy early evening air, Ben made his way towards the manager's house. Lights were coming on. Muffled sounds and voices competed with the beginnings of the noises of an African night. Ben found Rob sitting outside the living room fronting on to an area of mown grass. Two cold bottles of Tusker were slowly perspiring on a low table beside him.

"Good man; come and pull up a chair. We don't want the beer to get warm."

As Ben settled down Rob reached under his chair and produced a bowl containing assorted scraps of food. "They will be waiting for their meal," he said, obviously enjoying the surprised look on Ben's face. "And we really mustn't keep them waiting any longer."

Getting up, and walking over to the centre of the grass, he put down the bowl and then made his way back to his seat, a forefinger held to his lips.

They sat in silence, but for moments only. A rustling in the nearby bushes heralded the arrival of the dinner guests. Whiskery noses started to appear, twitching, sensing the air. And out came a dozen or so small, short-tailed reddish brown animals, a foot or so long, bright eyes set below neat ears.

"Mongooses," said Ben, taking in the scene unfolding before him.

"Yup, dwarf mongooses to be precise. They've taken up residence here, attracted no doubt by free meals."

The food was consumed with much jostling, shoving and darting about; quick, nimble, deft movement. Play became more vigorous, acrobatic but at times rough. They tumbled over one another, rolling and kicking, nipping tails and ears. And then, almost as quickly as they had come, they were gone, swallowed up by the surrounding bush in the gathering darkness. The show was over.

"Quite a performance," said Ben approvingly.

"Yeah, they're great little animals. I really like watching them. They live in these small packs, very gregarious, very loyal, although their play can get pretty rough. I've seen some nasty injuries; one of the pack nearly had his paw bitten off. And yet they're really kind of forgiving; whatever happens they still hang together and look out for one another. You have to admire them."

"And there are other kinds in the Park, I imagine."

"Hell yes. Large grey, black-tipped, white-tailed, banded. If ever you're lucky enough to see any of them out in the bush, give them some time; it'll be well worth it. The tourists are all fired up about seeing the Big Five, but I tell you some of the smaller animals really deserve interest. One of the greatest shows is seeing a band of mongooses take on a snake, no matter how big or poisonous. They can dance round, running rings round it, and pinch its eggs one by one. Bloody brave and bloody clever."

With more beer Rob waxed on through the evening, ever more lyrical, but informative and clearly passionate about the magic of this wilderness. Ben listened and absorbed, already beginning to feel that magic take hold. Later, in bed at last, he lay very still as tiredness crept up on exhilaration and thoughts merged into dreams.

Knock, knock, softly at first. Knock, knock again, slightly louder.

Ben tumbled and stumbled his way out of bed.

"*Hodi, Bwana, chai.*"

The door opened to reveal a young man bearing a tea tray, smiling brightly.

"*Asante sana.*" Ben looked at his watch. Just after five thirty, still dark and quite cold too. Rob had arranged for him to go on an early morning game drive to familiarise himself more with the Park. It was also, he had been promised, a Samburu experience not to be missed. A small touring party in a VW Kombi was going out that morning with their driver, but they had not booked to take a ranger with them, Rob thought unwisely. Anyway, there was going to be space up front for Ben. He had been exhorted by Rob to keep an eye on them, not to let them lean out too far from the hatch in the roof if they were near anything dangerous and, importantly, not to make too much of a bloody racket. With these instructions firmly in mind Ben finished dressing, pulling on his one warm sweater. Binoculars in place round his neck; he was ready to go.

The driver was already waiting by the vehicle and eyed Ben slightly suspiciously. They exchanged words in a mixture of Swahili and English. It quickly became clear to Ben that the man was far from being just a driver; he was also an experienced guide who knew the park well; probably why he felt able to go out without a ranger. Ben, for his part, wanted to make it clear that he knew a thing or two, but that he was not going to lord it in any way or be an interfering *mzungu*. He wanted to help; to work with him. He was pleased to think that he had got his message across.

"*Mzuri sana*," said the driver with a smile devoid of front teeth as he climbed into the driver's seat. The party had shambled into view, two German couples, one middle aged, one younger, and an older American with his slightly younger wife. Brief introductions revealed to Ben that the Germans spoke little English, with the exception of the younger man. The American woman had little to say, which was more than made up for by her husband. Everyone safely on board, Ben took his place up front. They were off.

As they headed away from the Lodge and around Koitogor

darkness was in gradual retreat. Rays of the early morning sun began shafting in above the eastern horizon, softly illuminating the wild landscape which shimmered and quivered into view. No one knew what would unfold on that great stage, that day or any day. The script was infinitely variable.

It was something which Ben wished that the American could understand. Showing little interest in the zebra, giraffe and impala they passed by, or even in a pair of gerenuk standing elegantly on their hind legs to reach foliage, he seemingly had only one thing in mind.

"We want to see lion. Yesterday we saw elephant and buffalo. Today it needs to be lion."

Ben just nodded, trying politely to avoid showing any sign of irritation. Such lack of understanding. This was no managed safari park with everything on permanent view, to be laid on when requested. This was the real thing for God's sake, at its very best.

The driver had seemingly picked up on his thoughts and was grinning.

"*Simba?*" enquired Ben, raising his eyebrows.

"*Baadaye kidogo.*"

A little later, well perhaps, thought Ben, hoping very much so. They might never hear the end of it otherwise. But any such thought was banished in an instant as his attention was drawn to a rocky outcrop. There perched high in all his magnificence the giant among eagles, a martial eagle, was scanning the plain from his vantage point, alert for guinea fowl or even a small antelope, a dik-dik perhaps.

The vehicle stopped. Binoculars were handed round and cameras readied for action.

"It's a bit far off," said the American adjusting his longest telephoto lens.

The young German looked rather smug as he removed from a case an even longer lens.

Pictures taken they moved on. The light was brighter, sharper now and the delicious coolness of the early morning was fast receding. Sweaters and coats were peeled off amidst a murmur of conversation. Silence again as all eyes looked out in eager anticipation.

"*Kifaru*," muttered the driver.

At first Ben could see nothing. Then he detected a shape of something, far off to the left, at the foot of a small hill. He trained his binoculars in that direction.

"Absolutely blooming right. Rhino."

Excitement rose in the back. "Where? Where? I can't see anything." And words to similar effect in German.

The American now had his binoculars to his eyes.

"Got it, got it!" he suddenly exclaimed. "Can we get closer?"

The driver had already turned off the dusty track and was carefully weaving between bushes over rough ground.

"Everyone sit down," commanded Ben. "This will be a pretty bumpy ride."

"I didn't see the driver using binoculars," said the American.

"No," was Ben's simple answer.

"But he could see the rhino when you spotted it through your binoculars."

"He'd actually seen it further back, I think."

"Goddam it, how was that possible?"

The driver was grinning as he deftly manoeuvred round rocks and small thorn trees.

"Difficult to explain," said Ben. "But I reckon it's something to do with being completely attuned to the landscape."

He was not sure that the driver understood, but he was nodding happily. He then said something in Swahili.

"Right," said Ben. "This is about as far as we can get. There's a sandy gully ahead which could only be attempted with four-wheel drive. But you've got a half-decent view at least from here."

The rhino was still some way off but had become aware of their approach, head turned scenting the air, eyes peering myopically beneath twitching ears. A great horn thrust upwards above the prehensile upper lip, for all its magnificence a potential death sentence. Cameras clicked amidst whispered words of wonderment.

"*Toto*," said the driver suddenly.

There was movement in the bush just beyond the rhino.

"Yes, yes," said Ben, struggling to keep his voice down as the baby rhino emerged.

There was just time for one good look before the mother put herself firmly between the line of sight and the baby, shielding it from view. With a sudden shake of her head she turned abruptly and crashed her two and a half tons away through the bush, shepherding the baby with her. The dust settled, the noise subsided and they were gone.

As they made their way back to the track Ben's mind reverted to the conversation with Rob the day before. Something has to be done to save these stupendous animals; his mind whirled; must, must, must be done.

An American voice cut into his thoughts.

"Now for lions."

Fortunately the driver had done his homework. The previous evening he had spoken to some rangers who had found a pride of lions with a kill a few miles from the Lodge, near the river.

Having rounded Koitogor they headed in that direction. After a few false starts, up and down tracks leading to the river, they spotted a zebra-striped VW van and a Land Rover parked on the edge of a large acacia thicket. A sure sign of something of interest and indeed they had been beaten to it. They crept closer and stopped a little way off from the other vehicles, being careful not to obstruct their view. And what a view; a large male lion and several lionesses stretched out, warming full bellies in the early morning sun. The remains of a zebra were being chewed intermittently by a few half-grown cubs. But they too had had their fill. Their main agenda was play. One ran off with the remains of a leg, two others in pursuit. Over they rolled, jumping and cuffing, stalking and biting; training for the seriousness of a later life. Mothers looked on indulgently; the father maintained aloof disinterest.

There was some jostling for space in the open roof hatch. A battery of cameras was brought into action. The American clicked and clicked away. Was he, wondered Ben, going to see anything other than through his viewfinder? Then suddenly he appeared to have had enough. Sitting down he consulted his guide book. Another animal ticked off in the pursuit of check-list tourism. But Ben didn't despair because his attention was drawn to the American's wife, a quiet, appreciative observer of the scene, serene and happy.

The excitement of the Germans was becoming rather too noisy. The male lion stood up, stretched and looked balefully in their direction. He took a few steps towards them.

"Right," said Ben quietly, but insistently. "Down now please and close the hatch."

Shortly after the other vehicles began a slow retreat and they followed. Back at the Lodge the Germans were first out, nodding and smiling,

"Good," said one of the men, taking advantage of a similarity in language.

The American grunted, Ben hoped in satisfaction. His wife, who had said very little, paused before following her husband and half turned towards Ben.

"Could there be a better start to the day? To any day?"

"No; no probably not," said Ben overcoming his initial surprise.

Pondering such thought he headed hungrily for the dining room. It was nearly nine o'clock. Eggs, bacon, a stack of toast and a cup of hot coffee. Breakfast had never tasted so good.

A little later Ben headed for the office. It was time to report for duty.

"Ah, there you," said Rob. "Hope you had a good tour."

"Yeah, really great."

"Good man; now for some work. I shall ask you to help out from time to time in the office here, general admin, dealing with booking sheets, typing menus, boring stuff I'm afraid. But you will also be out and about, checking the bar daily, overseeing the laundry, issuing supplies and generally keeping an eye on things; most importantly making sure that the visitors are happy."

"Sure. Where shall I start?"

"You need to meet the two main guys you'll be dealing with, Solomon, the bar man, and Jonathan who runs the laundry and oversees housekeeping. Jonathan is an easy-going old bloke, a Luo, rather a long way from home in Nyanza Province who has ended up here by some means. Solomon is a different kettle of fish." He have a hollow laugh. "Yes man, a Kikuyu; smart, sassy, fluent English, good at his job although I'm sure he's on the fiddle from time to time. I haven't been able to figure it out; good luck if you can. Typical bloody *Kuke*, he thinks that he's cleverer than me," he added hotly.

Ben thought it better to say nothing.

"And another thing to mention, he doesn't like white Kenyans like us talking to him in Swahili. He thinks that it smacks of neo-colonialism, or some such crap."

They set off, first to the bar. Solomon looked up from polishing glasses without much apparent interest as Ben was introduced. They chatted briefly about the tasks to be performed, morning stock checks, collecting up slips recording drinks signed for and counting cash. Ostensibly civil enough, but a thinly disguised air of insolence made Ben feel slightly uncomfortable, although all the more determined to make things work between them.

Jonathan was a different proposition altogether. The Hoopers had long employed a Luo house boy, Okumu, who had played a special part in Ben's life when he was growing up. He had frequently looked after Ben and looked out for him in a variety of ways. Not content with speaking only Swahili, he had taught Ben some Luo which had enabled Ben to play with Okumu's son, rather to the disapproval of Ben's grandmother.

They found Jonathan coming out of the laundry.

"*Amosi?*" enquired Ben.

"*Ber ahinya,*" was the astonished reply.

Rob looked somewhat surprised. The old man though laughed delightedly as he grasped and shook Ben's hand.

Reverting to Swahili, Ben asked for his Luo name.

"Ochieng," came the answer.

"Mine is Omollo."

There couldn't have been a more pleased reaction. Various people were called out from the laundry. Explanations resulted in much clapping, laughing and even some chanting.

Ben still had no idea why he was called Omollo. Africans had a knack of naming people in subtle ways which reflected their true character. Such names were readily understood whilst being beyond actual explanation.

"I think I can leave you safely to it," said Rob.

Ben was confidently under way. He already felt at home.

GIFTS

The most worthwhile gifts are those made precious by the giver

Ovid
Heroides XV11

"Who's that?" asked Ben sitting at the bar one evening with Rob. He indicated in the direction of a forty-something woman, tallish, slim, with short-cropped dark hair. She had just left the dining room and was heading off to her room. "An American, her name's Annie Meyer. She came in this morning and she's going to be here for longer than the usual visit; booked in for a whole week."

"So, not part of a tour?"

"No, she's doing her own thing. I believe her husband died not so long ago, brain tumour, and she's getting away from it all by doing some wildlife photography."

"Is she a professional photographer?"

"No, I don't think so, but she told me she's hoping to use the pictures for a book."

"Huh, good for her."

"She must have got some dosh. She's hired a four-wheel-drive Toyota with a driver."

"Well, I suppose she'd have to; she couldn't do what she's doing on her own."

"Anyway, what's the great interest? She's attractive, I know, but too old for you man."

81

Rob shook his head and laughed. "No way. Normally I would have fancied my chances though. But it's probably not the right time and actually I'm not sure she's my type."

Ben nodded while privately wondering whether Rob was her type.

The next day began at least with the usual routine. After breakfast Ben checked the bar under the sullen and watchful gaze of Solomon. All appeared to be in order. The reconciliation complete, the mood improved as Ben unlocked the store for further supplies to be brought out. Locking up again he helped move some crates and bottles and Solomon then began the process of re-stocking fridges and shelves. It was time to leave him to get on. Solomon smiled for the first time as he once again became master of his own domain.

Arriving at the laundry Ben had a very different reception. Jonathan always seemed genuinely pleased to see him and there were the usual exuberant greetings. The cheerfulness of the atmosphere helped mitigate the tediousness of the tasks in hand. Sheets and towels were checked in and out. The housekeeping staff set off to prepare rooms for the next influx. Fresh supplies of cleaning materials were issued for such purpose, in some instances in rather surprising quantities; something to keep an eye on. New supplies had just arrived on a truck and had to be unpacked.

Later, after lunch, was the quiet period. Guests had disappeared back to their rooms, waiting until the strength sapping heat of the mid-afternoon gave way to lengthening shadows, heralding the time for the spectacle of early evening game drives. In the meantime there was opportunity for relaxation and Ben was off duty. He made his way to the small swimming pool set back to one side of the buildings. There was only one person there, a woman in a black bikini lying on a sunbed reading a book. She looked up as he approached, smiled and nodded by way of acknowledgment. It was Annie Meyer. Ben smiled back, raising a hand in greeting. He then pulled up a sunbed at what he judged to be a respectful distance and settled down to read his book.

A short while later he became aware of movement. Looking up he saw suntan oil being applied to long, smooth brown legs and his eyes lingered. His gaze did not go unnoticed.

"Hi," she said, "you work here?"

"Yes." Slightly embarrassed. "That's right."

"Well, of course, I reckoned as much; I noticed you checking the bar this morning."

"Yup, part of my duties. I'm here temporarily helping out the manager."

"Great place to be."

"I know; I'm lucky to be here."

His eyes returned briefly to his book.

"Sorry to disturb you, but can you tell me what kind of birds those are?" She had finished oiling her legs and was sitting up looking across the pool. There pecking about on the ground were a few plump, short-tailed birds, in the sunlight brilliant metallic blue bodies separated by white bands from glossy chestnut bellies.

"Superb starlings," said Ben sitting up himself and squinting into the glare.

"I thought that they must be some kind of a starling. Hey, why don't you come over and join me? Pull across your chair."

Ben was quick to do so, although striving to maintain a nonchalant air.

"Hi, I'm Annie. Good to meet you."

"Thanks, good to meet you too. I'm Ben."

"So Ben, what do you do when you're not helping out here?"

"I've just left school and I'm biding my time, waiting to go to university in England, in October."

"Why, that's great; so you're off to college. What are you going to study?"

"Law."

"Impressive. Where will you be?"

"Bristol."

"Is that where you're from?"

"No, no I'm a Kenyan, born and brought up here. My family farm's not far away to the south, in Laikipia, and I went to school just outside Nairobi. I've only been to England once on a visit when I was quite young."

"Sorry," said Annie showing increasing interest. "I assumed that you were English, but I guess that some Kenyans are white."

"Yes, well," replied Ben feeling some strange confusion. "I do have English ancestry, although my mother was born in Kenya too; because of that I have Kenyan citizenship which is why I'm able to work here."

"Interesting," murmured Annie. "So going off to England is going to be quite a major departure for you."

"Suppose so," said Ben reflectively with a slight frown.

Annie noticed the book that Ben was clutching.

"What are you reading?"

"Oh," said Ben, his mind switching back to the present, "John Steinbeck, *The Pearl*."

"Great choice. Wonderful author. I'm particularly proud of him, as a fellow American of course. What got you reading him?"

"I studied him at school. English was one of my subjects for

Higher School Certificate, which is the equivalent of English A levels, if you've heard of them. One of the set books was *The Grapes of Wrath*; made a big impression on me, so I've gone on to read other Steinbeck books."

"So you should too; don't miss *Of Mice and Men* if you haven't gotten to it yet. But I'm interested that you were studying an American author. Were these Kenyan exams you were doing?"

"No, they were English actually, Cambridge Overseas, set and marked in England."

"OK, even more interesting. I know something about all this because I've been a teacher, of English and Drama, and for some of my studies I went to England. Then, at least, English literature in schools tended to be English authors."

"It was the same here, actually, until a new course was introduced for my year, called Literature in English, rather than English Literature. We still did English authors, but it meant that some works by non-English authors were also included, translated into English where necessary."

Ben felt this was all getting rather heavy, but there was no let-up because Annie was showing ever more interest.

"So, what were your set books, apart from the Steinbeck?"

"Some standard Shakespeare, of course, *Henry The Fourth Part One*. Thomas Hardy, *The Mayor of Casterbridge*. And then, for the non-English authors, we had another American, Arthur Miller."

"Which of his works?" Annie immediately interjected, without waiting to be told.

"*The Crucible*."

"Had to be. And?"

"Sorry, and what?"

"The other non-English authors."

"Oh yes, sorry. Russians, Dostoevsky, *Poor Folk* and Gogol, *Dead Souls*."

"Wow, impressive."

"And finally, an Irish work, *Juno and the Paycock* by Sean O'Casey."

"That was quite a heady mix; but nothing Welsh, no Dylan Thomas?"

"No, not as a set book, but our English teacher did a play-reading with us of *Under Milk Wood*; a great favourite of his he told us."

"Mine too," said Annie with an intensity which Ben found disconcerting. She removed her sunglasses and looked at him searchingly. "What did you think of it?"

"Well, I did enjoy it," he said choosing his words carefully, "but not all the parts were well read and there was a bit of larking about with odd accents."

"Which part did you read?"

"Um…" he struggled to recall. "Second Voice, I think it was, and a few minor parts. There was quite a lot of doubling up."

"Who did First Voice?"

"The teacher."

"So he kept the best part for himself." She gave a low laugh. "Why wouldn't he? Sure I would have done too. It's so special and not to be messed up."

Ben was slightly taken aback by the degree of her enthusiasm and unsure what to say. But he didn't need to bother. Annie was still in full swing, eyes shining.

"You know, we're really fortunate to have *Under Milk Wood*. Your teacher probably told you that Dylan Thomas died young, just after his thirty-ninth birthday, in New York actually where I come from. And he only just completed it within a month of his death, though he had worked on it intermittently for nearly ten years for God's sake." She sighed. "A masterpiece, even though he had no time for any final revision of the text."

The afternoon sun was now at its most relentless and the starlings, wide-beaked stretched their wings in the shimmering haze. Ben had removed his shirt during the mini-lecture.

"Great shape," said Annie suddenly noticing, looking him up and down with approval. "Do you work out?"

"No, not as such," said Ben a trifle embarrassed, but he had to admit to himself also rather flattered. "It wasn't all reading at school. Sport was a big thing and I did a lot of it."

"Yeah, I can see that." But she hadn't quite yet dismounted from her hobby horse. She had something else to add.

"Have you ever heard the BBC recording of *Under Milk Wood*, the all-Welsh cast with Richard Burton as First Voice?"

Ben shook his head.

"It's absolutely great because it does the work full justice. I think you'd really like it."

"Well, I'll look out for it and try to listen to it sometime," said Ben rather non-committedly.

"Hey, we can do better than that. I have a tape of it and I'd love to play it to you; if, of course, you'd like to hear it," she added seeing the rather surprised look on Ben's face.

"You have it with you?"

"Sure, I often listen to it."

"OK, thanks," he said ambiguously, keeping his options open.

They resumed reading their respective books for a while until Ben looked at his watch. It was time for him to get ready to go back on duty and he pulled on his shirt.

"I must get going."

"It's been great to meet you. I've really enjoyed our chat."

"Me too."

"Hopefully we can catch up with one another again. I'm here until the end of the week."

"OK, good."

"And remember my offer," she said smiling encouragingly.

"Yes, of course, thanks again."

He felt sure that she was watching him as he walked off in the direction of the office. His head was spinning rather, confused thoughts swirling round. What to make of the encounter? Surprised, wary to a degree, but excited too in some way which was unclear to him. And so, what to do, what to do indeed?

He didn't see Annie again that day, probably because he had dinner with Rob in the manager's house. The following day he saw her briefly in passing when he was busy with a group of visitors. There was simply time for them to exchange smiles. He hoped that she didn't think that he was trying to avoid her. There was no question of this the next day. After dinner Annie was sitting at a table a little way from the bar when Ben came in to have a word with Rob who was perched on a stool talking to Solomon. Annie raised a hand in greeting, but Ben didn't see her at first.

"The lady wants you," said Solomon ambiguously, with a salacious smirk.

Ben turned round in surprise.

"Oh, hi," and he dithered for a moment in a state of uncertainty, glancing from Annie back towards Rob.

"I can wait, you go ahead," said Rob, eyebrows somewhat raised.

Aware that he was being watched Ben walked over to where

Annie was sitting.

"Sorry if I'm interrupting, but I was hoping to catch up with you."

"No, that's fine."

"Great, do join me."

Ben pulled up a chair. They chatted for a while and then Annie glanced at her watch.

"It's still quite early. Would you like to listen to *Under Milk Wood*?"

Ben hesitated for a moment.

"Hey, sorry, only if you'd like to. You may have other things to do."

"No, no, not at all. I would like to."

"Well great, let's go then."

They got up to go and he followed her out, eyes still watching.

In her room, hastily and with murmured apologies, she tidied away scattered clothes, books and camera equipment. Two chairs were drawn up to a low table on which she placed a tape recorder. The tape was already on the reels and simply had to be re-wound.

"OK ,OK, we're all set." She was really up for this. "But first let me get you a Scotch. I have my own stash here."

"Um," more hesitation on the part of Ben.

"Oh God, sorry, I'm being pushy. I'm so excited to be playing this to you. But you probably don't drink Scotch. I do when I'm listening to it; somehow makes it sound even better, if that's possible."

"OK I'll join you; just a small one, thanks."

Two glasses and a bottle were brought out. She poured a small measure for Ben and a larger one for herself.

"Cheers, here we go." Glasses were raised and the play

button pushed.

Softly, smoothly, rhythmically the voice of Richard Burton filtered into the room and seeped into the consciousness, every word and every letter.

To begin at the beginning:

It is spring, moonless night in the small town, starless and bible-black, the cobblestreets silent and the hunched, courters'-and-rabbits' wood limping invisible down to the sloeblack, slow, black, crowblack, fishingboat-bobbing sea... And all the people of the lulled and dumfound town are sleeping now...

Just as the Second Voice took over Annie leant forward and stopped the tape. Partly re-winding she was set to listen again to certain passages.

It is to-night in Donkey Street, trotting silent with seaweed on its hooves, along the cockled cobbles... It is night neddying among the snuggeries of babies... going through the grave-yard of Bethesda with winds gloved and folded, and dew doffed; tumbling by the Sailors Arms.

"I tell you," she sighed, "it just damn well gets better every time you hear it; the words become music." Dreamily she poured some more whisky into her glass and, without asking, into Ben's too.

The tape started again and rolled on accompanied by the background night chorus of the Uaso Nyiro River filtering into the room.

Captain Cat, the retired blind sea-captain, asleep in his bunk in the seashelled, ship-in-bottled, shipshape best cabin of Schooner House dreamed of his long drowned shipmates, sucked down salt deep into the Davy dark. He moaned for his dead dears. In his dreams Mr Edwards, the draper, mad with love for Miss Price, dressmaker and sweetshop-keeper, scooped low over her lonely loving hotwaterbottled body. With the coming of the day, as with every day, they wrote letters of love and desire to one another, safe in the knowledge that they would for ever be happily apart on the separate islands of their contentment. Willy Nilly postman's wife whimpered at his side, begging teacher not to spank her, but every night of her married life she was late for school. The town was rising and raising its blinds. Frying pans began to spit, kettles and cats purred in the kitchen. The Reverend Eli Jenkins delivered his sermon to the dawn and then closed his front door.

And on and on, in that room in wild Africa, a day unfolded, far away, in a small Welsh town by the sea at the foot of Llaregyb Hill. The words swirled with the whisky. A coven of kettles hissed hot on Mrs Willy Nilly's range, always ready to steam open the mail. And there was hissing too, in the School House, in the prussic circle of caldrons in the mind's eye of Mr Pugh, cooking up a fricassee of deadly night-shade, nicotine, hot frog, cyanide and bat-spit for his needling, stalactite hag and bednag of a pokerbacked nutcracker wife. In contrast Dai Bread, the baker, dallied happily between Mrs Dai Bread One and Mrs Dai Bread Two, the one for the day and the other for the night. Captain Cat called hullo to Polly Garter; a cock crowed; too late, cock, too late he murmured. So the morning progressed into a sunny slow lulling afternoon which yawned and mooned through the dozy town. Captain Cat was dreaming again of his dead dear, Rosie Probert, seeing his name on her belly as he shipwrecked in her thighs. Polly Garter and children sang. Cherry Owen finished downing seventeen pints of flat, warm thin, Welsh bitter beer. The ship's clock in the bar of the Sailors Arms said half past eleven. Half past eleven is opening time. The hands of the clock have stayed still at half past eleven for fifty years. It is always opening time in the Sailors Arms. The day was drawing to a close. Organ Morgan made his way to the chapel to play the organ. Johann Sebastian, mighty Bach; oh, Bach fach. And as the music faded the thin night darkened. Suddenly the wind-shaken wood sprung awake for the second dark time that one spring day.

Click and the tape stopped. It was late, very late by now. Ben was floating happily in a sea of intoxication.

Annie leant forward and clasped his hands, her face glistening and shimmering in the pale light of the room.

"I'm so glad that I was able to share that with you. If you enjoyed it even a fraction of the amount I did, then it was so worth it."

Ben stood up, slightly unsteadily.

"I really did get into it; mind-blowing."

Without another word, and much to Ben's surprise, he was suddenly enveloped in Annie's arms. She hugged him close and he could feel the contours of her body.

"Sorry," she said, breaking quickly away, sensing his uncertainty. "I didn't meant to embarrass you. I got a bit carried away. It's been such a fabulous evening."

"No, it's fine, fine," stammered Ben. "I really enjoyed it too. But I must get going; work tomorrow."

"Of course, good night and sweet dreams. I'll see you around."

"Sure, good night to you too, and thanks again."

Slightly unsteadily Ben made his way to his room, barely noticing the blaze of countless stars, dazzlingly brilliant against the bitumen-black backcloth of the African night. Tumbling into bed he was lulled into sleep by echoes in his mind of the sweet voice of Polly Garter, singing a lament to her one and only true love who downed and died.

O Tom Dick and Harry were three fine men
And I'll never have such loving again
But little Willy Wee who took me on his knee
Little Willy Weazel is the man for me.

The song faded and he dreamed the dreams of blind Captain Cat, tossing on the jolly rogered sea.

"Late night?" enquired Rob, with a smirk.

"Yes, but not what you might think," replied Ben rather hotly. "You wouldn't understand."

"Try me."

"I was with Annie Meyer."

"I know, I saw you sloping off with her to her room, you sly bastard."

"Yes, but we just listened to *Under Milk Wood*."

"You did what?"

"Listened to *Under Milk Wood*, you know by Dylan Thomas."

"No, I don't know. You're right, I don't understand. I don't even know what the fuck you're talking about man. Sometimes I think that you're from another planet."

Duties resumed and another day passed. Ben did his best to concentrate on his job, but disconcertingly Annie was never far from his thoughts. He saw her around, but not to talk to until after lunch, the following day, when she loomed into view.

"Hi," she said, smiling engagingly, "you've been busy, I know, but it's good to see you."

"You too, how's things?"

"Well OK, until just now." She frowned. "My driver has just announced that he can't take me out on a game drive this afternoon. He muttered something about *mgonjwa*."

"Oh, that means ill. Does he look unwell?"

"He's certainly looking a bit sorry for himself and has blood-shot eyes."

"Probably too much *miraa* chewing."

"What?"

"*Miraa*, also known as *Khat*, which you might have heard of. The Somalis are really into it and it's grown in the Nyambeni Hills, not so far from here. I've seen your driver hanging around with a Somali guy near the staff quarters and they've probably been chewing away together."

"Yeah, I have heard of *Khat*. But isn't it some kind of stimulant?"

Ben smiled, remembering a Somali who had worked for a time on the farm.

"That's how it starts, for sure; can make a guy really pumped up. But then they don't sleep too well and often become pretty lethargic. Oh yes, and also suffer from loss of concentration."

"If that's the state he's in, then he probably shouldn't be driving."

"Hell no, not a good idea at all."

"It's so frustrating. I'm getting short of time. I only have one full day, after today, and I still haven't gotten all the elephant pictures I want."

Ben thought for a moment. "I could drive you."

"Really?"

"No reason why not. I passed my test over a year ago now, but I've actually been driving for years on the farm."

Annie's face lit up and she patted him on the arm. "I'd be really grateful."

"OK then, I could be ready by four thirty, so we could go out

94

for a good couple of hours."

"So, so looking forward to it."

"I know where your vehicle's parked, and I'll see you there."

They parted in a state of mutual anticipation.

Shortly after the appointed time Ben turned right onto the dusty road leading away from the Lodge, running parallel to the river. Annie, sitting beside him, was happily busy readying her camera equipment for action.

"Photography has become quite a passion of mine. I'll get back to teaching sometime, I know, but before then I'd really like to have a go at putting together some wildlife pictures in some format; if only I can get good enough ones of course."

Ben carefully avoided a flock of yellow-throated francolin, fluttering in the dirt.

"Sounds like quite a project."

"I've got some pretty good shots, particularly of the big cats from when I was down in The Mara. One, I'm thrilled with, is of a cheetah with three cubs. I had a print of it done when I was passing through Nairobi and I can show it to you if you'd like."

"My favourite animal, I reckon; so I'd love to see it."

"Good, that's a must then. But I'm still a bit short of good elephant pictures, so I'm really grateful to you for taking this time out with me."

"I'm happy to help. You probably noticed I didn't need much persuading." He glanced towards her and their eyes met briefly before he turned his attention back to the rigours of the road.

There was a thoughtful pause in the conversation before, looking out of the window towards the foot of Koitogor, Annie spotted movement in the vicinity of a small flat-topped acacia. Rob saw where she was looking.

"Gerenuk, two of them."

"Ah yes, so elegant with those long necks."

"Yup, the Africans call them *swala twiga* which means giraffe gazelle."

"Very appropriate. I've got some shots of them, but from rather a long way off."

"Yeah, they're very timid. If you try to get too close, they scarper."

"They stand up on their hind legs sometimes, don't they, to reach the acacia leaves?"

"That's right, and if there are two or more of them doing it at the same time, particularly with a small tree like that one, it looks for all the world as if they're sitting round a table."

"Wow, how I'd like a shot of that."

"Well, let's give it a try. We've got time before looking for elephants. I'll turn off the road and drive to the far side of where they are. We'll have to give them quite a wide berth and even then they're likely to retreat into that nearby thicket. But we can just wait quietly and hope for the best."

"Sounds like a plan, I'm up for it."

Twenty minutes later and quiet patience brought its reward.

"That was a great suggestion," said Annie. "Now let's see if we can get lucky with elephants."

They headed back to the road and followed it for a while towards the airstrip. Ben was looking out for the various tracks leading to the river.

"Let's try this one," he said, swinging the wheel to the right.

Ahead of them they could see the trees on the north bank. Slowly negotiating their way round ruts and rocks, they reached denser bush and acacia trees. Then in a small clearing among doum palms they stopped on a rocky ledge just above the river bank. The water in pools and small streams looked particularly sluggish in the softening light of the still, dry-season late afternoon. Ben switched off the engine and reached for his binoculars.

"Right, what have we got here?" He scanned up and down the river banks.

Large numbers of sandgrouse and doves were drinking gratefully, taking advantage of water which was becoming increasingly scarce. Directly opposite them a tiny pygmy falcon perched high in an acacia tree surveying the scene. Below and to one side two crocodiles lay completely motionless on a large flat rock, absorbing the last warmth of the day. But no elephants.

"What do you reckon?" asked Annie.

"Well, it's probably worth waiting a bit. I've heard from the rangers that quite a lot of elephants have been seen in this area. And this is the sort of time for their evening drink and bathe."

Minutes passed. Some bushbuck appeared, treading carefully and scenting the air before daring to drink.

"OK," said Ben after a while. "I think we should give it a go a bit further along."

"Agreed," said Annie. "I'm a bit concerned about time before the light fades."

Back to the road they went and along to the next track, carefully threading their way down to the river. Still no luck, no elephants at least. But repeating the process once more perseverance finally paid off. As the river came into view there, on the far bank, some way off to the left, a dozen or so elephants were making their way to the water's edge; a matriarch and her family.

"That's so great, just what I wanted," said Annie, selecting an appropriate lens for her camera and clicking into action.

"Now, what do we have here?" Ben asked himself, binoculars to his eyes. "Ah yes," he muttered, "apart from the big mama, three other adult females, I think, some adolescents, a couple of young males, and is that quite a small baby in amongst them? Yes, it damn well is."

"I see it too," said Annie excitedly. "Perfect."

The elephants drank and splashed, wallowing as best they could in the shallow waters of a pool. The baby could be seen intermittently, being gently nudged along between towering protective legs.

"I wonder if we could get a bit closer," said Ben after a few minutes. "There's another track a little further along which, I reckon, comes out almost opposite where they are." He checked his watch. "We've just about got time."

Annie needed no persuading. "That would be fantastic, if we could."

So, once more it was back to the road and on to the next right turn. As they drew nearer to the river bank, and scrubby bush began to give way to trees, there was sharp bend to the left. Rounding the corner Ben suddenly braked sharply.

"Oh, shit."

Standing defiantly, directly in front of them, astride the track, was a young bull elephant. He was not for one moment inclined to move out of their way. He was on guard and they were going no further.

"Shouldn't we back up?" asked Annie nervously.

"We could do," said Ben trying hard not to show his concern whilst considering options. "The problem is I can't reverse very fast and the first place where I could turn round is quite a way back. He could easily outrun us if he wanted to."

"And so?"

"And so we sit tight," said Ben resolutely, as he realised it was in fact the only thing they could do, before adding, "we must be as still and quiet as possible."

At that moment the young bull made as if to charge. Ears flapping he moved rapidly towards them, his huge shape looming up above the front of the vehicle. Annie gasped and grabbed Ben's left arm, harder and harder still; he felt her nails digging in as the elephant stopped just short and veered off to the left. Back he came and the same thing happened twice more.

Struggling to maintain composure Ben hissed, "We're going to be OK, really. I've heard elephant experts tell of these mock charges, particularly by young bulls."

But the show was far from over. For the next several minutes the elephant rampaged around, from one side to the other, ripping up bushes, smashing down small trees, stamping and snorting, trumpeting and bellowing, his head shaking and his trunk waving between two already finely developed tusks. It was a devastating display of immense strength and power. The message was unmistakeable. This was his world in which he reigned supreme. And then, with a final, disdainful toss of his head, he turned abruptly and crashed away through the undergrowth. These mere people were plainly not worth bothering with any longer. He was gone.

"Wow!" said Annie, slightly loosening her grip on Ben's arm. "That was terrifying for a while, but totally awesome."

"Quite something, pity you couldn't capture any of it on film." He gave a low laugh. "Not exactly a time for concentrating on taking pictures."

"No, but now that I've calmed down, I realise how privileged I've been to see something like that." She leant across and put her head on Ben's shoulder.

"And I'm so glad that I was with you."

He said nothing, but buried his face in her soft, fragrant hair.

Now it really was beginning to get dark; time to go.

Little was said on the way back to the Lodge but minds were saturated with thoughts. Unseeing eyes stared into the gloom, barely noticing the outline of a male impala, proud horned head held high, standing guard over his harem. A pair of duiker retreated before them, baleful eyes looking back momentarily illuminated in the beam of headlights.

Arriving at the Lodge Ben parked the vehicle and helped Annie gather up her camera equipment.

"That was quite some experience," she said. "Not one I'm going to forget in a hurry, perhaps never."

"Me neither," replied Ben, half elated, half relieved.

She studied his face for a moment. "I'm really kind of wrung out and also I need to start sorting out my stuff, so I'm going to retreat to my room and get something to eat there later."

Ben did his best to conceal any look of disappointment, not entirely successfully.

"Sure, I understand."

"But I want to make certain I see you tomorrow, to say good-bye; it's my last full day and I leave very early the next morning."

"Of course, I shall be around and I'll look out for you, without fail."

"Sounds good, well, goodnight then, and see you tomorrow."

Slinging her camera bag over her shoulder, Annie headed away to her room and was gone. Ben blankly watched her go, deflated by the sudden anti-climax to the day. A voice called out of the dark.

"Ben, is that you man?"

Turning, he made out the figure of Rob heading from the

office to the Lodge.

"Yeah, hi Rob, it's me." And he walked over to join him. Rob was frowning.

"Was that you I saw driving Annie Meyer's Toyota and heading off with her this afternoon?"

The tone of Rob's voice made Ben hesitate for a moment, but realistically there was only one answer available to him.

"Yup, I was helping out because her driver's sick."

"Christ man, are you out of your senses? That's not your job and you wouldn't have been covered on her insurance."

"Sorry, I didn't think of that."

"Clearly not, so I hope that you didn't do anything too risky."

Ben swallowed hard. He decided it was not the time to relate any tale of close encounters of the elephant kind. He just shook his head.

Rob was by now looking puzzled.

"Anyway, what is it with you and this woman?"

It was a question which Ben had already asked himself, several times. But he still had no clear idea of an answer. Mumbling an apologetic excuse he parted from Rob and was grateful to be swallowed up by the night.

Annie's last full day duly dawned, but it was not until the afternoon that she finally caught up with Ben.

"Hi there, I was hoping to see you. I still haven't shown you my cheetah picture. If you'd like to see it, pop down to my room before I finish packing up this evening, only of course if you would like to."

"I really would like to see it. Actually I'm free now."

"Great, let's go then."

Annie's room was in a state of upheaval, assorted clothes,

books, maps and camera equipment spread out in various places. A rucksack and a large zip bag were already half full. But a small table had only one thing on it, a good size black-and-white photograph, waiting to be viewed.

"Well, here it is."

Ben picked it up carefully and walked over to the window, studying it intently. There, in the sharp afternoon light, he saw the finely defined image of a female cheetah in her prime, sitting proudly on an old termite mound, head held high, surveying her territory stretching away over the vastness of the plains of the Maasai Mara. Around her, seemingly artistically arranged, were three cubs, sitting close to her, looking with interest in different directions. It took him a while to say anything.

"Wow, that's just a great picture. You've captured there, somehow, what's just so magnificent about these animals."

"I'm so, so glad that you like it. You had me worried there for a moment when at first you didn't say anything."

"I don't just like it, I love it."

"That means a lot to me, I can tell you, because I get a strong sense of how much the wildlife, in this beautiful wild country, means to you."

"Yup, and I've got a particular thing about cheetahs, as I've already told you of course."

"I know, I know, which makes it even more special that you like my picture." She spoke with a real intensity, taking the picture back from him, carefully laying it on the table, and then clasping him by both hands, looking deep into his eyes. As she then let go of him, for a moment Ben was uncertain what to say, until something caught his eye. Piled up by her bag, ready to be packed, was a set of small leather-bound books.

"Interesting-looking books. Are they old?"

"Yup, they are, as a matter of fact, early eighteen hundreds. There's a date in them at the front of each volume." She picked one up and opened it. "Yes, eighteen twenty-seven." She laughed. "The date's the only thing I can goddam read; they're in Latin."

Had he heard her correctly? "In Latin?" asked Ben in undisguised astonishment.

"They sure are. They belonged to my husband, Brett. He had studied classics and he went on to teach classics. That's how we met, teaching at the same college. Anyway, he picked up these books somewhere in New York, in a second-hand bookstore. He really treasured them and because they're small I carry them around with me, as something of him I suppose, a kind of talisman. "But—" she pursed her lips and her face clouded suddenly "—I have to admit that I only look at them occasionally, and it has to be said less and less frequently, because, let's face it, I can't read a word and they're completely meaningless really."

"May I?"

"Sure, go right ahead." She looked puzzled.

Ben picked up one and then several of the others, carefully holding each one in turn and examining them with reverential interest.

"The works of Cicero," he muttered.

"You know what they are?" Increasing surprise. "Can you read them?"

"To some extent. Latin was one of my other A-level subjects."

"You don't say; how did you do?"

"I was really lucky to have an inspirational teacher. He had been a pupil at my school, went off to Oxford to read classics, then came back to teach. There were only two of us who did Latin

A level, so it was almost like having an individual tutor. His enthusiasm fired me up to do really well. I owe him a lot. I probably wouldn't have got into the university I'm going to without him."

"And you're telling me you can read this stuff?"

Ben wondered whether he was being tested.

"Yes, some of it, certainly bits that I've studied. Let me see." And he quickly thumbed through a few of the volumes. "OK, here we are, speeches, yes, and defence speeches."

Annie was looking blank.

"Well, I'm sure you know that Cicero was a famous Roman politician, philosopher, teacher, writer and, especially, orator, probably one of the greatest orators ever. From time to time he defended people charged with offences. And here are some of his defence speeches."

"Do you know any of them?"

"Yes, certainly, let me see, this one in particular, *Pro Milone*."

"What?"

"*Pro Milone*, for Milo, this was a great favourite of my teacher's and we did a study of it with him. If I remember correctly, it was Cicero's last defence speech and maybe his finest."

"And you can read it?"

"Yes, look I'm sorry, I don't want to be a bore, but let me just tell you a little about it, because it's so great."

"OK then, shoot."

"Milo was a friend and ally of Cicero. He was charged with ordering the killing of Cicero's greatest enemy, Clodius."

"Had Milo done so?"

"Without doubt, and he was duly found guilty, but even so,

and although there was no real defence, Cicero managed to conjure up one of the greatest defence speeches of all time."

"How so?"

"I need to set the scene; it was quite something. Everything was stacked against Milo. The normal procedure had been changed somewhat, probably to make things more difficult for him, and there he was, brought before the Magistrate and a great array of jurors, originally eighty-something strong, if I remember correctly, then voted down I think to fifty odd. And standing on guard, all around, were soldiers. So it was pretty intimidating. And yet Cicero, the old fox, turned this to advantage in a great opening to his speech."

Annie was picking up on Ben's enthusiasm. She waited with interest while he looked for and read over to himself the particular passage.

"Yes, that's it, he said to the jury that he realised that it was a disgrace, when beginning a speech in defence of a man of great courage, to show fear for himself, particularly when the man in question was less concerned for his own survival than that of his country. But he went on to point out the alarm caused by the irregularities in procedure, and being surrounded by troops, rather than the usual spectators, meant that it was not possible to be free from fear. Great stuff."

There was a pause while Ben flicked through the next pages. "And an impassioned speech followed, but I particularly want to tell you how it ended. Here we are. There was almost certainly no more he could have said, but he made out that he was forced to stop. Let me try to give it to you, as literally as I can." Ben carefully read through the words to himself a few times, pausing and scratching his head occasionally. When seemingly satisfied he then said, "Right, I think I've got it, this is what Cicero said:

'But I must stop now. I can no longer speak for tears —— and my client has instructed that tears must not be used in his defence.' Quite some advocacy."

Ben looked up, his eyes gleaming.

"Totally awesome," said Annie for the second time in as many days. "I find it mind-blowing that I'm sitting here, in the middle of the African bush, having Cicero translated for me out of Brett's books. You just couldn't make it up for Christ's sake."

Pride and pleasure combined in Ben. "I loved doing it. Thanks so much for letting me see the books. Cicero has been really important to me." He looked suddenly thoughtful. "I think that he's part of the reason I've decided to do law."

"Wow, that's quite something." Her mind too was racing.

Ben looked at his watch. "I must be getting going; on duty again."

"Of course. Now look, I'm not going to say goodbye now because I'll see you after dinner, and I insist on buying you a farewell drink."

"That would be good. I'll meet you in the bar, and thanks, I've really enjoyed the afternoon."

"Me too, I tell you; it's been unreal."

Ben made his way back to work, treading lightly.

Shortly after dinner Ben found Annie waiting for him in the bar. Two drinks were on the table in front of her, creamy and dark brown in tall glasses.

"Hi Ben, come and sit down. We're all set up." And she gestured towards the glasses with an amused look. "They're Solomon specials and he recommended them as just the thing for a special occasion."

"Thanks, sounds interesting. What are they though?"

"Black Russians."

"Sorry, I'm none the wiser."

"Equal measures of vodka and Kahlua, served long over ice."

"Wow, sounds potent." He glanced towards Solomon who was making out to be busy whilst watching them slyly.

They clinked glasses silently, awkwardly, neither knowing quite what to say as their eyes met. Taking first sips there was the taste of smooth, rich coffee with a kick; dangerously refreshing, the sort of thing you could down too quickly. Then, relaxing into conversation, the talk was of Dylan Thomas, elephants, cheetahs and Cicero, photography too, but not of farewells. There was no inclination to contemplate their inevitably separate futures. One more round, for the road, slipped down cold, but with an increasingly warm feeling inside. Glasses at last drained, Annie looked very directly at Ben.

"I'm leaving really early tomorrow and I won't be able to see you then, but I have something for you. Do you mind coming down to my room now?"

"No, no, of course," Ben slightly surprised and a bit slurred. "I have just a few things to finish up here, locking up and so on, then I'll be there."

"That'll be just fine."

"Good, fifteen minutes, twenty max."

Ben gathered up the empty glasses and took them to the bar as Annie disappeared down the path beside the river leading to her room. Although Ben found himself hurrying, there were things to do and it was at least twenty minutes before he found himself knocking gently on Annie's door. No answer. Waiting for a moment he then tried the door and it half opened. As he did so, in the dim light of the room he saw Annie emerging from the bathroom. She was wearing a towelling robe, loosely tied and partly open. He froze.

"It's OK," she said softly. "Come in and close the door."

Waking from a late, deep sleep Ben shook his head, hoping to shift a dull ache, and then opened his eyes wide. On the low table beside the bed in his room was a single sheet of paper. He picked it up and read what was written on it. Rubbing his eyes he read it again, the words a voice in his mind.

Ben,

These are for you. I can't help feeling that you should have them. So, I'm totally committed to giving them to you to wish you well for your future, whatever it may be. I know that you will appreciate them in a way I never can. Also I feel strongly that Brett would have wanted someone like you to have them, someone who shares the passion he had and will treasure them as he did. And, selfishly perhaps, I hope that they may from time to time remind you of me. I don't think that I shall ever forget you.

My time here has been so unexpected, so beautiful.

Annie

Carefully folding the piece of paper Ben replaced it on the table before sinking back into his bed. He buried his face in the pillow for a moment and then turned to look across the room. His eyes fixed on a small pile of books on a chair. From the window a shaft of soft early morning light settled on soft brown leather. It was a new dawn.

A DAY IN THE COUNTRY

Oh to be in England
Now that April's there

Robert Browning

"You are invited," beamed Edward, striding into the common room and finding Ben preparing for a tutorial over a lukewarm cup of machine-vended coffee. "Spring is breaking out and it's high time you saw something of the English countryside."

"What do have in mind?" asked Ben, looking rather uncertain.

"Well, my parentals seem keen to see me, for some reason, and I have agreed to go home on Sunday for lunch. They asked if you would like to come too."

"How do they know about me?"

"Oh, they're fully briefed," chortled Edward, slapping Ben on the back. "They're really quite intrigued, and looking forward to meeting you."

"OK, well thanks then," said Ben, still somewhat uncertain.

"And, and, wait for it," grinned Edward, very much enjoying the moment, "Charlotte is going to be there too."

"Oh," was Ben's comment, determined to be nonchalant.

But accompanied." Edward was making the most of this.

"Really?"

"Indeed, by none other than the great El Lawrence."

Ben shook his head. "Sorry, I'm not with you."

"Charlotte's man, Lawrence, the one I told you about at the beginning of last term; in his last year at Oxford; seems like he's Charlotte's intended."

"Of course," said Ben quickly, wondering if anything in particular was revealed by his expression. Edward appeared to be studying him closely. "I remember now," he added, adopting a casual air, but steering clear of Lawrence for the time being, "you said something about your family knowing Charlotte's family and her being a friend of your sister."

"That's right, my sister's going to be there too. She wanted to see Charlotte and also to meet you; so it's all fallen into place." Edward rubbed his hands together.

Unsure what to say, Ben simply nodded and there was a reflective pause before Edward added, "It seems that Charlotte has spoken of you to Lawrence because he too is looking forward to seeing you; apparently he also is intrigued."

"Crikey," said Ben. "What for God's sake has he been told? I'm getting cold feet about this invitation. Seems like I'm going to be put under a spotlight and subjected to a series of tests of some kind."

"Nonsense, you should be chuffed that people are genuinely interested in you. And it's going to be a great day out with a bloody good Sunday lunch thrown in, courtesy of my mum. So we're on then, right?"

"Yeah, OK, I suppose so. I shall try to put on a good show."

"Settle down, dear boy, no need for any of that. It's going to be fun."

"Right, I'll just have to take your word for it. So, what's the plan?"

"I'm mobile now, so we can drive there. As I told you a couple of days ago, I have become the proud owner of a Mini

Cooper; second hand, but in bloody good nick and goes like a bomb. It takes a bit under an hour to get home, so I suggest picking you up outside Hall at around eleven thirty."

"I'll be waiting."

"Good man."

Another slap on the back for Ben and Edward departed to confirm arrangements. A day in the country pondered Ben, wondering just what might be in store for him.

As they cleared Bristol Ben began to take in unfolding views of countryside, rather flashing by the windows as Edward enjoyed picking up speed and putting the car through its paces. Soft, gentle undulating land stretched away beyond hedges and stone walls, but seemingly not very far. And dotted about nearly everywhere could be seen signs of man, houses, cottages, churches, barns and other farm buildings, bridges, electricity pylons, fences, gates, more fences, more gates, signs saying 'Private' and 'Keep Out'. For all its rural prettiness it seemed to Ben cluttered, so different from the rugged wide-open spaces he was used to, untamed land stretching in every direction towards distant views, mountains and hills, forests and lakes, and the seemingly endless expanse of the savannah under the big African sky. He was particularly struck by how little distance there was between the towns and villages they passed through; so unlike the many miles at home from one place to another

"Good to see signs of spring," said Edward encouragingly, glancing in Ben's direction and momentarily wondering what lay behind the thoughtful expression on his friend's face. "Are you OK? You're very quiet."

"Yeah, I'm fine; just taking it all in."

"Glad to hear it. It's good to get out of the city on a day like this. The country looks great and the sun is shining; can't be bad."

"Yes," nodded Ben, "I must admit I'm particularly pleased to see the sun; it's been in rather short supply recently."

"Yup, but hopefully we shall now start seeing more of it."

"I hope so too. I long for the feeling of warm sun on my back."

Enough of the weather. It was time, Edward felt, for a heads-up on the day.

"Now, I've told you who's coming to lunch."

"Yes, you mentioned your sister."

"That's right, Julia, we call her Jules. She's home for the weekend from the UEA, that's the University of East Anglia in Norfolk where she's studying history of art. She's in her second year."

"Oh, so you're quite close in age."

"She's two years older, but only one year ahead of me at university because she had a year off after leaving school when she spent time in Italy and then went to Israel where she stayed on a kibbutz, not that we're Jewish."

"I wouldn't mind if you were."

"No, no, of course not; can't think why I said that." Edward looked rather cross and embarrassed.

"And I think you mentioned Charlotte will be there," said Ben, moving quickly on.

Edward visibly brightened. "Indeed, with Lawrence. I know I've told you a bit about him before. He's in his last year at Oxford, doing PPE; likes to think of himself as an intellectual socialist. But underneath all that crap he's actually a good bloke; ferociously clever which, it seems, is the attraction for Charlotte."

"I see," was all Ben could manage, although he didn't really see at all.

"You'll like my dad, I think. He's extravert and fun; lives life full on, although perhaps a bit too much sometimes." Edward paused for a second. "Can be quite a handful, but Mum's learnt to cope with it."

"What does he do?"

"Marine insurance. Works in the City; either commutes or stays up in town during the week, depending on work commitments."

"And does your mum work?"

"She doesn't go out to work." Edward laughed before adding, "But she hates it when people say 'oh, so you don't work'. As far as she's concerned she never stops working, looking after us lot in the family, keeping up the house, maintaining a beautiful garden, doing umpteen things in the village, singing in a choir, and so on and so on. Oh, she also somehow finds time to paint; she's a bloody good botanic artist. She's probably the most talented member of the family in truth."

"She sounds great."

Edward laughed again. "I've really talked her up, but she's lovely too and I know you'll like her and she'll like you. And boy you're in for a treat when it comes to her Sunday lunch."

They were coming into a village, quintessentially picture-perfect of the kind Ben had only seen before in books of 'the old country' as Kenya settlers liked to refer to it. "That's where I play cricket," said Edward pointing to the green, "and we adjourn afterwards to the pub over there." Passing the post office they turned into a small lane leading to the church. Not far beyond lay their destination. Edward swung the car through some open gates bearing the sign 'The Old Rectory' and up a gravel drive between banks of rhododendrons. "Well," he said grinning, "here we are," as he pulled up by the front door of an imposing but handsome double-fronted stone house.

"Edward, there you are!" boomed the voice of a man emerging from a room leading off the spacious hall. "And you must be Ben, the old colonial, we've heard so much about you; welcome."

Ben shook the proffered hand of a smiling man sporting plum-red corduroy trousers and a checked shirt; an older version of Edward, with thinning hair.

"Thank you, sir, and thanks for inviting me."

"You're most welcome, dear boy; and so polite, good old-fashioned manners obviously still thrive in the colonies, less and less so here more's the pity."

Ben didn't feel it was appropriate to correct his genial host. He just smiled and out of the corner of his eye he could see Edward giving his father a warning look which was totally ignored.

"Now come along, everyone else is here."

Stepping through the open door Ben found himself in a large, but warmly comfortable sitting room. Sofas piled with assorted cushions flanked a stone fireplace with logs burning in the grate. Assorted chairs provided other seating amidst tables bearing magazines, framed photographs and cut-glass tumblers. On the walls hung several portraits, interspersed with pictures of hunting scenes, horses and birds. One picture, strikingly different from the others, briefly caught Ben's eye; a finely painted watercolour of an artichoke plant in full flower.

People were rising from their chairs. Edward hugged a young woman who hardly needed introduction to Ben because she was clearly his sister; another strong family resemblance, tallish, handsome rather than pretty, brown hair swept back above soft brown eyes in a kind face.

"Hallo Ben, I'm Jules," and, rather to his surprise, she leant forward and kissed him gently on the cheek.

"Hi, good to see you," he managed rather lamely.

"And this, of course, is my mum," said Edward as a woman in her late forties stepped forward, elegant and poised with matured good looks.

"We're so glad you could come, Ben; we've been looking forward to meeting you."

"Thank you, Mrs Brooke, it's great to be here."

Ben turned to the remaining two people in the room, standing together to one side. Charlotte looked particularly fine, smartly casual with knee-high black leather boots. "Hallo Ben," she said. "This is Lawrence."

Ben couldn't help but scrutinise him carefully: about his height, but slim; a high forehead and glasses; clever-looking undoubtedly; hints of studied eccentricity in his collarless shirt and checked waistcoat. "So this is the man I've been hearing about," he said, shaking Ben's hand and looking at him rather searchingly.

"Indeed, well I've heard about you too, of course," responded Ben with matching determined friendliness.

Edward's father intervened. "What's your poison Ben, G and T, wine, beer?"

"If you have a lager that would be great."

"Of course, I got some in specially, in anticipation."

"Thanks, I appreciate it."

"Right, coming up."

Charlotte and Lawrence had turned away and were talking to Jules. Edward was mixing himself a gin and tonic from an array of drinks on a side table. His mother caught Ben's eye and he moved over to join her standing by large French windows looking out on to extensive lawns and flowerbeds.

"Lovely place you have here Mrs Brooke."

"Thank you, we've been here a number of years now and so we've had plenty of time to get it the way we want it."

"Have you had much to do?"

"A fair amount. The house needed renovating, rather than anything structural. But the garden had been neglected for years and I almost had to start from scratch."

"So, you've done all this," said Ben with a mixture of surprise and admiration as he gazed out of the French windows. "But surely you've had a lot of help?"

"Some," she smiled, "certainly initially when there was a lot of grunt work to do. Now I just have a man who comes in once a week for a few hours to do the heavy stuff. Edward's father mows the lawns. The rest I do myself."

"Impressive." Ben was still looking out over the expanse of the garden, but further away, a long way away in his mind's eye. Then quietly, almost to himself, he found himself saying, "It reminds me of my aunts' garden."

"Oh, whereabouts in England is that?"

"No, not in England." He half turned towards Mrs Brooke. "In Kenya."

"Gracious, a garden like this, a very English sort of garden, in the middle of Africa? How extraordinary." She was anxious not to appear rude and did her best to temper any tone of incredulity.

"Yes, absolutely, it may sound crazy." Ben was excitedly warming to the subject. "But they live up at Limuru."

"Oh?"

"Twenty miles or so from Nairobi, on the edge of the Rift

Valley escarpment. They're seven and a half thousand feet above sea level."

"Your beer and your very good health." Edward's father appeared thrusting a pewter tankard into Ben's hand.

"Thank you, sir; and thanks again for the invite."

"You two seem to be having a jolly conversation. What's the subject?"

"Gardening," replied his wife, amused to take him by surprise. She was not disappointed.

"Crikey," was the response, eyebrows raised. "I think I'll leave you to it." He retreated towards the gathering by the fire place.

Ben was not finished. "You see, at the sort of altitude which I mentioned, the climate at certain times of the year is rather like an English climate, in spring and summer at least, I suppose."

"Tell me about your aunt."

"Aunts, my great aunts actually; my grandfather's two sisters. They both lost their fiancés, killed in the First World War. Afterwards, left rather high and dry, they decided to join their brothers in Kenya. My grandfather and the elder brother of the family had already been there a few years by then."

"I see, and they stayed."

"Yes, neither married, but they are devoted to each other. They have their lovely house and garden and are really active in the local community, playing golf, making music, charity work, you name it."

"Presumably they're getting on a bit by now."

"Yes, but they keep going; they're great."

"Did you see much of them when you were growing up?"

"A fair bit, at family gatherings. There was also a tradition that we would all go to them for New Year. On New Year's Day itself they would always lay on an incredible lunch. Then there would be fun and games in the garden. As children, me, my sister and cousins had such good times, running wild, hiding in hedges and great banks of blue hydrangeas, chasing through the orchard."

"So it's a big garden?"

"Oh yes, five acres, partly garden and partly vegetables and fruit."

"That must take some upkeep."

"Yes, the aunts do a lot of it themselves; they're demon gardeners; but they also have a couple of *shamba* boys." Seeing Mrs Brooke look puzzled, he added:

"African gardeners."

She smiled. "I wish I had; what a luxury."

"Not really, not there; it's rather expected that you provide local employment."

"Interesting. And I'm fascinated that it's an English-type garden, rather than a tropical garden; it must mean that the weather can be quite cool."

"Not just cool, cold at times, particularly during the rainy seasons, even though it's only a little over a hundred miles from the equator. We used to sit by their log fire eating homemade scones just out of the oven." Turning away and looking through the French windows into the distance he said softly, to himself really, "I'll never forget the taste."

She studied him thoughtfully for a moment. "It all sounds idyllic; there's a lot for you to miss."

He turned back towards her. "You're right; I'm realising that more and more; things I've always taken for granted I suppose."

Stepping away from the French windows, Ben's eyes were drawn once again to the painting of the artichoke. Looking at it more closely he could see the letters "SB" in the bottom left-hand corner. "If you don't mind me asking, are those your initials?"

"Yes," she smiled, "Susan Brooke, that's me."

"Wow, it's really beautiful; Edward told me you painted, but I didn't realise you're that good."

"Thank you, I'm just an amateur really, but I do enjoy it."

"It caught my eye because it's very like the sort of work my grandmother does. Oh heck, sorry, here I go again; another reminder of home."

"Is she a professional artist?"

Ben laughed. "She'd probably like to have been; no, but no way; she never went to art school, or anything like that, and she was far too busy as a young woman being the wife of a pioneer farmer. Still she has a real talent."

"I would have liked to have gone to art school too."

"Why didn't you?"

"My father didn't approve. He was old fashioned in his views. So for me it was to finishing school." With a rather hollow laugh, she added, "To prepare me to marry 'the right sort of man'."

Ben quickly decided against asking any follow-up question.

"Right," she said briskly, "I'd better go and see to lunch."

"Of course; can I help in any way?"

"No, that's sweet of you, but I'm fine. You go and talk to the others. I've rather been monopolising you I'm afraid, but I have enjoyed our chat."

"Me too."

Halfway to the door she turned back towards Ben. "I'm so glad Edward has you as a friend."

Before Ben could think of an answer she had vanished in the direction of the kitchen.

"Come and join us," called out Edward. "My goodness, you and Mum seem to have been getting on like a house on fire."

"She's a lovely woman, your mum."

"I know; didn't I tell you so? Now come and sit down; here, there's space for you on the sofa next to Jules."

As he sat down, Jules got up, causing Ben to look a bit taken aback, which she immediately picked up on.

"Nothing personal," she said with a laugh. "I'm just going to let the dogs in; they should have dried out after their morning walk. Are you OK with dogs?"

"Very much so; they're animals I'm particularly fond of actually."

As Jules left the room Ben caught Charlotte's eye. She was sitting on the sofa opposite with Lawrence who was deep in conversation with Mr Brooke, sitting the other side of him in an armchair. Edward was refreshing people's glasses. Ben smiled, but before he could say anything the door burst open and in rushed two black Labradors, tails thrashing causing imminent danger of things being swept from low tables. They were swiftly followed by a stocky and perky Jack Russell. The dogs did their rounds of the people in the room, pushing noses into laps and being greeted with return pats, except from Lawrence, as Ben noticed out of the corner of his eye.

A moment or two later Jules was back and took her place on the sofa again next to Ben. One of the Labradors immediately came and sat at her feet and the other by Ben's feet.

"Lovely dogs," he said, scratching each one in turn behind their ears as they raised their heads approvingly.

Jules beamed at him. "I'm so glad you like them and you seem to have made quite a hit. This is Dougie and that's Daisy; they're brother and sister."

"How old are they?"

"Eight, nearly nine; so they're getting on a bit, but still really fit, thank God."

"And they keep us fit too," intervened Mr Brooke. "So often, on a cold or wet day when I'm trudging the fields with them, I realise that if it wasn't for them I'd be slumped in my chair at home."

"Too right," added Edward, "and when I'm here I take them running with me. After a few miles I'm knackered, but they look at me as if to say they're only just warming up."

Laughs all round. Ben switched his attention to the Jack Russell sitting on the floor beside Charlotte. She was fussing over him and muttering words of affection. Her dog, presumably, but he felt he'd better ask.

"Yes," she replied looking up. "This is Jock."

"Bloody good name for him," retorted Edward in a flash. "He's full jock most of the time; randy little bugger."

"Oh, shut up Edward," said Charlotte in the midst of the general ribaldry which followed. Lawrence was smirking and, as Ben noticed, was inching his feet further away from Jock. As voices fell, Ben made a strange low noise from somewhere in the back of his throat. Immediately he had the attention of all three dogs. Jock trotted over and sat right in front of Ben, gazing up at him."

"*Mbwa mzuri sana*," he said softly.

Heads went to one side, ears pricked and tails wagged.

"H'm, good working knowledge of Swahili."

A rather surprised silence in the room was broken by Charlotte.

"Be careful with Jock; he can be a bit snappy, with men in particular for some reason. Lawrence can't really have anything to do with him."

Ben looked over to Lawrence. "Do you like dogs?"

"No, not much. But," he added quickly, "Jock doesn't know that; I've always been unfailingly nice to him."

"Oh, he knows all right," said Ben. "You can't fool dogs about such things. They watch us all the time, read our body language and absorb our feelings."

"That's going a bit far, isn't it?"

Ben didn't say anything further in response. He simply looked down at Jock who promptly jumped onto his lap, turned round and sat down, looking triumphantly, possibly even defiantly, at those on the sofa opposite him. Glancing up his eyes met Charlotte's, scanning him searchingly.

"Do you have dogs?" asked Jules, patting a happy Jock on the head.

"I did have two, until recently; now just one, Brutus who's half Great Dane and half Rhodesian Ridgeback; one hundred and twenty pounds of muscle. He's fiercely loyal and a great guard dog, although he only goes for—" Ben stopped short with a sudden stab of shame.

"What happened to the other dog?" asked Jules quickly.

"Ah, Albie," sighed Ben. "He was a terrific little dog, a terrier-cross, a bit like this fellow on my lap. Unfortunately his hunting instinct got the better of him in the end; catching rats was fine, he was bloody good at it, but he was as brave as hell and would also go after more dangerous things."

"Is that what did for him?"

"Yes, just before I left, he dashed out one night, barking like mad, and was taken by a leopard."

Jules put her hand up to her mouth with a pained expression amid general murmurs of regret. Her hitherto jovial father looked suddenly thoughtful. "Sort of thing that makes one realise what a different world you come from, Ben."

At that moment the door opened. "Lunch is ready," announced Mrs Brooke. "I hope you're all hungry."

Charlotte was quick to stand up and she leant forward to pick up Jock off Ben's lap. In doing so their hands touched with a slight lingering pressure, just for a moment. Neither spoke as they joined the others and headed off in the direction of the dining room, dogs trailing in their wake.

A door across the hall led into a dignified, partly wood-panelled room. Light from a lead-paned window fell on an impressive array of fine English porcelain and crystal glasses on the long table. Opposite the mahogany sideboard bore serving dishes steaming on a hotplate under a painting of pheasants lying on a table in a rustic seventeenth-century kitchen. At the end of the room a large mirror above the fireplace reflected the assembled company waiting to be seated.

In through the door at one side Mrs Brooke emerged from the kitchen bearing a good-sized joint of beef on a platter which she put down at the far end of the table. "Right dear," she said glancing at her husband, "you can start carving. I shall sit at the other end. Ben, you can be here on my right, with Jules next to you. Edward you sit the other side of me, opposite Ben, with Charlotte in between you and Lawrence. Yes, I think that works."

There was general conversation as people took their allotted seats. When Mrs Brooke prepared to sit down, Ben jumped up and helped push in her chair.

"You smoothie," remarked Edward with a grin.

Ignoring her son, Mrs Brooke inclined her head towards Ben. "Thank you, Ben," she said with an appreciative smile. "Thank you very much."

Warm plates of sliced beef, slightly pink in the middle, started to come round.

"There's gravy and horseradish sauce on the table," said Mrs Brooke, "but it's probably easier if you all help yourself from the sideboard to potatoes, Yorkshire pudding and vegetables."

"And while you're doing that, I shall dispense wine," said Mr Brooke. "It's quite a good Wine Society claret; I take it that you would all like to imbibe."

There were murmurs of assent. Wine was poured, plates were filled, seats were taken and the room was enveloped in a warmly appreciative hubbub, clattering and clinking overlaid with happy voices and laughter.

"Well Ben," said Mr Brooke looking down the table, "what do you make of the roast beef of old England?"

"Really good, thank you." Turning towards Mrs Brooke he added, "It's delicious; the best meal I've had, by far, since coming to England."

"Come off it, you old flatterer," interjected Edward "You've only been on a student diet so far."

Sensing Ben's embarrassment, Mrs Brooke reached out and put a hand on his shoulder. "Well, I take it as a great compliment, thank you Ben."

"Yes indeed," said Mr Brooke. "You can't beat a traditional English Sunday lunch and Ben is quite right to appreciate it."

Lawrence was looking across the table at Ben. "Do I understand correctly that you've never lived in England before?"

"That's right. I visited once, as a young kid, for a short time, but otherwise I've always been in Kenya."

"And," Charlotte added, "you're second generation because, as you've told me, your mother was born there too."

"Yup," Ben nodded.

"Interesting," said Mr Brooke. "So what's struck you most about good old England?"

Ben's brow furrowed as he thought. "It's a very different type of life here, in so many ways, big and small I suppose; it's quite difficult to compare."

"What particular differences would you say you've noticed most?"

"Well," thinking, but wanting to tread carefully, "it's struck me particularly how small the country is, how close together everything seems to be, how many people there are everywhere, and it all appears organised, cultivated, rather tame. Sorry, I don't mean that rudely, but compared to the wildness and wide open spaces I'm used to."

"And you bang on a bit about the weather," interjected Edward.

"Yes, I'm afraid I probably do; but, of course it's a given that the weather is quite different here, and I expected that."

"Except, perhaps for high up on the Rift Valley escarpment," said Mrs Brooke, enjoying her moment of imparting special knowledge.

"Good Lord, dear, how can you possibly know about that?" asked her surprised husband. She simply smiled contentedly.

"You know, Ben," said Mr Brooke, "I take on board what you've been saying, but you shouldn't judge the country simply by what I imagine you've seen here in the south. There are big open spaces up in Yorkshire, the Lake District, the Pennines, and Scotland of course."

Whilst having to admit to himself that he hadn't seen such places, Ben remained dubious. He doubted whether they could really compare to the great plains of the Mara, stretching to the vast Serengeti and beyond, or the seemingly endless expanse of the wild landscape of the NFD.

Perhaps sensing doubts, Mr Brooke added, "And let's not forget the hills and valleys of Wales." Ben nodded rather blankly, but decided against saying that he had heard that the whole of Wales would fit into the Tsavo National Park.

"And, let's not forget either good old Norfolk, where I'm at university," volunteered Jules. "It's much less crowded there, flat, but that means big open skies of the kind I Imagine you're used to."

"Sounds good," said Ben turning towards her.

"Well, you should come and visit me sometime."

"Thanks, maybe one day," he replied non-committedly, half distracted by what he thought was an odd look Charlotte was giving Jules. But his mind was also moving on.

"A whole host of other things have struck me, some probably obvious, but I just hadn't thought about them before I came here."

"Such as?" asked Lawrence.

"White people driving buses, working as gardeners, mending roads, emptying bins and doing all sorts of jobs which are only done by black people in Kenya." He sensed he was getting on to more sensitive issues.

"Well," said Lawrence, "that difference in Kenya is a product of the colonial regime; black people serving white people as a ruling class."

"Yes," said Ben, "but you have to understand that there has never really been a white working class in Kenya. White people came to Kenya as colonial administrators, and some to work as professionals, doctors, teachers, engineers and the like, others to run businesses, and many, way back, like my grandfather, as settler farmers."

Lawrence though for a moment. "That may well be so, but the result was the country being divided by race."

"In the same way, perhaps, that this country is divided by class; and also by race for that matter."

"No, no, hang on, I don't think for one moment that there is any real comparison here; not on proper analysis, whatever divisions, admittedly, we do have."

"Really?"

"Do, please, all help yourself to some more," said Mrs Brooke brightly. "There's plenty left over."

"No thank you," said Lawrence, "I've done very well."

Ben looked uncertain, but Edward wasn't holding back. "Well, I'm going to have seconds, come on Ben, join me."

"I'm certainly going to," said his father and the three of them went over to the sideboard to help themselves.

Lawrence, not eating, was looking thoughtful, even watchful, as Ben sat down again. "Tell me more about your grandfather."

"Well," said Ben, wondering rather where this was going and how much detail to go into without being a bore, "as I mentioned he was a settler. Having fought in the First World War, and been fortunate to survive, he decided to take up the opportunity provided by what was called, I think, a 'soldier settlement scheme'."

"Yes," said Lawrence, "I've read of these schemes; they were a way of finding things to do for a mass of de-mobbed soldiers; send them to the colonies, provide them with farms on very favourable terms and develop agricultural economies. But, of course, there was a huge downside to that for the local African people."

"Why ever?" asked Mr Brooke, sensing perhaps that he

needed to come to the rescue.

"Because," said Lawrence, not prepared to be deflected and still looking at Ben, "it, of course, resulted in a colonial land grab; many Africans were dispossessed."

"Not necessarily in all cases," said Ben, feeling defensive, but anxious to avoid being provoked into arguing the unarguable. "I do know, from my Kikuyu friends, that this happened a lot in what became known as the White Highlands, where my grandfather's brother went actually, but my grandfather was up in the north-west, in the Cherangani Hills, near a place called Kitale."

"Still, must have been have been tribal lands of some kind," suggested Charlotte.

"All I can tell you," said Ben, "is that my grandfather carved his farm out of virgin bush and woodland."

"Yes," said Edward brightly, "from what you've told me before it was real pioneering stuff, as recently as fifty years ago; incredible really."

"That's right; luckily he was a very practical man; he'd trained as a civil engineer before the War. Anyway, he built his own house out of local materials, dammed a river to make a reservoir, built a small church and even a rudimentary school for a missionary teacher who taught the children of the farm labourers."

"Had he married your grandmother by then?" asked Jules.

"Yes," Ben smiled, turning towards her, "fortunately for him he had. She had also gone out to Kenya, after being a nurse during the War. Her brother was running a sawmill and she went out to be with him, to be a kind of housekeeper I suppose. Anyway she quickly met and married my grandfather."

"So she took to the life there?" said Mrs Brooke, beginning

128

to clear away plates.

"Very much so, what a godsend she was too; very resourceful, made things for the house out of old packing crates and anything she could get hold of, grew vegetables, kept chickens and various animals, tended to the sick and injured, helped run the farm; oh, of course, and brought up her children, my mother and her sister, in the middle of nowhere."

"Quite a woman," remarked Jules.

"Remarkable, and a real inspiration to me."

"Oh, in what way?" asked Jules.

"In a number of ways, but particularly because she embraced life there, she made it her business to get to know the people, their languages, customs and traditions." Enquiring faces made him continue. "So, for instance, as a nurse she knew a certain amount about medicine, European medicine, but she also wanted to learn about African cures. She became a great expert in herbal remedies. Often she would help the women and work with them, particularly in healing sick children."

"But," said Charlotte, "I don't suppose she socialised with them in any sense."

"No, there was no question of that, certainly in those days; it would never have been expected, or I suppose, accepted."

"There was a racial barrier," interjected Lawrence.

"To an extent, yes, but more complicated than just that; there were such huge differences of nearly every kind." Ben thought for a moment. "Despite this barrier, as you put it, what I can say is that the Africans clearly respected my grandmother, perhaps even had affection for her; they called her *Mama*."

"And what about your grandfather, would you say he was respected too?" asked Lawrence.

"Yes," said Ben firmly, "I would say that. In return for their work they were all allowed by him to occupy and cultivate parts of his land, as squatters, which they appreciated. This system of having squatters was the way things worked on many farms during colonial times."

"Squatters, squatters," expostulated Lawrence. "They were on African land taken away by the British."

"You know what I've said about that already," said Ben quietly, through slightly clenched teeth. "In answer to your original question, I would repeat that there was respect, I would say on both sides. My grandfather looked after his workers and their families in so many ways. He didn't pay them much, because he never had much money himself and, as he saw it, in those times, they didn't so much need to be paid as provided for; which is precisely what he did."

"So it was really a sort of feudal system, a twentieth-century feudal system," mused Lawrence. Catching Ben's eye he added "I'm sure benevolent in the case of your grandfather and probably some others too." He looked away again. "But almost certainly not, I expect, in a lot of cases."

"And you know what my problem with this is, Ben," added Charlotte, "because we've discussed it before. These Africans, working on British-owned farms, in a state of feudalism, were being denied their own opportunities."

"Yes, of course, I do know what you say about this, and, as I've said before, I understand the argument," said Ben quietly, almost to himself, as he felt all eyes were on him. Looking directly at Charlotte, he said more firmly, "But you remember, I'm sure, what I've also said. It isn't nearly as simple as you make out because there just weren't the opportunities you seem to think there were, not in those days."

"They were being held back," insisted Charlotte.

"From what? There were no other jobs or job prospects. Let's be frank, these people, primitive people, were peasants working the land; there was nothing else for them to do; all they could do if they weren't employed by my grandfather, or other settlers, was to go back to the land."

"Ah," said Lawrence quickly, "but therein lies the critical issue; that it was no longer their land to go back to."

"And, surely Ben," added Charlotte, "you must recognise the importance of education and opportunities, for everyone. I know you can't always see where this may lead, but it's bound to broaden horizons."

"As a matter of interest," asked Mr Brooke, "what has happened with your grandfather's farm?"

"As independence was coming, he felt he could sense which way the winds were blowing and so he sold; not for very much; he was quite bitter about it."

"His workers must have seen it as the dawning of a new age," said Lawrence, perhaps with just a hint of triumph.

"Some perhaps," nodded Ben. He waited for a second until he could look Lawrence directly in the eye. "Many others wept."

Edward pushed his chair back slightly and clasped his hands together saying, "Fascinating, but really quite heavy for Sunday lunch."

On cue, once more the lighter touch was swiftly applied by Mrs Brooke. "Pudding everyone."

The sun was now shafting through the large lead-paned window of the dining room. It had become lighter and warmer, outside and in. Delicious traditional puddings had been served. Ben had been easily persuaded to have both the blackberry and apple crumble as well as the sherry trifle. Conversation flowed with more wine and coffee. There was talk of politics, student unrest, blood sports and other issues raised mainly by Mr Brooke, egged on by Edward, somewhat mischievously, to provoke generally good-natured debate with Lawrence and Charlotte. On the other side of the table there was lighter fare; talk of families, places visited and to be visited, holiday plans and Jules' forthcoming skiing trip. No, as Ben explained, he had never experienced snow, although he saw it nearly every day at home, particularly in the early mornings and evenings when the veil of clouds lifted to reveal Batian and Nelion, the twin high peaks of Mount Kenya, towering over seventeen thousand feet above the equator.

"Ben," asked Mrs Brooke, "I know your mother was born in Kenya, and has always lived there, but, am I right in thinking not your father?"

"Yes, that is right. My father was born and brought up in England. He was in the army during the Second World War, after which he stayed on with his regiment and served in various places before coming to Kenya, where he met my mother."

"But presumably he wasn't able to stay indefinitely; he would have had to move on with his regiment."

Ben smiled. "Oh, it was all pretty whirlwind. They were engaged within a short time, but Mum made it clear that no way was she leaving Kenya. So Dad took the plunge; he arranged to leave the army and they were married later that same year." Pausing for a moment he added shyly, "And I arrived not long after."

Jules' interest had been aroused. "It all sounds very romantic. But what did your father do, having left the army?"

"He joined the colonial service for a while, as a district officer, which did him well because he got to know the country and its people." Ben grinned. "And it made him knuckle down to learning Swahili."

"And after that?" asked Mrs Brooke.

"He went into farming, first with my grandfather, who needed help as he got older, and then he branched out with his own farm, a ranch really, on the Laikipia Plateau, which has been our main home ever since."

"You say your main home. Do have another home?"

"Sort of; my mother owns a farm, near a place called Nyeri, not too far, by Kenya standards at least, from Laikipia. It's run by a farm manager, but there is also a family house there which we go to sometimes."

"Gosh," said Jules looking surprised, "why did your mum want to buy her own farm?"

"No, no," said Ben turning towards her, "she didn't buy it; she inherited it from her uncle, my grandfather's brother."

"Oh, did he have no family of his own?"

"Not by the time he died, no; it was very sad really. Uncle Tom had been married, to Aunt Mary, and they had two sons, my mother's first cousins, John and David, who she was very close to; they were brought up together as kids."

"And what happened to them?" asked a concerned-looking Mrs Brooke.

"John, the elder one, was presumed killed in the War. He was listed as missing in action, fighting the Italians in Somaliland. They never really found out what happened to him which made things worse in a way."

"And the other boy?"

"David died, not long after. He was still at school in Nairobi and went on a scout camp. Shortly after he got back he became very ill. They thought it might have been typhoid which did for him."

Mrs Brooke gasped. "How awful for your uncle and aunt. I can't think of anything worse than losing a child. But to lose both your children, within a short space of time, is unbearable."

"You're right, because Aunt Mary never really recovered. She became involved in spiritualism and was obsessed about trying to contact her lost boys. And then a few years later she became seriously ill and died."

"Your poor uncle, or great uncle I suppose he was to you."

"Yes, he was a broken man and then he also died, quite young."

Mrs Brooke looked thoughtful for a moment. "I suppose your mother inheriting the farm rooted her even more to Kenya, if that was possible."

Seriousness began to drain away from Ben's face with the onset of happier thought. "She has always been pretty firmly rooted; she would never want to leave and, hopefully, she'll never have to."

"Has she ever spent time in England?" asked Jules.

"The odd visit only. Oh, and a short spell at school here." Ben laughed. "A very short spell."

"Where was she?"

"Somewhere near a place called Weymouth, if I remember correctly from what I've been told. This was back in the thirties. My grandparents decided that my mother and her sister were running too wild on the farm and they needed a more formal education. So they were packed off to England and there are photos of them in a family album, wearing their new school uniforms, looking forlorn."

"But it didn't last?"

"No way; by Christmas they were begging to leave and they were home at Easter. Mum vowed never to leave again."

"Gracious," said Mrs Brooke, "it really is a country which gets a hold of people."

"Yes, and then, as my grandma says, you can never truly get it out of your system."

Charlotte had seemingly disengaged from the conversation the other side of the table. But Ben had the distinct impression that she was listening in.

SAVING THE DAY

With courage, nothing is impossible

Sir William Hilary
RNLI motto

Lunch was over and all had helped with clearing away. Following well-earned and well-deserved compliments Mrs Brooke had retired to the sitting room to read the Sunday papers. Mr Brooke was busying himself in his study. All others headed out for a walk, urged on in the spring sunshine by enthusiastic dogs. The back door led out to a patio with a broad swathe of lawn beyond, bordered by flowerbeds. Off to one side, behind a hedge, Ben noticed fencing round a grass tennis court. At the far end of the lawn they streamed through a gate to a field and the dogs fanned out excitedly ahead of them. The field sloped down and then up again to a ridge on the far side, crowned with a lone tree.

"That's where we're making for," pointed out Edward, looking across to Ben who was chatting with Jules. "Should help us work off some of that almost too good lunch."

"What's beyond?"

"Another field, leading down to the river."

Edward produced a ball out of his pocket and whistled the dogs. Having quickly gained their attention, he threw the ball a good way down the slope. The Labradors led the charge, Jock doing well on his short legs to be not far behind. Dougie was first to the ball, a nose ahead of Daisy. Triumphantly he ran back towards Edward, head held high, holding the ball just out of the reach of Jock leaping round him, barking excitedly. The process was repeated several times, everyone taking a turn at throwing. Edward teased the girls about what he termed 'girl throws'. Ben was rather pleased that he threw the ball further than anyone else.

"Poor Jock," said Charlotte after a while. "He can't really compete. One or other of the Labs gets the ball every time."

The ball was with Ben again. The Labradors were a good way in front of him. He made as if to throw over their heads and they began to set off. But he still had the ball in hand which he quickly showed to Jock, waiting near his feet. Then he skittled it away low to the ground, in the opposite direction, with a very happy Jock fast behind it. The big dogs, suddenly realising that they had been duped, wheeled round and also gave chase. The head start, however, proved enough. Jock, ball firmly in mouth, did a lap of honour, growling slightly. Laughter and congratulations followed. Charlotte caught Ben's attention with an appreciative smile. Edward wrestled to free the ball from Jock's mouth, eventually succeeding. "Our turn," he said firmly, and he shied the ball at Ben who, somewhat taken by surprise, fumbled and only just managed to hang on to it with one hand.

"Bit slimy," said Ben, wiping the ball on the grass. He then whipped the ball back to Edward, straight at his midriff. Game on. The ball was thrown at varying speeds from one to the other, whilst the dogs followed the action, hoping to pick up from a dropped catch. Edward did his best to tease the girls, throwing high and low alternately, or just out of reach. Sometimes this got the better of Jules, but rarely Charlotte who combined determination with swift, deft movement. Ben was impressed. As she took one particularly sharp chance, he clapped. She spun round in his direction, panting slightly, glowing, hair flung back, shining blue eyes flashing, challenging, tempting. It was an image which seared into his consciousness with as much force as the ball coming at head height in his direction. Reflexes to the rescue brought hands to the ball, just in time. He threw back firmly to her. She returned harder and to one side. He flipped back lower, to the other side; and back it went even harder, and back again harder still.

"Hey," called out a rather peeved sounding Lawrence, "if I may interrupt your private contest, there are others who would quite like to join in."

Charlotte turned swiftly and flung the ball straight at him. He was far too slow to react and the ball bounced off his chest, to the outward amusement of Edward and the inward satisfaction of Ben. To add to Lawrence's discomfort, one of the dogs promptly ran off with the ball. It had, of course, to be Jock.

They had crested the hill and were heading down the other side, towards the river. Edward pointed off to the left. "We shouldn't get too close to the weir, just beyond those trees with the thicket on the bank. It's running fast after the recent rain and we need to keep the dogs well clear." So that's what they duly did, the Labradors running well ahead and Jock trotting happily around assorted feet. Then suddenly a rabbit appeared, running fast diagonally from right to left, making for the cover of the very thicket to be avoided. Needless to say, the Labradors gave chase and Jock peeled off in hot pursuit. Loud calling from Edward, Jules and Charlotte had no immediate effect. But the Labradors, being gun-dog trained, pulled up just short of the river on loud blasts of the whistle on the cord round Jules' neck. It had no such effect, however, on the terrier in Jock. He crashed full tilt into the thicket and disappeared from view. In the moment of horrified looks and an anguished cry from Charlotte, Ben set off, sprinting fast down the slope towards the thicket. Edward shouted at Jules to put the Labradors on leads, throwing the one he was carrying in her direction, and set off at full speed after Ben. "Come on," he shouted over his shoulder to Lawrence, "we may need your help too."

Ben had reached the thicket and was on his knees, peering through the tangle of undergrowth. As Edward reached him, with Lawrence a little way behind, Ben jumped to his feet. "I've seen him, over the far side, dangling over the water's edge; I think his collar is caught on something, but, if it breaks free, he'll be down in the drink."

"Christ," expostulated Edward, "then he will go over the weir. What the hell can we do?"

"It'll be too difficult to get through to him from here; there's only one option!" shouted Ben as he rounded the edge of the thicket on the far side of the weir and headed for the bank.

Edward's call to be careful coincided with a splash as Ben launched himself into the swirling water, grabbing at branches of the thicket overhanging the river to stop himself being swept away. The shock of the cold water was counteracted by an adrenalin-fuelled determination to hang on for all he was worth.

"For God's sake, this is far too dangerous; you must get out now; here, grab my hand," said Edward, down on one knee on the bank and leaning out as far as he dared.

"No," Ben shook his head. "We can bloody well do this. But I need your help to hang on to me while I go under the thicket."

"You must be fucking mad."

"Just get in here for Christ's sake. Hold on to the branches, like I'm doing. I can't reach you otherwise. Then Lawrence will have to do the same, but keeping close to the bank and holding on to that low branch sticking out there. We can then form a human chain to pull each other out."

"You're a bloody maniac," said Edward grimly. "You absolutely must get out now and I'm going to help you." But he still couldn't reach Ben from the bank. Time and options were running out, so in he went, grabbing frantically at branches, then latching on to Ben's outstretched left hand. Twisting back towards the bank he focused on a stunned-looking Lawrence. "Come on man, quickly, you heard what Ben said; we need your help to get out."

The urgency in the voice caused Lawrence, if not to jump in, at least to slither down the bank into the water. He reached up for the overhanging branch and edged along it until he was in touching distance of Edward. "Right," said Edward to Ben, "keep hold of my hand and I'll hang on to Lawrence; we can then inch back to the bank."

"That's the plan," said Ben. "But first there's the rescue." He shook his hand free and to the shocked amazement of those in the water and on the bank ducked under the thicket. Bobbing up and down and weaving between branches, holding on to whatever came to hand, Ben worked himself towards a struggling Jock. He could see now that the dog had been fortunate indeed to be snagged by the collar, but only on a slender offshoot of a branch which was sagging dangerously and about to break off at any moment. The pull of the water was becoming stronger and Ben was having to hold on ever more tightly. He was just in reach as he saw the branch holding Jock begin to break. Gripping on to an overhang as hard as he could with his left hand he lunged with his right and grabbed the dog by the scruff of his neck. Holding him tight to his body, he pulled himself one-handedly back the way he had come, suffering double scratches from the thicket and Jock's claws as he kicked and squirmed in panic, particularly when being briefly submerged on a couple of occasions. A final lunge and he was clear, gripping Edward's outstretched hand. The sudden tug on the human chain nearly caused Lawrence to lose his hold on the branch, but he hung on with all the effort he could muster as Edward pulled himself along the branch with Ben clinging on behind him. Latched on to the branch, one by one they reached the bank and scrambled and clambered their way up to safety, declining the girls' outstretched hands for fear of pulling them in. Ben did, though, thrust Jock up to the waiting Charlotte before levering himself on to dry land. For a moment he paused on all fours, breathing hard, dripping wet, freezing cold, scratched and sore, but with an overriding feeling nevertheless of exhilaration. As he stood up he felt an arm round his neck. Charlotte, still clutching Jock under the other arm, drew herself against him. He felt slight tremors as she sobbed softly.

It was a hurried return to the house, wet clothes hanging heavy and increasingly cold, shoes sloshing and squelching. The Labradors, let off leads, were allowed to run ahead. Jock, though, was kept firmly in check by Charlotte as she and Jules mulled over what had happened and speculated, in hushed tones, about what might have been.

"I'm at a loss for words," said Edward walking quickly beside Ben, with Lawrence a few paces behind. "I just don't know what I should say really; whether I should be bollocking you or singing your praises. What you did was dangerous, bloody stupid actually, but by hell you pulled it off all right and saved the day."

"It was OK really," said Ben quietly, beginning to shiver. "I reckoned there was a fair chance of getting him out, so I went for it."

"Charlotte will be forever in your debt," said Lawrence over

141

Ben's shoulder. Did he sound rather peevish wondered Ben? He just shrugged by way of response.

As they reached the back door Jules ran in ahead of them with news of what had happened. Her parents then both came rushing out, looking most concerned.

"Goodness," said Mrs Brooke, "you lads must get out of those wet things as quickly as possible. Into the kitchen with you and strip off in front of the AGA. I shall find you some towels. Charles?" she called out to her husband. "Run up to Edward's room and find some dry clothes for them." She thought for a moment. "I'm not sure about shoes, though."

"*Tackies* would do," suggested Ben.

"Sorry, what dear?" queried a puzzled Mrs.Brooke.

"*Tackies.*"

Still a look of puzzlement. Crikey, thought Ben. What do they call them here? Oh yes, a rueful smile: "Gym shoes," he blurted out. Lawrence was looking uncomprehending. Edward was quietly sniggering.

"Was that a Swahili word you used, Ben?" asked Mrs Brooke.

"No, no, but I didn't realise it's not an English word either. But anyway," he added quickly, anxious to move on, "please don't worry; size may be a problem and we can easily pad about barefoot while our shoes dry out."

A short while later three naked men were gratefully absorbing the warmth of the Aga, almost dry and about to make selections from the shirts, trousers and jerseys left for them on the kitchen chairs. The door swung open, framing for a brief moment Jules and Charlotte who just had time to take in the rear view of three bodies, two white, varyingly smooth and hairy, one golden brown and toned with a mere flash of white buttocks. In

142

amongst the surprised looks all round two pairs of blue eyes met for an instant across the room before the door was hurriedly pulled shut by Jules. "Sorry guys," she called out. "We thought you'd finished changing." And she leant against the door, trying to stifle laughter.

"Sure you did," called back Edward. "Very funny; well, that was your cheap thrill for the day."

Jules nudged Charlotte. "Well worth a view, don't you think? Crikey me, quite an Adonis."

"I'm not sure what you mean," said Charlotte rather curtly.

"Oh, come off it; your eyes were riveted in one direction only."

Mrs Brooke was calling out from the hall. "Tea in the sitting room when you're ready."

"See the conquering hero comes," chanted Mr Brooke as Ben came into the room and took a seat by the fire.

"OK, Dad, that'll do just fine," quickly intervened Edward.

"Now," said Mrs Brooke, carefully putting down a large plate on a side table, "while you were out I made some scones, particularly to bring back happy memories for Ben." She looked up, caught his eye and smiled. "I do hope they compare."

"What on earth are you referring to?" inquired a mystified Jules.

"Ah, inside knowledge," was the only reply.

There was visible relaxation with the warm comfort of afternoon tea round the fire; time to sink back against plumped-up cushions, dogs ranged around, stretched out on rugs. Happy conversation went back and forth as plates were passed round and cups filled and re-filled. There was no more talk of the drama of the day, but, perhaps inevitably, a turning full circle brought them back once more to the subject of Kenya.

"Your grandparents must have had a high old time in Kenya," said Mr Brooke, looking across to Ben. "You know what I mean, I'm sure, the Happy Valley Set and all that, non-stop partying and socialising, looked after by servants, plenty of time for enjoying pretty well anything you fancied."

"Yes, they had a great time." Ben paused for a moment, thinking carefully about what to say next. "But they were never part of the Happy Valley Set; in fact they didn't have a good word to say for them."

"Oh really?"

"No, you see, those in that Set were really only a small minority of settlers, mainly aristocrats, some with plenty of money behind them, who formed a kind of clique. They lived pretty scandalous lives. As I grew up I got to hear the stories about orgies, drinking and drug taking, going off with other people's wives and husbands and so on."

"Sounds pretty good to me," interjected Edward, prompting pained looks from Charlotte and Lawrence.

"For a few maybe," said Ben with a brief smile, before wrinkling his brow. "But my grandmother, in particular, and many like her, thought they were a complete disgrace."

"And your grandfather?" asked Mr Brooke.

"Well, he was more broad-minded. His objection was that they brought the colony into disrepute, as he used to say, with the assumption in many circles, back here in England and elsewhere, that this was the norm for the settler community, which was far from the truth when it came to him and most of his friends; so it made him pretty pissed off; sorry, excuse me." A brief embarrassed pause provided Ben with the opportunity to have a mouthful of scone before continuing. "He also used to get

144

particularly fed up with the old jokes which used to go round, 'Are you married or do you live in Kenya?', and all that sort of stuff."

Mr Brooke started to chortle and then thought better of it. "Sorry, I'm sure your grandfather was out of a very different drawer."

"Yes, very much so." Ben was getting pumped up. "He worked bloody hard, actually, frequently with the odds stacked against him. In the early pioneering days it was very much experimental farming; he often didn't know, until he tried, what crops would really work, or what animals would survive tick and mosquito-borne disease; and then, even as time went on, there were always perils to be faced; bush fires, locusts, and wild animals trampling crops, sometimes just before harvest. He didn't have capital behind him, like some of the bloody Happy Valley lot, so he often had to go cap in hand to the bank manager to tide himself over for another year, until another harvest, or until animals could go to market. And that is how it was for many."

There was rather a stunned silence in the room. Speech over, Ben sensed the need to lighten up. "Grandpa did, though, get a kick out of the Happy Valley Set in one respect."

"Oh, what was that?" queried Mr Brooke.

"The Erroll murder." Ben grinned, seeing quizzical looks, but let his rather cryptic answer hang in the air as the scones were being passed round again.

"Do have another," said Mrs Brooke. "They're still warm."

Ben took a mouthful and shut his eyes for a moment. "It makes me imagine I'm back with the aunts." More quizzical looks, but a knowing smile from Mrs Brooke.

"Let me think now." Mr Brooke was scratching his head,

dragging up a vague memory. "Erroll was the chap who was bumped off in Kenya and a fellow aristocrat was accused of his murder. It caused quite a sensation, if I recall correctly, with wide press coverage here as well."

"That's quite right," said Ben, no longer feeling defensive and beginning to enjoy himself again. "It's even been called the murder mystery of the century."

"So, who was the man who was murdered?" asked Jules.

"Josslyn Hay, the Earl of Erroll; he was one of the leading members of the Happy Valley Set. He was having an affair, the latest of his affairs I should add, with a very glamourous woman, Lady Diana Broughton. They had been out together one night, having previously had dinner at the Muthaiga Club with the woman's husband no less, Sir Delves Broughton; incredible stuff really." Ben was really warming to this. "Anyway, after Erroll took Diana home to her husband, in the early hours of the morning, he drove off and that was it."

"What do you mean?" queried Edward.

"He was found later, not far away, slumped over the wheel of his car. He had been shot dead at point blank range."

"Yes, of course, I remember now," said Mr Brooke. "It was Broughton who was then charged with Erroll's murder."

"Right, but he got off. There was a sensational trial, full of scandal, people couldn't get enough of it. Broughton was defended by a hotshot lawyer from South Africa and he was acquitted."

"He must have been a happy man," mused Edward. "Presumably he had been on trial for his life."

"Well, here's the thing which got everyone going again. He later went back to England and committed suicide."

"Gracious," said Mrs Brooke, "doesn't that rather suggest he

146

was guilty?"

"Possibly, but as my grandma says, any number of others could have been queueing up to do him in, 'jealous husbands and jilted lovers' is how she puts it."

"But it was your grandfather's reaction, which you mentioned, which got us onto the subject," Mr Brooke reminded Ben.

"Oh yes, he felt the whole thing provided some light relief from all the gloom of the War. He also had no sympathy with Erroll, not just because of the Happy Valley business, but also because Erroll had fascist leanings."

"Crikey," said Lawrence sitting forward and taking more interest than he had shown hitherto. "That must have been pretty controversial in a British colony during the War."

"Absolutely, there's even some theory that this is why he was bumped off."

"Ben, how do you know so much about all this?" queried a rather puzzled-looking Charlotte. "You say it happened during the War, which was long before you were even born."

Ben laughed. "Easy, because it's still talked about and debated in Kenya, even to this day. Lots of people have their own theories and some claim to have inside knowledge, including my old history teacher, actually, who was at Muthaiga Club on the night in question when Erroll was with the Broughtons."

"Well," said Jules leaning forward and clasping her knees, "I think it all sounds incredibly exciting; makes life in good old England seem rather dull by comparison."

Tea was being cleared away and watches looked at. Jules had a train to catch early evening. Charlotte was off to spend a night with her parents and Lawrence was returning to Oxford. Edward was muttering about getting back to Bristol in time to prepare for a tutorial which he should have done days before. There were grateful thanks all round to Mrs Brooke for such a good lunch. And great relief was expressed at the outcome of the events of the afternoon. It was generally agreed that it had been quite a day. But Lawrence hadn't quite done with Ben. There was still a little time before they had to leave and there was something in particular he wanted to find out.

"Ben, I hope you don't mind me asking, but I've been really interested hearing about your family and, I'm intrigued to know, how have they reacted to independence?"

He had to think for a moment; although he was tiring, there were a few things important enough, he felt, still to say. "It was hardest for my grandparents, at first at least. Grandpa was pretty negative in the period leading up to independence. He used to say that although he hadn't exactly expected the British Empire to last a thousand years, he had never thought either that it would end in his lifetime. It was a real shock to him. He had devoted so much of his life to the country."

"Did he fear for the future?" asked Lawrence.

"He did actually. He was living with us by then and he was a man of strict routine." Ben permitted himself a brief smile. "Every evening, shortly before six o'clock, and you could set your watch by this, he would appear in the sitting room. There would be the sound of him tapping out his pipe, followed by the whoosh of the soda siphon for his glass of brandy, and then the click of the radio to come on just in time for the pips before the news. He used to sit in his chair listening intently. Then, as soon as the news was over, he would switch off the radio, tap out his pipe again, and leave the room saying, as he went, 'the country's finished'. Yup, that was about it, every evening."

"And what about your grandmother?" queried Lawrence.

"She was really afraid, that we would be thrown out of the country or even, as she used to say, 'murdered in our beds'."

"That was most unlikely, surely?"

"You're probably right; it's certainly easy to say now. But, at the time, there was real fear, particularly because of what had happened elsewhere."

"Where do you mean?" asked Mr Brooke, rising interest drawing him into the conversation.

"The Congo, which had become independent a few years earlier. Belgians had to flee for their lives from the violence. Properties were seized and looted, people were murdered and women were raped. I remember, when I was growing up, some of those who escaped coming to Kenya, as refugees, and having to be provided with shelter, clothing, food, you name it; they had nothing."

Ben could see that Mrs Brooke was really quite shocked. "Well, thank goodness," she said, "that things turned out differently in Kenya."

"Yes, as my parents thought that they would. They were more positive about the future than my grandparents. They had their concerns about independence, sure, and braced for it, but they were also, as they used to say 'cautiously optimistic'; and they have since adapted well."

"And you, Ben?" asked Jules, sitting well forward on the sofa next to him. "How did you feel about the coming of independence?"

"Ah well, here's the thing; for me it was completely different."

"Why so?"

"Well, you see, I lived it in a way, I suppose." His voice took

149

on a certain intensity as his brow furrowed. "It was part of my upbringing, through my formative years. There were big changes which came quickly, at school, in the town and cities, in the country, everywhere. One of my teachers said that we were seeing history in the making and I realise now that he was right and I feel privileged, in a way, to have experienced it." He paused for a moment. "Sorry, I'm not sure if I'm explaining it properly; it's quite difficult to put into words. But there was so much anticipation and excitement about it all, particularly with the Africans I was growing up with, a sense of expectation and feeling that their future was now in their hands; I got caught up in it I think." There was another pause, but he clearly was thinking of something to add, something important, waited for silently. "I suppose it comes down to this; I was born in colonial times, but I grew up as a Kenyan, first and foremost, and I'm proud of it."

All eyes were on him, no one moved and there was not a sound in the room until the silence was broken by Edward. "That was quite a speech, Ben."

Charlotte's mind was racing back to something. "Ben, I was interested that you used the words 'at first' about the coming of independence being hard for your grandparents. Does that mean there was then a change?"

"Yes, over time, they came to accept, a bit reluctantly, even a bit grudgingly at first, that things were working out better than expected, or, at the very least, were not nearly as bad as they had feared that they might be."

"What did they put that down to, do you suppose?" asked Mr Brooke.

"'Reconciliation' was the word my granddad had for it. There was a spirit of reconciliation between the Africans and the

Europeans, and the Asians too, not to dwell on the past, not to kick out people who were rooted in the country, but to move forward together in the new national interest; *harambee*, let's pull together, became the country's motto. Grandpa gave Kenyatta full credit for this; he came to see him in a wholly new light."

Charlotte was still looking thoughtful. "I suppose it was a great relief to your grandfather, whether or not it really made him happy in the end."

Ben looked across at her sitting on the opposite sofa. "I can tell you that he was content at least, with the way things finally worked out, but above all he was really grateful for the life he had had there."

"Did he say as much?"

"What he said to me, shortly before he died, last year, was that although he had never made any money, despite having worked hard 'had nothing to show for it', as he put it, still, given the chance, he would do it all over again."

Mrs Brooke had immediate cause for thought. "I suspect that not many people end up being able to say that. Do you have any idea why he felt the way he did?"

"I think that meeting the challenges which he had to face gave him a lot of satisfaction, but, above all, I reckon, he just got such a kick out of his life there." Looking round the room, at the expressions on people's faces, he was uncertain whether he had really explained it properly or whether, indeed, it was capable of any simple explanation. "I don't know," he said, running his fingers through his hair, "it's difficult to put into words; man, you have to see it, feel it, breathe it." Looking down he noticed that his fists were tightly clenched.

Jules put a hand gently on his shoulder. "It sounds as if you feel just as your grandfather did."

Ben shot her a grateful smile, but then directed his attention back to Lawrence once more. "In answer to your original question, there's just one final thing I should add."

"Oh, really?"

"One of the last things Granddad said to me was that he had been wrong about Kenyatta; he reflected about this saying 'to think that I used to say that he should have been strung up with Kimathi'."

"Who on earth was Kimathi?" asked Edward.

"One of the main leaders of the Mau Mau uprising; probably the cleverest, and certainly the most ruthless and most feared of all. He was eventually hunted down, captured, tried and hanged." There was a moment of stunned silence. "But since independence he has come to be regarded as a hero," Ben added quickly. "There is even a street in Nairobi named after him."

Lawrence had leant well forward and it was his turn now for fists to be clenched. "I have read about Mau Mau. At the core of it was the land question we were talking about earlier. This was an insurgency by the dispossessed. More and more is coming to light about it; I know of people researching it further and, I can tell you, other books will be written about it." It was evident that he was becoming increasingly worked up. "It has already been shown to be a dark stain on British colonialism." He paused before adding grimly, "And I think it will be proved to be the darkest stain of all."

"Right, time out," said Edward quickly. "That's quite enough for one day; I'm sorry I asked the question."

But there was no need for the intervention. Ben had already retreated into silence.

The light was fading as the early spring warmth seeped from the day. They gathered in the hall for final thanks and farewells. Mr Brooke slapped Ben on the back and wished him well. Mrs Brooke, for her part, kissed Ben on one cheek and then leant back, placing her hands on his shoulders, seemingly scanning his face. "It's been a really fascinating day," she said. "I'm so glad you were able to join us."

Jules stepped forward telling Ben that if he didn't visit her in Norfolk she was jolly well going to come and see him in Bristol. He nodded blankly, not knowing quite how to react. He was just aware of Edward and Lawrence catching each other's eye and smirking. But he was careful to avoid looking at Charlotte, until she appeared in front of him. "See you next week, Ben," she said softly. She hugged him tightly, just for a moment. "I'm really grateful, you know, for what you did for Jock."

As she turned away Lawrence clasped Ben's hand and shook it, surprisingly firmly. "It's been good to meet you and really interesting talking to you. I apologise if I've appeared challenging at times."

"No, that's fine, really. Both you and Charlotte have given me a lot to think about."

Releasing the handshake Lawrence smiled. "I think it's fair to say you have given us a lot to think about too."

Damn, thought Ben, Edward's right. Lawrence is actually a good bloke.

SINS OF THE FATHERS

The soul that sinneth, it shall die. The son shall not bear
the iniquity of the father, neither shall the father bear the
inequity of the son: the righteousness of the righteous shall
be upon him, and the wickedness of the wicked shall be upon
him.

Ezekiel XIX, 20

The drizzle of the grey, damp rainy season Saturday afternoon
was easing somewhat as the boys trooped off the rugby pitch.
Ben paused and leant forward, hands on knees, panting and
steaming slightly. He dripped mud and it was difficult to make
out the actual colours of the Duke of York School first fifteen kit.
He stood up straight as Joe approached, equally bespattered, but
with a triumphant air. They slapped one another on the back,
rejoicing in a hard won victory to which each had contributed
individually and in combination.

"I didn't see your folks," said Joe scanning the crowd of
spectators still milling round the touchline.

"No, they couldn't make it. Have you got anyone here?"

"Yes, my aunt, Grace." He pointed in the direction of a slim
African woman in her late thirties, swathed in a plastic mac, but
sporting a colourful headscarf under an umbrella still held aloft.
He laughed. "She doesn't really understand this *mzungu* game,
as she calls it, but she is keen to support me and so she comes
anyway."

Ben had, in fact, met her briefly before, at end of term events. They waved to one another before Ben turned towards Joe saying, "Well, I'll leave you to it; see you back in the House later."

"No man, come and say hallo; I'm sure she'd like to see you again."

As they approached her she smiled warmly. "I'm glad to see you boys are still in one piece. This game of yours seems to involve some kind of warfare."

"This is Ben," said Joe.

"Yes, of course; I've met him before; and, anyway, you're always talking about him."

Joe looked slightly embarrassed, but Ben felt rather pleased.

Grace took a step back as she put down her umbrella, shaking off the accumulated drops of water. Looking again at the two bedraggled figures in front of her, she laughed and shook her head. "I would not want to have to do your *dhobi*; no way." She made them turn round for further inspection and laughed again.

"Where are you parked?" asked Joe.

"Outside your boarding house, near the dining hall."

"OK, well let's walk there together." And they set off, the boys still dripping and squelching. They chatted away, mainly about school, what the boys had been doing and how they were getting along. Grace was particularly keen to be assured that in the midst of all the sporting and other activities, about which they enthused, that they were also working hard towards their Higher School Certificate exams, now only months away at the end of the following term.

"I can promise you I shall be doing my best for the exams. My father would never forgive me otherwise; and I wouldn't forgive myself," said Joe with a concentrated frown.

"He will work hard, I know," said Ben supportively, "even though he'll also be a star player in the football first eleven." He slightly regretted the last remark when he saw a quizzical look on Grace's face.

"And you," she asked, "will you also be spending time playing football with Joe?"

"No, actually, I shall be playing cricket, which takes rather longer; so I'll have to be disciplined about my study time."

"Ah, another *mzungu* game," she mused, "five years after independence. But I suppose some colonial traditions will live on," she added matter-of-factly.

"I like football too," said Ben brightly. But you can't do both; you have to choose one or the other, and I think I can make more of a contribution playing in the cricket team."

Joe gave him a friendly shove. "You probably wouldn't even get into the football first eleven."

Ben grinned. "It pains me to admit that you might be right." And he shoved him back. "You see," he said, turning to Grace, "there's such talent now, some coming up through the junior ranks of the school. There's a Luo boy in our House, only in the third form, and he'll make the team for sure; what a player."

Joe nodded in agreement. Ben nudged him in the ribs saying, "He can even run rings round you."

"No way," said Joe, without much conviction, and smiling happily enough.

They had reached the House, but before there were any goodbyes there was talk of plans for the following day, an exeat Sunday.

"I'll pick you up here tomorrow," Grace said to her nephew.

"Yes, I'll be ready waiting, at the usual time. What are we going to do?"

"Nothing too exciting I'm afraid. But I'm going to cook you a good lunch, better than this school *chakula* here." She laughed. "It looks as if you could do with some feeding up."

Joe turned to Ben. "Are your parents taking you to lunch at the Norfolk Hotel?"

"No, not this time."

"Where then?"

"Actually, I've had a message from the house master; they can't make it this weekend; something's cropped up at the last minute."

"So, what will you do?"

"It's been too late to make any other arrangement, so I'll stay here and catch up with some work, I guess."

Grace was looking concerned. "Excuse me one moment," she said to Ben and she took Joe to one side where they put their heads together and exchanged a few hushed words. Joe then turned and stepped back towards Ben. "Aunt Grace wants to know if you would like to come to lunch with us. She didn't want to just ask you in case it caused any embarrassment, but, knowing you, I said it would be OK, to ask at least."

Ben would have to admit to himself that he was taken aback at first, but he was not slow to accept, gratefully, and with an increasingly warm feeling.

"Thank you, thank you so much. I shall have to get the house master to phone my parents for permission, but I know that it won't be a problem."

"Very good, then see you tomorrow."

The rain clouds began to disperse on Sunday morning, the sun winning the battle to break through, illuminating and warming the landscape as it did so. Ben was sitting in the back of Grace's small car, with Joe in the front seat next to his aunt. They headed down the long stretch of the Ngong Road towards central Nairobi, then cut across to Uhuru Highway, running along one edge of the city centre. In between chatting Ben gazed out of the window; it felt good to have a change of scene after the repetitive rigours of the school routine. Initially Ben was somewhat uncertain as to how to address Grace, not wanting to be too formal, but also anxious not to cross any bounds of familiarity. Being perceptive enough to sense this, she quickly put him at his ease saying, "Please, do call me Grace." She seemed particularly interested in pursuing further a topic from the previous afternoon, asking a lot of questions about the boys' studies and how hard they were working, giving the distinct impression, at times, that she rather disapproved of the potential for too many distractions. Ben discovered that she had been to the University of Nairobi, as a mature student, graduating with a history degree. It was clear that she was justly proud of this achievement, the first in her family ever to go on to higher education, and it was plainly a matter of great importance to her that Joe should make the most of his opportunities and follow in her footsteps; not that he was going to do history. "I'm so proud," she said, "doing the three sciences so that he can go on to medical school. Ah, to have a doctor in the family; what an achievement that would be." Joe looked rather embarrassed, or bashful perhaps, as Ben nodded and murmured words of understanding and agreement. They then both reverted to looking out of the window again.

The buildings of Grace's *alma mater* came into view on the right as they neared the end of the highway. At the roundabout by the National Museum they branched off up the hill, past the International Casino, and on into the suburb of Westlands. A side road led to a small block of flats, one of which, on the first floor, was where Grace lived. She parked the car and the boys followed her up the stairs.

"Come in boys and make yourselves comfortable. There are some newspapers and magazines to read, if you're interested. I must just go to the kitchen and finish off preparing lunch."

Ben looked round the small, rectangular living room. It was somewhat sparsely, but adequately, furnished; comfortable in its own way. There were double doors at one end opening on to a little balcony bedecked with pots of African violets. In the room itself were two armchairs and, in one corner, a table and plastic chairs. On the walls were a slightly lurid oil painting of an African scene and two interesting photographs of President Kenyatta surrounded by rather distinguished-looking Kikuyu elders; perhaps, Ben wondered, including members of Joe's family. But what impressed Ben most was a bookcase covering an entire wall with every shelf filled, including some books stacked on top of others: history, politics, biography, classics, religion and other topics too; serious reading. Joe was sitting in one of the armchairs flicking through a newspaper. Ben picked up a *Time* magazine and made himself comfortable in the other chair.

A voice called out through the door of the adjoining kitchen. "I know you boys are old enough now to drink Tusker; but I don't touch alcohol and there's none in the flat I'm afraid."

"No, that's fine," chorused the boys.

"But I can offer you Pepsi; there's some in the fridge, Joe. Come and help yourself."

He got up and returned shortly after holding two full glasses, already beginning to glisten with condensation. The boys drank the ice-cold liquid thirstily. As they continued their reading, commenting on the material intermittently, they became increasingly aware of aromas of cooking and the clattering of plates and pans. Lunch was imminent and taste buds had become aroused.

"Right boys, come and sit up." Grace appeared from the kitchen holding a large steaming pot. Joe and Ben took seats at the table while Grace shuttled back and forth bringing out more food: rice, sweet potatoes, mealies and beans. The boys lost no time in applying themselves to it with relish.

"The stew is really good," said Joe after a while, as Grace helped him to another generous spoonful.

"Well, I know it's your favourite from home." She smiled, looking affectionately at her nephew. "I hope it's up to standard." His mouth full, he nodded vigorously.

"It's delicious," said Ben, "such a welcome change from the usual Sunday lunch at school." He paused. "I know they try to do their best, but I smell the vegetables cooking as early as after breakfast." There was laughter all round.

"You know, I don't actually do a lot of cooking," said Grace. "But, when I do, it gives me pleasure to see it being appreciated. Ben, you must have some more too."

They filled up contentedly, leaving just enough room for some fruit and the final treat, choc ices, bought in specially, and retrieved from the small icebox at the top of the fridge with eager hands. Grace had done them proud.

After all had finished, Grace accepted help in clearing the table, but was adamant that the boys should do no washing-up. They settled back into the armchairs, warm, comfortable and full. There was a somnolent air in the room when, after a while, Grace re-joined them. But Ben immediately became alert and jumped up, offering Grace his chair.

"No, thank you Ben, you stay where you are. I'm quite

happy on one of these chairs from the table." She pulled one up and sat down opposite the boys.

"It's great that you live in Nairobi and can see Joe and take him out," said Ben.

"Yes, it is fortunate because, as you may know, his parents live quite a long way away. And, as you may have realised, I follow his progress quite carefully." She laughed and leant forward, placing one hand affectionately on Joe's shoulder. He raised his eyebrows slightly, but nodded and grinned.

Ben was looking thoughtful. "I think, Joe, I've only seen your dad at school, briefly, on a few occasions. I'm not sure about your mum."

"She has been, but only a couple of times." Joe had begun to look a bit uncomfortable.

Sensing this, perhaps, Grace intervened, feeling possibly that Ben, as a good friend, deserved some explanation. "It's not easy for them to come; it is, as I've said, a long way. But, to be completely frank, there is another factor here. My brother is not entirely comfortable with the school. Even though it has changed so much in the last few years, since *uhuru*, he still sees it as part of the old *mzungu* establishment."

Ben looked shocked and worried, Joe embarrassed. Grace wondered whether she had said too much. But having come this far, it was not something to be left hanging in the air. Ben had a follow-up question. "Does he not really want Joe to be at the school?"

"No, he does, it's something he has had to wrestle with, within himself, because whatever his feelings may be, he is very keen for Joe to have the best possible education. And I support him absolutely in that."

Ben still had a worried frown. "And *mzungu*, generally, is

that a problem for him?"

"Yes and no; it's complicated. There has been a very bad problem in our family from what happened to our brother, Joe's uncle, Mwangi, and his wife, during the time of Mau Mau."

"No, no Aunt, please," said Joe, showing some signs of distress, "we should not talk of this."

She took his hands, saying firmly, but kindly, "Sometimes hard things have to be said, so that there can be proper understanding; so much about Mau Mau has been swept under the carpet."

"It must have affected your brother very badly," said Ben thoughtfully.

"Yes, me too, although to a lesser extent. I'm much younger and perhaps that has helped me come to terms with it, to some degree. But, make no mistake, it has left a deep wound which cannot heal easily."

"I do know," said Ben, "that bad things happened, but to Europeans too."

"Yes, they did, and those are the ones you will have heard most about. The British made sure of that."

Kinangop, Kenya — 24 January 1953

It had been just another day on the farm for the Ruck family. Roger was a hard-working farmer of British origin, but a popular and established member of the settler community. He was in his early thirties, as was his attractive and sociable wife, Esme. Their young son, Michael, aged six, had been brought up to an African life, a life among Africans, in that lovely part of the White Highlands. He liked to roam free and to play with the children of the Kikuyu workers who lived near the farmhouse.

But these were dark and worrying times. The Mau Mau

uprising had started in earnest some months previously, in 1952, and an Emergency had been declared by the colonial government. Attacks on settlers had begun and people had been murdered. Instructions had been issued to settlers to take extra safety precautions, to be on their guard and to arm themselves in their homes. The murders continued nonetheless. Two men had been hacked to death as recently as New Year's Day 1953, as they sat having dinner in their home that evening. They had both been armed, but neither had managed to fire before being overpowered by fifteen or so Kikuyu men who burst into their dining room. There was a further attack on a settler farm the very next night. But on this occasion two elderly, but formidable, ladies had been diligent in following the advice of the police. They were armed and had moved their table and chairs so that they were well clear of the entrance to their sitting room. They suspected something was wrong because their house servant was behaving nervously and they readied themselves. As the first member of the Mau Mau gang entered the room, Raynes Simpson shot him dead. She then fired at another attacker, while her companion, Kitty Hesselberger, blasted off with her shotgun. The attackers retreated to the kitchen, but other danger was still close by. The ladies heard sounds from the bathroom next to the sitting room. They aimed their guns at the thin dividing wall and fired a salvo of shots, killing two Kikuyu men lying in waiting. Attack turned into retreat. The men fled, leaving three dead. The ladies had prevailed and were heralded as heroines. There was wide reportage in the press in Kenya and elsewhere. Kitty Hesselberger was even interviewed on BBC radio. Robust and resolute she had no regret about anything, except only for the death of her dog shot by accident. There was so much in this to be admired, by the settlers, and, they hoped, by the wider world.

Perhaps Roger Ruck felt as well prepared as he could be to deal with the known threat at a time of heightened awareness. He was in his prime, young and fit, and had undergone security training as a member of the Kenya Police Reserve, the KPR. His reputation was as a man of 'strong views', firm but nevertheless fair with his workforce and thought to be liked by his domestic staff and the thirty or so squatters who lived with their families on the farm. He was resourceful and self-sufficient. He had to be. The farm was in a remote part of the Kinangop, many miles from the nearest police post and even further from the nearest town of Naivasha in the Rift Valley. And Esme, too, was well regarded and respected. She had put her medical training to good use, running a clinic on the farm where she treated the workforce and their families, and even squatters from the surrounding areas. It was in these very areas where there had been recent trouble. The local commander of the KPR had been shot at, only the previous evening. Roger knew that Mau Mau were active in the vicinity and had posted extra guards at outbuildings and to watch over his cattle. But what he didn't know was that Mau Mau had already infiltrated his workforce. There had been a recent turnover of workers. Strangers were on the farm and oaths had been administered. The strangers and some of the squatters had made a plan. In the darkness of that night lurked extreme danger.

"I'm going to get Michael to bed now," said Esme. The family had finished their evening meal and the table was being cleared. She took him to his bedroom upstairs. As he undressed, she noticed that he still had a few bruises from the fall from his pony a few days before. It could have been worse. Fortunately a trusted servant had rushed to his rescue, comforted him and carried him home to the arms of his mother. When he was snuggled into bed Esme tucked him up with his teddy bears. She then kissed him goodnight before stepping carefully over his toy trains, strewn over the floor, on her way out of the room. She turned off the light and shut the door, locking it behind her as part of their increased security measures.

Downstairs the domestic staff had finished clearing away and had left the house. Esme joined her husband in the sitting room. Glancing at her watch she noticed that it was just on nine o'clock. There was still time to enjoy the relaxation of the evening. At that moment any such thought was instantly banished by one of the farm workers shouting outside that he had caught a Mau Mau intruder. Roger snatched up his Beretta pistol and cautiously let himself out onto the veranda. In doing so he at once fell into a carefully laid trap. He was grabbed from behind with his arms pinned to his side. Although he struggled to free himself, to try to use his weapon, before he could do so another attacker slashed at his legs with a *panga*. As he fell to the ground his assailants hacked at his head and back, inflicting terrible injuries. Inevitably Esme heard his loud screams. She grabbed a shotgun and rushed out to the aid of her stricken husband, ready to fire. It was no doubt an instinctive reaction on her part, but one doomed to failure. As soon as she emerged from the house she too was hacked down. The same fate befell a loyal farm worker who came running to try to help the Rucks. After the screams had subsided three lay dead on the front lawn.

The assailants poured unchallenged into the house. Rampaging around they were in search of guns, ammunition, money, clothing, food even, anything of use or value to them. But there was still one more horrific act to follow. Upstairs they came upon a locked door behind which lay the terrified young Michael. Smashing down the door they surged into the room and hacked the little boy to death as he cowered in his bed. At last a deadly hush descended and the quiet of the night was restored. The attackers began to disperse. One of their number lingered for a moment, wide-eyed, in Michael's room, blood dripping from his *panga* onto a teddy bear and the toy train. He was the trusted servant who days earlier had so tenderly carried the boy home.

When the news broke the following day the outcry in the settler community became a bellow which echoed around the colony and reverberated against the walls of Government House itself. By mid-morning a huge throng of over fifteen hundred settlers and other members of the white community was surging through Nairobi to the official residence of the Governor, Sir Evelyn Baring. The policemen guarding the entrance had no way of stopping them. A tidal wave of furiously energised humanity swept all before them onto the lawn in front of the imposing main doors. The African police on duty hastily formed a line on the terrace, linking arms to bar the way. If anything, this inflamed the crowd even more. There were shouts for the 'nigger police' to be removed and loud, angry demands for the Governor to come out. The crowd continued to press forward. The police struggled to hold the line, even as lighted cigarettes were pressed against the naked flesh of their arms.

The Governor was within, closeted in the Cabinet Room with Michael Blundell, a leading settler politician and member of the Kenya Legislative Council, and other settler leaders. But he was far from inclined to face the mob, heard to be baying outside. When one of his aides came hurrying in to warn that the situation was rapidly getting out of control, he retreated to the safety of his study. It was left to Blundell and his colleagues to deal with the escalating situation. By now the crowd had reached the high front doors and were hammering against them with all their might. On the other side of the doors staff were rapidly pushing furniture into place to form a defensive barricade. Blundell found his way out of the building and emerged round the corner. There were shouts and cries as the crowd recognised him. He urged them to get back on the grass below the terrace, but they were so worked up that initially they refused to do so. He gambled, boldly, persuading the commanding officer to dismiss the line of African police. Only then did the surging crowd begin to subside.

Blundell climbed onto a chair and did his very best to gain attention and to be heard. It was a daunting task in a still highly-charged situation. The crowd milled around in an angry, emotional mass. Many were armed and there was a distinct lynch-mob mentality. They wanted to see Mau Mau culprits hang and were making it clear that they would do the job themselves if the government had no stomach for it. Men and women were shouting about 'fucking niggers, bloody bastards'. There were calls to 'put the troops into the Kikuyu villages and shoot them all, men, women and children'. A man with a beard clutched his pistol aloft as he shouted and raved. Another, a normally quiet scholarly man, a musician and scientist, was crouched down by the terrace, so beside himself that he was foaming at the mouth as he uttered a blistering cascade of words.

Eventually, with the help of a colleague, Humphrey Slade, Blundell managed to be heard and to restore some measure of control. He assured the gathered assembly that action would be taken, that Baring would indeed introduce sterner measures, and that there would no need for them to take the law into their own hands. They began to disperse.

The backlash was not slow in coming. Within days Baring completely reorganised Kenya's security services under military control. The British assault on Mau Mau was underway.

Grace looked across to where Ben was sitting, reflecting upon their discussion. "But you know," she said, "only thirty-two Europeans actually died during the Emergency." Seeing a look of shock on Ben's face she added, "I say 'only' because African deaths numbered in the thousands."

Ben frowned. "I think my dad has said that not all African deaths were caused by the British, but that many were killed by Mau Mau."

"He's right, to an extent. Nearly two thousand, mainly Kikuyu, were killed by Mau Mau."

"So, that wasn't the fault of the British?"

"Ah," she gave a deep sigh, "this is where you need to have some knowledge of colonial history. I think you've mentioned before, Ben, that you're doing history for your higher school cert."

"Yes, English and European history, 1815 to 1939."

Another deep sigh was followed by a look of exasperation on Grace's face. "Interesting, I'm sure; but here we are in 1968, coming up for the fifth anniversary of independence, and still your school is doing English, Cambridge exams. It's about time they started teaching Kenyan history, of the nineteenth and twentieth centuries up to 1963 would be a good place to start, although I appreciate that learning materials have to be produced and made more readily available for this purpose."

"I suppose," was all Ben could manage, rather doubtfully.

Joe was shifting around in his seat, looking uncomfortable. "I think, Aunt, they will move in this sort of direction, but it will take time."

Grace ignored this remark. She was thinking of how to throw some further light on the matter for Ben. "There were, in fact, several root causes of the dissatisfaction which led to the Mau

Mau uprising. Of course, there were the issues of lack of proper democratic rights for Africans, low fixed wages to benefit European employers, restrictions on movement, the *kipande*, racial discrimination and so on. But, at the heart of it all was the land question and it came to a head, particularly for the Kikuyu, with the squatters."

"Surely though," Ben protested, "the squatters had land on European farms, like my grandfather's farm."

Grace pulled a long face. "Leaving aside the question of people having been dispossessed in the first place, there was then a very bad situation after the Second World War."

"Oh, why?"

"Because the effect of the War was to stimulate the farming economy. The European farmers made big gains and from then, and in the years following, they developed more and more of their land. This led to many, many squatters being evicted, particularly from large areas of the White Highlands."

"Where did they go?"

"Ah, now we come to the crux of the matter. Thousands, up to, it is thought, one hundred thousand, if you can imagine that, were forcibly repatriated into central Kenya, the Kikuyu heartlands."

"Well, that was the land reserved for the Kikuyu."

"Yes, indeed, but there was not room to absorb all these people. There was not sufficient land there for the needs of so many. The result was that the returning squatters were not welcome."

"So there was trouble?"

"Oh yes, bad trouble brewed over time. The Kikuyu already established in the reserve had the land, but also were given preferential treatment by the British."

"Such as?"

"Positions of authority of various kinds, licences for market stalls to sell produce, permits to operate taxis and conduct other business, and so on and so forth. Some were very rich. Many had also become Christians. These were the 'Loyalists' and the British relied upon them for support, particularly when the Mau Mau uprising came. These Kikuyu even formed the so-called 'Home Guard' to protect themselves and supplement the British security services."

Ben was doing his best to take all this in. "This must have led to resentment on the part of other Kikuyu, the ex-squatters."

Grace leant towards him. "So much so that these were prime candidates to be oathed and recruited by Mau Mau. They then turned on the Loyalists, murdering some leaders and others, before the situation worsened even further."

"More killings?"

"Massacres even. Have you heard of the Lari Massacre?"

"No, I don't think so."

Grace shook her head. "No, you were too young at the time, but these things have never been taught to *mzungu* like you when you were growing up. It was an attack in the Kikuyu heartlands when Mau Mau killed many Loyalists, women and children too, whole families hacked to death; more than seventy dead; it was very bad."

"So, this was Kikuyu against Kikuyu."

"Yes, yes, yes." Grace was wringing her hands and her eyes were beginning to moisten. "Mau Mau was not just an uprising against the British, not just a race war, it became a vicious civil war among the Kikuyu themselves."

"That must have caused a very serious situation."

"Ah yes, but while Mau Mau divided the Kikuyu, it united

170

the white settlers as never before."

Joe decided it was time to intervene. "Can I make some *chai*?" he asked brightly.

"No, no let me do it," said Grace getting to her feet. "Sorry, I've been going on too much about these things." And she patted Ben gently on the shoulder as she passed him on the way to the kitchen.

"I hope you're not embarrassed," said Joe quietly. "Aunt Grace is very passionate about this history, which she has studied, and continues to research."

Ben smiled. "*Hakuna matata*. She's taught me things I didn't know, but probably should know, as a Kenyan, even if my family is *mzungu*."

"Biscuits?" came the call from the kitchen.

"Yes please," chorused the reply.

Soon she emerged with a tray bearing three mugs of milky tea and a plate of Baring biscuits. The tea was ready sugared, with no questions asked; hot and sweet as required. They sipped and munched in reflective silence for a while. Glancing up from his mug Ben noticed that Grace was looking at him with watchful interest. For his part he was not quite done with their previous conversation. He had something further to say or, more precisely, to ask. "How many Africans, in total, is it reckoned were killed during the Emergency?"

"That is the very question which is still being researched," replied Grace nodding appreciatively. "The official figure is eleven thousand, including the one thousand and ninety hanged by the British. But it is suspected that because of the large numbers killed by the army and security services the total is many times more than this; thousands and thousands more. The problem is that so often deaths were not recorded; there were extrajudicial killings on a large scale; often people 'disappeared' and their bodies were never found. And the killed were not the only victims. Others were tortured or maimed and huge numbers, I'm talking again many thousands, were detained in very bad conditions."

Ben was almost beginning to regret having asked the question. But he nodded grimly. "And your brother and his wife were caught up in this?"

"Yes, in the backlash after the murder of the Ruck family."

Ben immediately picked up on the name. "My grandfather had a cutting from an old newspaper with a picture of the little boy lying dead in his bed, covered with blood."

"Yes, it was very shocking to see. But the deliberate release of that picture went beyond news. It served to whip up the storm which followed."

Nyeri District, Kenya — early 1953

It was seemingly just another ordinary day in the life of the small village. Shafts of sunlight reflected off corrugated iron roofs and illuminated columns of dust kicked up by boys playing with an improvised ball made of discarded *posho* bags. Some younger children were chasing after hoops, two old bicycle wheels, expertly keeping them rolling along with the aid of short sticks; a bare-bum young *toto* grizzled in their wake, unable to keep up. A few men stood talking outside one of the rudimentary buildings. Women chatted as they hung out washing, intermittently laughing happily, some with babies bobbing up and down on their backs in colourful cloth slings. An old man, one of the village *mzee*, laboriously heaved about a sack of charcoal. Two tethered goats foraged for whatever they could find under their scrubby bush. Chickens scrabbled in the dirt under the watchful, beady eye of a shiny cockerel. A lone dog sat scratching behind one ear. Just another ordinary day.

Mwangi was busy mending a puncture in the front tyre of his bicycle. He looked up and smiled as his young wife, Esther, appeared on the path leading to their small *shamba* where she had been tending their crop of vegetables. At that moment there was a noise of vehicles approaching fast down the track to the village. A Land Rover came into view followed closely by a truck. The vehicles stopped abruptly in a cloud of dust as the villagers froze in watchful silence.

The doors of the Land Rover swung open. Out stepped two white KPR officers. One was a tall, muscular man in his early thirties, a standard issue revolver in a holster at his waist. The other younger, shorter man sported several pistols hanging from his belt. A number of Home Guard were jumping down from the back of the truck, rifles strung over their shoulders, *kibokos* and *rungus*, heavy sticks and clubs in hand. The older officer barked out an order in Swahili. "Round up the men you can find, and throw in a few women too for us to enjoy later."

Some of the villagers began to scatter. They were immediately hunted down by the Home Guard and beaten into submission before being dragged to the truck. The younger officer strode over to where Mwangi was standing in shocked silence. He had taken up one of the pistols from his belt which he prodded into Mwangi's stomach. "You too, move you bloody nigger." Frozen with fear Mwangi did not move quickly enough to avoid being beaten about the head with the butt of the pistol. He sank to his knees bleeding and battered. Through a mist of semi-consciousness he suffered the added painful anguish of just being able to see Esther being pulled away past him. He didn't remember himself then being tied to the bonnet of the Land

Rover to be displayed as a trophy on the return journey.

Not long after the vehicles departed with their cargo of human misery. A little way down the track three adolescent boys had the misfortune to be emerging from a forest path at precisely the wrong moment. The young officer sitting in the passenger seat of the passing Land Rover spotted them and immediately pulled out one of his pistols. He fired several shots in the direction of the boys fleeing back towards the cover of the trees. "Any luck?" called out his companion.

"I think I might have hit one."

"Shall we stop and take a look?"

"No, it's not worth the bother; but hopefully that's one less of the buggers."

Laughing they lit cigarettes and drove on.

A while later Esther was at the mercy of the two KPR men, but there was no mercy to be shown. She was pushed around from one to the other, slapped and humiliated. Her clothes were torn off and she cowered and shivered in the shame of her nakedness as she was prodded and taunted. Unbuttoning themselves they took her in turns. With humiliation heaped upon humiliation she became limp and defeated, but her crying continued to pierce the sullen stillness of the day. It was the first sound heard by Mwangi as he regained consciousness where he was being held nearby. Finishing with her, one of the officers stubbed out a cigarette between her breasts before handing her over to the Home Guard. Her ordeal was far from complete.

Mwangi's ordeal was also set to continue. On the orders of the KPR officers he was taken to a nearby compound where they were waiting in a room to interrogate him. Two of the Home Guard dragged him in and deposited him on his knees. The taller officer stepped forward. "Right, you black bastard, a little *ndege* has told us that a Mau Mau gang came to your village last week for an oathing ceremony. I want you to tell us all about it."

Mwangi shook his head, but said nothing.

"Well?"

Still nothing, so they beat and kicked him until he began to splutter.

"Did you say something at last?"

"*Bwana*, I was not in the village last week."

The shorter officer kicked Mwangi in the stomach, shouting at him, "You lying nigger!"

"Don't try to bullshit us that you know nothing about the oathing," added the other officer, looming menacingly over Mwangi, fist clenched.

"I did hear something when I returned to the village; that a Mau Mau gang had come."

"And there was oathing, right?"

"Only, I was told, because it was forced on some people who feared for their lives and their families, even for their children."

"You know all about this because you were bloody well involved in the oathing."

"No, sir, I was in Nyeri town; you can check with my employer."

"Don't you tell me what to do, you fucking liar. We know what has been going on; you're bloody well implicated, in it up to your neck with Mau Mau."

"No *bwana*, no *bwana*, no, no, no," his voice tailed off in despair as he slumped forward in a kneeling position, blood dripping from his face onto the concrete floor.

The two Home Guards who had brought him in were called back. "Right," said the taller KPR man, "turn him over and pull off his trousers." It was impossible for Mwangi to resist as he was put onto his back, naked from the waist down.

"OK, now hold his legs, firmly."

The shorter officer was at the ready, holding a large pair of pliers. "Here goes," he said. "At least we can put a stop to him breeding."

Supreme Court sitting at Nakuru, Kenya— April 1953

The trial was under way of twelve Kikuyu accused of the murders of the Ruck family. It appeared from the evidence that Mau Mau had been active in the area and that a gang had been hiding out on an adjoining farm for some time prior to the attack. These so-called strangers had planned the attack, recruiting and, perhaps, in some cases at least, compelling Ruck farm labourers to take part. However, the Mau Mau gang had fled back to the forests after the murders. None had been apprehended. Farm labourers alone stood accused in the dock.

The defendants' case was that the evidence against them had been obtained by duress, as a result of violence, intimidation and coercion. It was clear that the local KPR commander, the first European to attend the scene of the crime, was greatly affected by the shock of what he found, especially when he discovered the appalling sight of little Michael hacked to death in his bed. However, what had happened next was seriously in issue before the court. The KPR commander's evidence was that the farm labourers were rounded up for questioning and that the investigation proceeded in a proper, orderly manner. But the Africans questioned gave a starkly different account. They claimed that they were taken into police custody where they were beaten repeatedly, including with sticks. Systematic beating continued, they said, not just during questioning, but also while they were waiting in turn to be interrogated. Various officers were involved and even some settlers were said to have been present to watch. The consistent account by the labourers was of being beaten on the legs with heavy sticks. Even one of the Africans called as a witness for the prosecution, one of the Rucks' domestic servants, gave a vivid account of such beatings during the investigation. But, almost inevitably, the police themselves completely denied the allegations.

The defence evidence of the beatings was directed towards showing that statements relied upon by the prosecution were obtained by the police under duress. Such statements had been formally put on record before the district officer and magistrate in Naivasha. But some makers of the statements claimed that the statements had been dictated to them. Others said that they had been made to put their thumbprints on blank sheets of paper. Two of the defendants described how they had been forced to hold certain items when blindfolded, items which were then put in evidence by the prosecution as things retrieved from the Ruck house bearing prints of the men in question.

Justice Paget Brooke, the trial judge, was having none of it when it came to these defence allegations. He took great care in his judgment to list and dismiss them all. "There is not a vestige of truth on the view I take of the evidence in any of these allegations," he said. "The investigation of the case was in charge of British European senior police officers, in particular Superintendent Steenkamp, who I am satisfied went out of his way to ensure that the accused were decently treated."

Having criticised the defence for having put forward such allegations, the judge had something further to say. "In all my time upon this bench I have happily not met with a case in the charge of a European police officer that was not investigated with considerable fairness to the accused. This case is no exception;

the police have behaved decently and fairly and in all the revolting circumstances with a commendable restraint, though, to be sure, such is only to be expected from them."

Two of the accused were acquitted, but the remaining ten were convicted of murder. Three of these, juveniles under the age of eighteen at the time of the crime, had sentences automatically commuted to detention at the Governor's pleasure. The law took its course for the other seven.

Nderito Kikaria, Mbogo Githari, Githai Kiama, Kangethe Kihara, Macharia Magondu, Ndirangu Kariuki and Burugu Kungu were transferred to Nairobi Prison to await their fate. There they were hanged.

No one ever faced justice for what happened to Mwangi or Esther, or innumerable others like them.

DOWN THE RIVER AND BEYOND

Summer afternoon, summer afternoon, to me
those have always been the two most beautiful
words in the English language.

Henry James

Edward was waiting for Ben on the steps of the Victoria Rooms, beaming as brightly as the warm summer afternoon sun. Moments later when Ben appeared Edward clapped him on the back. "Thank God, last exam over; summer's on." And he rubbed his hands with glee.

Ben nodded, but said nothing.

"Are you OK?" asked Edward giving him a friendly nudge on the shoulder.

"Yeah, yeah, just knackered and rather shell-shocked I suppose. God it's been a slog. Don't know about you, but I was up half the night, yet again, doing last-minute revision, trying to cram in some more of those damn case names."

"Me too, and a couple of questions I really expected didn't come up. My bloody tutor sold me a dummy. But who cares? Nothing I can do about it now; they're over, that's the main thing, and it calls for a celebration before we go our separate ways for the summer."

"Sure," replied Ben, loosening up and looking brighter.

"I've already begun hatching a plan; I'll tell you about it on the way back to Halls."

A bus heading in their direction, up Whiteladies Road, was about to leave a stop just ahead of them and they hurried to jump on. Settling into their seat upstairs, Ben half noticed two girls sitting on the other side, diagonally opposite them. As the bus set off, the girls glanced in their direction, exchanged whispers and stifled giggles. It was all rather conspiratorial and Edward picked up on it too. "Shop girls," he whispered, Ben felt rather too loudly.

"What do you mean?" hissed Ben.

"Well, working class, anyway; they don't know quite how to react to chaps like us; think we're toffs or hooray Henrys who might be no good in bed."

"For God's sake, man, keep your voice down."

But the girls were still taking furtive looks in between sniggers and Edward was well into it. "I think they fancy us, unless of course they take us for a couple who fancy each other; actually, that may be it. Come on, let's mob them up; snuggle up and I'll put my arm round you."

"No way," said Ben between clenched teeth, relieved to see that the bus was by now crossing the Downs. It was time to get up to go down stairs in readiness for the next stop. He carefully avoided looking at the girls as he did so. Edward was unable to resist a wink. Ben did though glance up as he dismounted. The girls were peering down at him from their window. One was holding up her hand, but not waving. Was that one or more fingers raised, Ben for a moment pondered?

Edward's mind had already moved on. "Now, I mentioned a plan for a celebration."

"Oh yeah, what have you been cooking up?"

"A day on the river, no less, followed by a party back at Liz's flat in the evening."

"The river?"

"Indeed, dear boy, there's a place just near Bath where we can hire boats."

"What sort of boats?"

"Just rowing boats, but they're good fun. We can take a load of grub and booze and row off down the river, find a place for a picnic, soak up the sun with the girls, and who knows how the day may end up."

"Girls, which girls?"

"Jennie, naturally; as you may have noticed we've become an item."

"I had clocked it."

"Then there will also be Hugh with his girlfriend, Katie."

"Who's she?"

"I'm not sure if you've met her; she's doing French and German; got together with Hugh on some language course they were doing together."

"Anyone else coming?"

"Certainly, Nick, but he's not bringing a girl of course."

"Why 'of course'?"

"Because, as I would have thought you'd realised by now, he's not into girls; he has his friend Mike."

"Oh yes, sorry, I've been a bit slow on that one." Ben had a sudden rush of foolish embarrassment and felt the need to say something else, in a matter-of fact sort of way. "Well that's fine, is he bringing Mike?"

"No actually; they're still a bit coy about their relationship. What's it been, now? Three years since it was legalised by the 67 Act, but I think it's going to take a long time for a lot of people to feel comfortable enough to come out; there's still a stigma, jokes and so on."

"I suppose." A bit rich thought Ben, casting his mind back to the performance on the bus.

"But Liz will be there; she definitely wanted to come when she found out that I was inviting you."

"Bollocks, stop taking the piss."

"No really, I'm serious. You need to get your head out of your arse and wise up about that girl; she's crazy about you."

Ben looked uncertain for a moment, even a bit flustered. "So, that's the boating party then."

"Not quite; there's one more."

"Oh, who?"

"Charlotte." He let the name hang in the air.

As forecast, it was the perfect summer day. Late morning Ben appeared outside Churchill Hall, refreshed and relaxed, revelling in being able to wear shorts and a T-shirt, a sweatshirt thrown over one shoulder, a light rucksack over the other. He didn't have long to wait. Edward's car swirled into view and pulled up abruptly beside him.

Edward was already in ebullient mood. "Chuck your things in the boot and jump in the back!" he called out through his open driver's side window. Jennie was in the front with him. Glancing in Ben saw a smiling Liz sitting behind them. He slid onto the seat beside her. She leant over and kissed him gently on the cheek. Edward and Jennie exchanged brief meaningful glances. Then they were off.

It took a bit of time to clear the Bristol traffic and to creep out of the city, past Temple Meads station, and onto the road to Bath. But no one minded. They matched the champagne quality of the summer air with their own fizz of laughter, banter and joyful companionship. Edward's left hand, when not changing gear, tended to rest on Jennie's knee and from time to time they inclined their heads towards one another. Liz inched closer to Ben until their legs touched, lightly at first, then with rather more pressure. The traffic thinned somewhat and the countryside began to reveal itself, laced with old stone walls. They were nearly there and the river beckoned.

The others were already waiting for them in the small boatyard. Hugh introduced Katie, open and friendly, crowned with flaming red hair. Charlotte and Nick were examining the waiting boats. There were greetings, hugs and kisses all round. Ben clocked that Charlotte's white cut-off jeans were topped off by a T-shirt the colour of the sky, very like his own, making blue eyes look bluer still.

"Right, how shall we do this?" asked Edward after a while, keen to get going. "We shall need two boats, four in each. Jennie and I could go in one; Ben and Liz in the other perhaps; Charlotte, you could come in my boat and..."

"No Edward," said Charlotte intervening swiftly and decisively, "I'll go with Ben, and Liz of course, with Nick making up the four. Hugh and Katie, as a couple, can then be with you and Jennie. I think that works well."

There were nods all round. Ben, playing it cool, did his best to conceal his delight. Boats were selected, bags loaded and they were off, Edward rowing one and Ben the other. Charlotte, sitting opposite Ben, watched him with mild surprise, but approvingly, as he handled the oars well, pulling the boat smoothly through the water. "I wouldn't have thought there was much rowing where you come from."

"Ah, you see, we have the Rift Valley lakes and various reservoirs, so I've been able to do a bit of it, from time to time."

Charlotte turned to where Liz and Nick were sitting in the

stern behind her. "What about you two?"

"No, no, not me," said Liz quickly; "never done it."

"Well, it was quite big actually at my school," said Nick. He paused, surveying expectant faces before laughing and adding, without a hint of embarrassment, "but I was complete crap at it." More laughter followed.

There was laughter too in the other boat, a little way off. They were taking it in turns to row in various combinations of pairs. Much to the amusement of the boys, when the girls were rowing together one of them dropped her oar into the water. It was eventually retrieved, only after narrowly avoiding either the boat being capsized or one or more of its occupants falling overboard.

Shortly after the boats drew level. By this time Edward and Hugh were rowing together. Ben was still rowing alone. Edward called out to him, "How about a race? Get Nick to pair with you."

Nick opened his mouth to protest, but Charlotte had already seized the initiative. Moving forward from her seat, she swiftly and deftly slotted in beside Ben, taking one of the oars from him.

"Come off it!" shouted Edward, "we want a proper contest."

Ben glanced at Charlotte, without anything being said detecting excited determination on her part. "We'll give you a contest all right," he called back. "You might even need a head start."

The challenge had become irresistible. The race was to be some way down the river to the next bend, a lone tree on the far bank picked out as the finishing post. Manoeuvring into position they were ready for the off. Nick was to call the start. "Ready, steady" and a shade before "go!" Edward and Hugh were pulling away.

"Bloody hell, they've jumped the gun," shouted Nick. But

there was no stopping them. Ben and Charlotte gripped their oars tightly and set off in pursuit. At first they were unable to catch up. Edward and Hugh remained a few boat-lengths in front, but at least they were not gaining any further; Ben and Charlotte were holding their own. Ben sneaked a quick, admiring look at Charlotte, pulling determinedly beside him. It was not long before they slipped into a smooth, efficient rhythm and began to draw closer and closer to the boat in front. Edward and Hugh became aware of this, looking over their shoulders from time to time, checking progress. Nervousness began to set in, causing them to pull harder. Their extra effort, however, was unrewarded and became counter-productive. They each began missing strokes and the boat was not always moving straight. Ben and Charlotte saw their chance. As Edward and Hugh started to veer to one side, Ben nodded to Charlotte and they both pulled strongly, guiding their boat through the open water in front of them. Edging past as the tree came into view, Ben and Charlotte finished a length ahead.

Shipping their oars, Ben and Charlotte half turned to face each other, panting hard, beads of perspiration on their brows. Charlotte raised her left hand. Ben grasped it with his right, holding it tightly; shared exhilaration. There were mixed reactions elsewhere. The occupants of the other boat were momentarily stunned. Nick was laughing delightedly. Liz appeared to be rather put out.

The boats had drifted round the bend in the river. A particularly inviting grassy bank came into view, partly shaded by tall trees on the edge of a field shimmering in the heat of the languid, lazy summer afternoon. It was time for a long, late lunch.

Boats safely moored, two large rugs were spread out. From

bags and rucksacks came quiche, veal, ham and egg pie, potato salad, crunchy lettuce, large ripe tomatoes, taramasalata, pitta bread and olives, succulent strawberries and plump cherries. Ben felt slightly embarrassed by his crumpled, and by now rather greasy, paper bag containing sausage rolls. He felt more confident adding his large bottle of dry cider to the collection of wine and beer. But he was almost immediately trumped by Edward producing a bottle of champagne. It was Charlotte, though, who provided the pièce de résistance: a freshly baked, long crusty baguette and a little wooden box containing oozing honey comb.

"Where on earth did you get that?" Jennie demanded to know.

"A little shop in Bath I know of; we stopped off on the way. The honey's to die for."

Lolling back on the rugs they ate and drank, talked and laughed, happy companionship, relaxed and contented. Long summer months of living and loving lay ahead; an unspoken sense of precious days to be long remembered, perhaps for ever. The bread and honey were proclaimed to be "divine". Hours passed without being of any relevance to the timelessness of that treasured afternoon.

"Right," said Edward, standing up at last, brushing away crumbs, "Jennie and I are going for a wander." And she was pulled, uncomplainingly, to her feet. Hand in hand they headed off to the field, Edward with a sly backward glance. Hugh and Katie were on the move too, although not very far. Dragging one of the rugs into deeper shade, they lay down together, bodies entwined.

Liz was lying back with her eyes shut, eating cherries. "I feel like Elvira Madigan," she murmured softly. "You remember the scene in the film when she and her soldier lover are on the run and she eats fruit with him, can't remember quite what, but it was in a field, I think, in an idyllic country setting on a perfect summer's day, just like this." She snapped her eyes open and looked searchingly at Ben sitting beside her.

"Nope, sorry, haven't seen the film."

"Well, you must try to one day; stunning to look at, sad but in a beautiful kind of way; and the music, oh my God the music, I can't hear it enough. I have a record of it which I can play for you when you come to the party at my flat this evening."

Ben was still taking this in when Nick announced that he was going for a walk along the riverbank, hoping to see a kingfisher. "Any takers?" No immediate response, but then Charlotte decided she needed to stretch her legs and elected to join him. As she got up to go, Liz edged closer to Ben, now lying down propped up on one arm facing her. Their heads inclined towards one another and their lips touched. Charlotte, following Nick towards the river bank, stopped suddenly and looked back over her shoulder. "I've something to tell you, Ben." Surveying the scene she paused for a moment. "But it can wait till later." Turning away she quickened her step to catch up with Nick.

Ben had sat up. He turned back towards Liz, but the moment had gone and it was beginning to cloud over.

It was late by the time Ben made his way through Cotham to the flat. The enduring light of that midsummer day was finally yielding to a darkening sky, pinpricked by the first stars of the night. He pushed open the partly closed door and was enveloped into a party in full swing. The living room was a sea swell of bodies, dimly lit by two lava lamps, swirling to an insistent beat of music. Che Guevara stared out from the large poster above the fireplace, seemingly presiding over the revelries. A tide of bodies flowed in and out, down the narrow passage to rooms leading off and to the kitchen beyond.

A glassy-eyed girl eased herself past Ben in the crush, then paused and turned to face him. She passed him the joint she was smoking.

"No thanks. I don't smoke, not even fags." God, no need to sound defensive, he found himself thinking.

"No sweat." Slightly unsteadily she was looking him up and down. "You look a bit square, but no offence because you also look kinda…" she struggled for a moment, but then could only come up with "nice." She rolled away saying, "see you later."

Ben made his escape, pressing through the throng of the living room. Edward loomed into view, well away, one arm draped over Jennie, clutching a bottle of vodka in his other hand. Ben declined the proffered bottle and forced his way to a table in the corner containing an array of drinks. He plonked down his contribution of a six-pack of beers, breaking one free for himself. Surveying the scene he began to pick out in the gloom a few familiar faces. Hugh and Katie, with a number of others, were swaying to the sound of the Beatles' *Let It Be*. Occasional glimpses of the far corner revealed Nick, with his friend Mike on this occasion. Why hadn't he brought him to the river picnic earlier, wondered Ben? Perhaps it was easier for them to be together in a crowd. And there, of course, was Charlotte. She and Ben circled the room for a while, or perhaps circled each other, never quite meeting. Was she avoiding him? Or was he avoiding her? Perhaps they were avoiding each other. Questions criss-crossed in their minds.

"There you are, at last. I was beginning to think you weren't coming." Liz had appeared, threading herself into the room towards Ben. Any annoyance almost immediately gave way to pleasure as she pulled him towards her. Arms around his neck they swirled into the undulating mass. After a while, taking him firmly by one hand, she led him out of the room and down the corridor.

"This is my room," she said, perhaps by way of rather unnecessary explanation, shutting the door behind her, muffling somewhat the noise of the party.

"Great," said Ben slightly uncertainly. He took in a rumpled bed facing the window, a desk piled with books and files, an old-fashioned wardrobe, doors partly open, posters and photos on the walls, things scattered here and there; bits and pieces of student clutter.

"You remember what I said earlier?"

"Sorry, you'd better remind me."

"Elvira Madigan."

"OK." He was clearly struggling, but this went unnoticed by Liz in her haze of excitement. She was busily putting on a record to play. As the music began she settled down on some large floor cushions, bidding Ben to join her.

"Do you know this?" she asked.

Ben shook his head. He had heard very little classical music.

"Mozart Piano Concerto No. 21, quite simply sublime." She snuggled into his neck as they sank down into the folds of the cushions.

Was it the occasion, was it the mood of that special day, or the sheer lightness of feeling in the close warmth of that summer evening, or was it, perhaps, just the unmistakeable sound of genius? Whatever it was, Ben soon came to realise he was hearing music the like of which he had never heard before. More intoxicating than even the strong cider of earlier, it began to permeate the innermost reaches of his conscious feeling. Liz was stroking his hair. Their lips met and hands began tentative exploration. A brief knock and the door opened framing Charlotte in the dim light.

"Oh God, not good timing, I'm interrupting again; but as I mentioned earlier I have something to tell you, Ben, and I might not see you before I go."

Disentangling himself from Liz he was sitting up, looking startled. "OK what, what is it?"

"I'm coming to Kenya."

There was a stunned silence in the room, apart from the music of Mozart. But down the corridor the party rumbled on to the sound of *The Long And Winding Road.*

A CHANGE OF PLANS

The best laid schemes o' Mice an' Men
Gang aft agley

Robert Burns
To a Mouse

Ben hadn't been slow to volunteer to accompany his father on a trip to Nairobi. There they were saying with friends. His father had business to attend to in the city. Ben had mainly one thing in mind. He mulled over and over what he had been told by Charlotte, to his astonishment and delight which he had found hard to conceal, shortly before he returned home. Her godmother, it transpired, was married to a man who worked in the Foreign Office who had recently been posted to the British High Commission in Kenya. Charlotte had been invited to spend a few weeks with them that summer. She had arrived a week before and was staying with them at their house in Muthaiga. For the umpteenth time Ben checked he had the piece of paper on which she had written down the telephone number where she could be contacted. He had done his best to play it cool, saying he was sure that she would be busy with her godmother, who had doubtless planned all sorts of things for them to do, but that if she had any free time, perhaps they could meet up because he was in Nairobi on occasion; but, really, if it didn't work out he would quite understand. For her part, she had certainly expressed interest in seeing him; he hoped that he had detected that she was even discreetly pleased at the prospect. Unbidden, it was her idea to provide the telephone number.

Carefully smoothing out the piece of paper, Ben dialled the number. After a few rings, a woman's voice answered.

"Hallo, is it possible to speak to Charlotte, please?"

"Yes, she's here, but may I ask who's calling?"

"My name's Ben Hooper; I'm a friend of Charlotte's, from university, but I live here in Kenya."

"Ah yes, of course; Charlotte's told me quite a lot about you. She said that you might be in touch. Let me hand you over."

A moment later there was a distinctive voice on the line. "Hallo Ben, I wondered if you'd call."

"Hi Charlotte, of course, I was going to; welcome to Kenya, the place I've always been banging on about. Now you're seeing it for yourself."

"Yes, here I am indeed, having a great time. Where are you phoning from?"

"I'm in Nairobi for a couple of days. Any chance of seeing you?"

"Let me just check with my godmother."

"Of course, I don't want to muck up any plans she may have for you."

"No, no, I'm sure we can arrange something; just hold on a sec."

Ben did so, also holding his breath.

"Yes, that'll be fine; I could see you tomorrow morning. Alice, that's my godmother, has to go into town and she's offered to drop me off somewhere. Any suggestions?"

"Yup, The Thorn Tree."

"Where's that?"

Ben laughed. "It's a famous meeting place; she'll know."

"OK," said a rather doubtful sounding Charlotte. But then, brightening up, "What time shall we say?"

"Eleven would be good; looking forward to seeing you."

"I'll be there; looking forward to seeing you too."

They rang off, minds racing.

Ben arrived at The Thorn Tree slightly before the appointed hour. He found a table and sat facing outwards, so he had a good view of people coming in from various directions. He didn't have too long to wait. Charlotte came round the corner from Kenyatta Avenue and stood, looking uncertain for a moment, in the midst of the busy café. Ben jumped to his feet and waved in her direction, catching her attention. Stepping towards him she removed a broad-brimmed straw hat and pushed sunglasses up onto her forehead. Inclining her head towards him he kissed her on the cheek. There was some confusion as to whether he was then going to kiss her on the other cheek. Their heads bobbed about and they brushed noses. It caused amusement rather than embarrassment. Laughing, they sat down.

Charlotte tossed her hair over one shoulder. "I can hardly believe I'm here."

"Me neither, but I'm glad you are."

She smiled as their eyes met and there was a pause. "Anyway," she suddenly said briskly, "here I am in what I understand is a famous meeting place."

"It is indeed, for locals and tourists; and even for people travelling across Africa who arrange to meet here or leave messages for one another. It's a kind of crossroads in a way."

A waiter had sidled up to the table. "*Jambo, Memsahib, Bwana.*"

"Now," said Ben, "Kenyan coffee is a must."

Charlotte nodded.

Ben gave the order. "*Kahawa mbili.*"

"I'm quite thirsty, so I'd like some orange juice too, if that's OK," chipped in Charlotte. There was no need for Swahili; the waiter, of course, understood perfectly.

Ben was keen to find out what Charlotte had done so far in the week since her arrival and, importantly to him, what were her impressions, thoughts, even feelings. Deep down, he realised, it really mattered to him.

"Alice and her husband, Uncle Eric we call him in the family, though not of course an uncle at all, have been very good to me. We've been all over Nairobi, been entertained right royally, had dinner at the Muthaiga Club, and..."

In her slight pause for thought Ben had a question. "What did you think of the Club? If you didn't know before, you probably now realise it was a real bastion of the colonial establishment."

Charlotte wasn't sure if she was being tested, but she had no hesitation in answering. "I thought it was fascinating and very atmospheric; a link, perhaps, between the past and the future."

Typical sharp mind, thought Ben, wishing it had occurred to him in that way.

"Did you have the chance to have a good look round?" he asked.

"Oh yes, most interesting things to see, and to be told."

"Really, what were you told?"

"All sorts of things; such as, one example which has really stuck in my mind, was finding out that there's stuff in the left luggage store which has been there since the thirties, maybe even the twenties; the imagination boggles."

"Yes, quite a thought."

"And, I remembered what you'd told us at Edward's house."

A puzzled look. "What was that?"

Charlotte smiled. "I'm not surprised you can't immediately recall because you had a lot to say that day." Seeing him look slightly wounded she put one hand on his arm outstretched on the table. "It was your account of the Erroll murder which came back to me, as I was looking round. I tried to imagine Erroll and Diana sitting there, with her husband Delves Broughton, on that fateful night."

Ben was by now nodding in agreement. "You're absolutely right, of course, it's no ordinary place."

The coffee and orange juice arrived with the cheerful waiter. Charlotte tasted the coffee. Ben watched her closely, really wanting her to appreciate it, and feeling warm pleasure when she obviously did so. Now he had other things to find out.

"Have you been out of Nairobi yet?"

"Yes, but not very far. We went to a place called Thika, I think, and had lunch at the hotel by the waterfall; can't remember its name."

"Blue Posts. Where else, have you seen any wildlife yet?"

"Absolutely, in the Nairobi National Park. We saw lots of animals, including lions on a kill, and, all in sight of the city. I could hardly believe it; so exciting."

"Did you also visit the Animal Orphanage, by the main gate to the Park?"

"Yes, we did. I really liked seeing animals close up and, hopefully, some of the photos I took will come out well, even though my camera is pretty basic."

"Yeah, I know what you're saying, but there is, of course, a dark side to it."

"Why so?"

"Because of it being an orphanage, with young animals being brought there, often because their mothers have been poached."

Charlotte frowned. "How much of a problem is poaching?"

"It's becoming a big problem and it's likely to get bigger still. Yeah, I reckon in my lifetime there will be a battle to save some of our greatest animals from extinction, elephant possibly, rhino certainly." He gave a deep sigh. "I often wish I could become involved in some way, to help to do something about it."

"Are there people trying to do something about it?"

"Fortunately, yes; particularly some dedicated people in the Game Department. For instance, in Tsavo, our biggest national park, there's an amazing couple, David and Daphne Sheldrick. Apart from trying to combat poaching, they've been working out how best to rescue and, eventually, rehabilitate orphan elephants and rhinos. It's a hell of a challenge, even keeping the very young ones alive. Daphne Sheldrick has had to experiment with various types of milk to feed the babies."

"What an amazing task." Charlotte was brooding, both shocked and interested.

"Anyway," said Ben, sensing the need for a positive switch, "the wildlife here is still fantastic and I hope you get the chance to get out into the real bush." He laughed before adding, "Without meaning any offence to the Nairobi park."

"I believe I shall," said Charlotte brightening visibly. "There's a plan to go to Amboseli, on our way to the coast next week."

"Pretty good; you should see some great animals, including big herds of elephants against the backdrop of Kili; stunning."

"Kili?"

"Sorry, Kilimanjaro, the highest mountain in Africa, as you

may know, but less well-known is that it's actually the highest individual, free-standing mountain in the world; not being in a range of mountains, if you see what I mean."

"Yes, I've seen a photo of it, a huge snow-capped dome."

"That's it, the main peak, Kibo, over nineteen thousand feet."

"Must be quite something to climb."

"It's certainly an experience. I've done it, in a school party."

"I didn't know that you're a mountaineer."

"I'm not really, but that's the thing; you can in fact walk up it, or scramble up rather on the steep final slope where you slip around in the scree. It's not to be underestimated, though, the altitude and decreasing supply of oxygen really get to you; it makes some people sick and they have to turn back and go straight down."

"But you made it?"

"I did. I have a photo to prove it and a little wreath of everlasting flowers given to me by the guide."

"I think I saw that in your room in Bristol."

"Yes, that's right; but I don't think I've ever shown you my photos. Apart from the one at the top, there's another looking east as the sun rose above the second highest peak, Mawenzi, crowned with a perfect halo of cloud; the sun rising above Africa, seen from its highest point. Awesome, man, truly awesome." Charlotte was watching him closely as he sank deeper into innermost thoughts, before snapping out of them with momentary embarrassment.

"Sorry, sorry, I'm banging on again. But I'm really glad that you're going to Amboseli; I only wish…" He broke off, thinking better of what he had been tempted to say about the rugged beauty of the vast landscape stretching north from his home in

Laikipia.

Simultaneously they sipped coffee and reflected. Glancing at his watch Ben then said, "I have a surprise for you." For his own reasons he had wanted a bit of time with Charlotte alone first, but he had asked someone then to join them. Standing up he gestured to a young African man approaching from the street. Charlotte half turned in her seat.

"This is Joe," Ben told her.

"And you must be Charlotte; no please, don't stand up." They shook hands as she settled back into her seat. Charlotte took in a young man, slightly shorter than Ben, but of a similar athletic build; rather more smartly dressed. But what she noticed most were his dark brown eyes, kind, thoughtful, all-seeing eyes. Ben was sitting down again and Joe pulled up a chair opposite. He signalled to the waiter and ordered a coffee.

"I've heard of you, or course," said Charlotte, immediately putting Joe at his ease. "Ben often speaks of you."

"He has also spoken of you to me, when we met up the other day." He smiled shyly and glanced in Ben's direction.

Wondering what might be coming next, Ben intervened swiftly. "Joe, like me, is just back from university; we had a lot of catching up to do."

"Oh, really, do you go to university in England, like Ben?"

"No, my father... eh... it was decided I should go to Makerere."

"Sorry, where's that?"

"In Kampala, Uganda. There you can do degrees from the University of London; so it's very good."

"And what are you studying?"

"Medicine actually."

"Oh really, that's great."

"Charlotte's doing law, like me," chipped in Ben.

"You told me," replied Joe patiently, catching Charlotte's eye and smiling.

"It was quite a surprise Charlotte coming here," said Ben. "But I'm really glad she has. I've told her so much about the country."

"Yes, it's really good to see it for myself, and to meet people like you, Joe; and to form my own views, I suppose."

"Charlotte and I have had some lively debates about things," said Ben, rather ruefully, but not shying away from discussion.

Joe became quietly serious. "Well, that's good." He turned towards Charlotte.

"It's been the same with me. Ben, of course, comes from a colonial background. I have challenged him a lot about things which he took for granted and there has sometimes been resistance on his part."

"I've tried to understand, to adapt in a way."

"I believe you, *rafiki*, but I know it has sometimes been hard because of what is deep-seated within you."

Charlotte was looking thoughtful. "It can only be to the good to air these things, to come to a proper understanding."

"Of course, almost exactly what my Aunt Grace has said when she has given this history boy a lesson or two in Kenyan history." Joe was smiling now, lightening the mood with friendly teasing. Ben remained rather tight-lipped.

"To be fair," said Charlotte, "I've also had to rethink some things, where perhaps there have been misconceptions."

"Me too," agreed Joe. "The great thing is that Ben and I have grown up together in a period of great evolution." He looked rather pleased with this last remark, but Charlotte was having to puzzle it out.

"I think I follow you…"

"The coming of independence," added Joe swiftly.

"Of course. And, if I may ask, has this brought you what you wanted, what you hoped for?"

"No, at least not completely, not yet."

"Oh?"

"Change has, of course, come and continues to come; but not always as quickly as people would like and expect."

"It's bound to take time," mused Ben.

"Yes, but I have another deep concern."

"What's that?" asked Charlotte.

"Too much ending up with too few; it's happening already."

"Why do you think that is?"

Joe sighed. "The big man syndrome. I have to admit it's very much part of the African way. You have big men who control things, with major landholdings, extensive business and commercial interests, and so on and so forth. They benefit people who support them, but in this way they also exercise power over them."

"Paternalism, of a sort," suggested Charlotte.

Joe permitted himself a rather hollow laugh. "Oh yes, it's not something the British have a monopoly of."

"I suppose not."

"It's also a system which is tailor-made for corruption, particularly when these big men get into government and become even more powerful. The risk is of some kind of dictatorship, or at least rule by an autocrat. This is going to be a major problem for us to face."

The waiter was back at the table. Ben and Joe ordered more coffee. Charlotte was content with her orange juice. She looked around and noticed for the first time the tree growing up in the centre of the café; of course, she thought, that must be the Thorn Tree. People were coming and going all the time; busy, yet somehow relaxed. She was more than happy to linger as the boys caught up with one another's news. Joe brought her into the conversation. He wanted to know more of how Ben was fitting in to life in England. She regaled him with stories of how he was in some ways and not in others, partly exaggerated in certain instances for the sake of amusement, but with some more serious points thrown in. Ben intervened at times. There was laughter interspersed with thoughtfulness. Charlotte, for her part, was interested to learn more about Joe, his time at school with Ben, and life for him now as a student in Uganda. She carefully, and she hoped politely, probed to draw him out on his hopes and aspirations for the future when, as she discovered, he intended to return to Kenya as a doctor. The conversation took a more serious turn when it reverted to the challenges facing the country.

"I just hope," said Ben, "that democracy can be made to work well for us."

"Why ever wouldn't it?" asked Charlotte, eyebrows raised. "Surely that is one of the good things to have come from British colonialism."

"In theory, yes." Ben was scratching his head, thinking how best to justify what he had said. It was, on the face of it, a controversial, even provocative, remark. "The problem to be confronted and, don't get me wrong, hopefully overcome, is tribalism. But already we are seeing people voting on tribal lines which is divisive and not necessarily in the best interests of the country; in fact it has already shown it can lead to trouble."

Charlotte was not prepared simply to accept this at face value. While Joe was looking rather uncomfortable, she pressed further. "But surely there are political parties. People vote for candidates from those parties depending on their policies, rather than which tribe they're from."

"I wish they would." Ben forced a rueful smile. "There are two main parties vying for power. KANU, that's the Kenya African National Union, mainly a Kikuyu party voted for by Kikuyus and their supporters; this is the party of President Kenyatta, who is, of course, a Kikuyu. Then there is the opposition party, KADU, the Kenya African Democratic Union, the party of the Luo chieftain, Oginga Odinga. Inevitably, I suppose, this is essentially a Luo party, voted for by Luos and their supporters. So, you see, Western-style democracy is not necessarily a good fit."

"Is there no cross-over?"

"I couldn't say none. But what I can tell you is that when it happens it can lead to real trouble."

"What sort of trouble?"

"At the highest level, political assassination." Ben felt it important to draw Joe into the conversation. He looked at him pointedly. "You know what I mean, don't you?"

He nodded sadly, saying quietly just one word. "Mboya."

"Exactly."

This meant nothing to Charlotte, without further explanation. "Who or what was that?"

"Tom Mboya," said Ben, lowering his voice slightly. "He was a Luo who became a minister in Kenyatta's government, a very able man, but he was bumped off last year, shot just near where we are now, in Government Road which runs parallel to the street outside the café here."

"Have they caught the person who did it?"

"A man was arrested, not long after," replied Joe.

"Presumably he has been tried by now?"

Joe looked uncomfortable. "No, he died." Seeing the look on Charlotte's face he added, "We don't know why."

"No," said Ben grimly, "but it is rumoured that after his arrest he asked 'why don't you go after the big man?'; it doesn't look good on any level."

"And who do you think 'the big man' may be?" asked Charlotte, wrinkling up her brow.

"There are competing theories," said Ben. "My dad thinks it may a Kikuyu in the Government who didn't like a Luo within their ranks becoming so prominent."

"But there's no proof of that," interjected Joe. "My aunt thinks that it may be someone in KADU who regarded Mboya as having deserted the Luo cause."

"Whoever it was, my God they caused trouble," added Ben. "There were serious riots in Nairobi and other places, just before I left to go to England. My Mum and I got caught up in them here when we were getting ready to go to the airport. It was pretty scary. I remember Mum saying that she felt that it was like a smouldering bushfire that could ignite and get out of hand at any moment."

"But it didn't," said Joe firmly.

"No," agreed Ben, "fortunately not. After the funeral and requiem mass, at which the President gave a very well-thought eulogy, things calmed down. But there is still suspicion that this was a high-level political assassination."

Joe was keen to move on the conversation. "I hope that, with time, we shall overcome these difficulties. Personally, I'm more concerned at the long-term prospect of a population explosion getting out of hand."

"Is it beginning to happen?" asked Charlotte.

"Oh yes, and it's going to get worse. As someone going into

medicine I worry about it."

Ben leant over the table and put one hand on Joe's shoulder. "Despite what we've been saying, we shouldn't leave Charlotte with the wrong impression. Look at you and me; you an African, me a white from a colonial background, good friends who, despite everything, believe in the future of this country."

Joe turned towards Charlotte. "Ben is not a *mzungu* in the ordinary sense; he is a Kenyan, like me." There was rising passion in his voice as he continued. "Not all black Kenyans think the way I do; and not all white Kenyans think the way Ben does; particularly older generations. But I like to think that people like Ben and myself, coming together, we are the future. This is the way the country must go to be strong and stable and it is our choice because we are free. *Uhuru* has placed our destiny in our own hands and it must be seized." His fists had become tightly clenched.

Startled for a moment, Charlotte looked from one to the other of the two young men sitting with her. She then nodded her head. "I've certainly come to realise, Ben, how much this country means to you."

As he nodded back in agreement, Joe had the final emphatic word on the subject. "He's a part of it and it's a part of him. I hope he comes back after university. Kenya needs people like him, but the longer he stays away the more risk of him not returning." With a meaningful look from one to the other he added, "There's been too much displacement in this country already."

A contemplative silence followed for a moment before Charlotte glanced at her watch. "I'm afraid I must go; Alice is picking me up shortly from where she dropped me off earlier. It's been really interesting talking to you, and so good to meet you,

Joe." She turned towards Ben. "I'm going to have a lot to tell Lawrence." A frown of concentrated thought gave way to a smile. "We often think we know it all in England; but we clearly don't." As she got up, and they did too, she wondered whether to kiss them, but some instinctive embarrassment held her back; embarrassment for whom? She felt confused for a moment and rather cross with herself.

"Is there any chance of seeing you again?" asked Ben. "I'm not going home until late tomorrow afternoon, so I could show you around a bit, perhaps in the morning; I have the use of a car."

"What's tomorrow?" mused Charlotte. "Oh yes, Friday. I don't think anything's planned for me until the evening. But I'll have to check."

"Yeah, of course. Why don't I phone you first thing in the morning to see how the land lies?"

"That would be good." She smiled and turned to go with a wave of her hand. As she walked away Ben's eyes followed her departure. Joe was watching him closely.

The following morning the phone at the house in Muthaiga was answered with a tremulous voice before being handed to Charlotte. Something was clearly wrong and Ben was immediately concerned.

"Have I phoned at a bad time?"

"There's been a terrible drama; I'm afraid Uncle Eric had a stroke last night. He's in Nairobi Hospital. Alice has just got back. She's going to call the hospital shortly for an update."

"Oh God, I'm so very sorry. How bad is it?"

"Pretty bad, although he is expected to pull through."

"I wish I could do something to help. Where does this leave you, if you don't mind me asking?"

"Well, of course, there's no question of me staying on. All future plans for my visit will have to be cancelled and I shall have to go home early. In fact I've already phoned BOAC, first thing this morning, to change my ticket and they can get me on a flight next Wednesday evening." Her voice was beginning to crack.

"What about the next few days?"

"I shall just have to hang on. I'd like to be of some help to Alice, although I'm not sure what I can do really. I expect she'll spend a lot of time at the hospital and going to and fro. She's concerned about me, but I'm doing my best to reassure her that I'll be fine. After all, she's got more than enough to worry about, poor woman."

Ben's mind was racing. "Look, I'd better get off the line; but I have an idea, and I'd like to call you back a little later, if that's OK."

Taken by surprise, Charlotte hesitated slightly before responding. "Yes, eh, yes, I suppose so. If the line's engaged, Alice will probably be talking to the hospital."

"Of course, don't worry, I'll just try again if necessary. Good bye for now."

"Thanks, bye."

Now Charlotte's mind was racing too. Ben's heart had begun to beat faster than usual.

Immediately after Ben had rang off he tracked down his father and there was an urgent discussion. This was followed by a call to his mother in Laikipia. There were a few practical considerations and discussion of domestic arrangements to be made, if required. But there was no hesitation whatsoever in agreeing to the plan proposed by Ben. It couldn't have been more warmly welcomed, and by God he loved his parents for their support, as ever.

A short while later Ben picked up the phone again, nervous, but with hopeful excitement. It was answered, almost immediately, by Charlotte.

"Hi, it's Ben again. Is it OK to talk?"

"Yes, Ben, fine. Alice has just set off to the hospital."

"Any further news about her husband?"

"Not really; he seems to be fairly stable now, thank goodness; but they're still trying to assess what damage has been caused."

"I see; well here's hoping it won't be too bad."

"Yes indeed, thanks."

"Now I have a proposal."

"Sorry, what?"

Ben was a bit flustered. "An invitation, I mean, for you to come and stay with me and my family in Laikipia for the few days before you fly back to England." Following a short stunned silence at the other end of the line, Ben quickly added, "I've talked to my parents and they would be really happy to have you to stay; they're so sorry to hear what has happened."

"Well, that's really kind, Ben, um, sorry, sorry; I'm just trying to take it in; I don't know what to say."

"I just think that it would be such a pity, a crying shame in fact, if after coming all this way you only got to see Nairobi and surrounding areas. There's so much more to the country and, well, I'd really like to show you something of it."

"I can't tell you how much I appreciate that Ben and I'm so grateful to you, and your family, for inviting me. The thing is I'm rather overwhelmed by the situation in which I find myself and I'm trying to get my thoughts clear."

"Yeah, of course, I understand, and I don't want to pressurise you in any way."

"No, no, not at all; it's not a question of that; you're being so kind. I just need to see if I can properly clear things at this end."

"Sure; I see."

"Can I phone you back as soon as possible?"

"Certainly; we're not leaving until late afternoon, so you have a fair bit of time."

Having given Charlotte the number, Ben rang off. But he didn't move far from the phone. He paced up and down the room, subliminally sympathising with how a caged animal must feel. The minutes dragged and he felt as if there were a clock ticking in his head, triggering a memory of lines from *Under Milk Wood*: 'Time passes. Listen. Time passes.' A little over an hour seemed much, much longer. The phone gave only one ring before Ben snatched it up. He took a deep breath.

"Ben, I'm on."

"You can come to stay with us?"

"Yes, yes; Alice is really grateful, even probably relieved, because it means she can concentrate on Uncle Eric, without having to worry about me. I think the poor woman was feeling so guilty about cancelling our plans; so it's a weight off her mind in a way."

"I'm so glad that it has worked out that you're going to come to Laikipia. Oh God, sorry, that was really thoughtless of me. Please don't think I meant to imply that I'm pleased with what has happened to Uncle Eric; it's just that I got carried away, I suppose, with the thought of being able to show you round a place which means so much to me; sorry."

"Ben, there's absolutely no need to apologise. It's so obvious that you're trying to make the best out of a bad situation, acting out of kindness."

"OK, well thanks."

"And I should say that I'm not only grateful; I'm now really looking forward to coming to stay with you."

Palpable relief and a rising sense of anticipation combined in Ben's senses, but he forced himself to think clearly of immediate practicalities. "Right," he said, sounding, he hoped, brisk and efficient, "I'll pick you up at about three, if that's OK."

"That'll be fine. What do I need to bring?"

"Just enough for the next few days; casual clothes, but something warm for the evenings when it can get a bit chilly; oh, and some fairly good walking shoes, if you have them; more than just *tackies*."

"*Tackies*, what are they?"

Ben laughed, remembering that he had been caught out about this before. "Sorry, Kenya terminology; gym shoes to you."

"Anything else?"

"Sun hat and, of course, most importantly, your camera; there should be some great opportunities for good pics."

"Right, I shall go and start packing. But first you need to know where to collect me. The house is near the Muthaiga Club."

"I know where that is, of course; so just give me directions as from the Club."

The directions were easy for Ben to follow; he didn't even need to make a note of them. The call ended to be followed by a whirl of activity with minds racing.

Ben had no difficulty finding the house, an imposing two-storey building typical of some of the grander residences in Muthaiga. He knocked on the large wooden door. It was opened promptly by a slim, fair-haired woman with tired eyes in delicate, refined features.

209

"You must be Ben; I've heard a lot about you. I'm Alice."

"It's good to meet you," Ben was stammering slightly, "Though I'm so sorry to hear about your husband."

"Thank you; it's been a terrible shock, of course, and so awful for poor Charlotte to be caught up in it."

"How is he doing, if you don't mind me asking?"

"So-so. He is fairly stable, thank goodness, but we still don't know the extent of the paralysis. The aim is to get him back to the UK when possible."

At that moment Charlotte appeared, coming downstairs carrying a hold-all.

"Hallo Ben; as you can see, I'm ready for the off."

Stepping forward promptly, he took her bag.

Before they departed Alice wanted to confirm arrangements. "Now your flight back to England's on Wednesday evening and you will need a bit of time to pack up here before I get you to the airport."

Charlotte looked enquiringly at Ben. "Will that be OK?"

"Yes, I've spoken to my dad about this already. You will be dropped back here round about midday."

"That'll be fine," said Alice taking a step towards Ben and smiling for the first time. "I'm so grateful to you and your family for doing this for Charlotte. It's an enormous relief that she's going to have such a wonderful experience before flying home, because we've had to cancel the plans we had for her which was so disappointing."

"I'm really glad we can help."

Charlotte stepped forward and kissed Alice. "Give my love to Uncle Eric and I hope there's some slightly better news by the time I get back."

Alice nodded. "Yes, hopefully, as you say; but, in the

meantime, you go off and enjoy yourself; I'm sure you will. I haven't been fortunate enough to get up to Laikipia, but I've heard how lovely it is."

Walking out onto the drive, Ben put Charlotte's bag on the back seat of the car and then opened the passenger door for her. Going round to the driver's side he got in and started the engine. Alice had followed them out onto the drive. She waved and blew a kiss. They waved back and then they were off. Driving back into Nairobi there was happy chatter. Charlotte wanted to know more about Ben's family and Laikipia. He was full of ideas and plans for the next few days. Reaching Uhuru Highway, they headed south past the city centre. Charlotte became curious about the journey.

"We've got some way to go haven't we? How long is it going to take?"

Ben smiled broadly; he had been keeping this part of the plan as a surprise. "If we were going by car, it would take several hours and we wouldn't be there until well after dark; but we're not doing that I'm glad to say."

"Oh?"

"No, we're flying; it's a little over a hundred and twenty miles by air; should take perhaps an hour and a quarter or so, maybe slightly longer depending on the conditions."

"Flying? Who's flying us there?"

"I am."

Ben enjoyed the moment of genuine astonishment on Charlotte's face.

"You're kidding me."

"No, really, we have our own plane and there's an airstrip on the ranch."

"And you can fly?"

"Yup, I passed my PPL, that's my private pilot's licence, nearly a year ago now and I'm getting up my hours." Seeing a look on Charlotte's face which he interpreted as being tinged with concern, he added, "But don't worry, my dad will be up front with me and he's an experienced pilot."

They passed the railway yards and headed towards the industrial area before branching off on the road leading to Wilson Aerodrome. Pulling up outside one of the buildings they got out of the car to be greeted by a man wearing a dark green polo shirt and khaki trousers. He was well built, but fit looking, with deep blue eyes in features made rugged by years of African sun, fair hair swept back, greying slightly at the temples. There was no mistaking him. Charlotte realised at once that this could only be Ben's father. He shook her hand warmly.

"I'm really grateful, Mr Hooper, for inviting me to stay."

"You're most welcome; I'm so glad that we're able to salvage something of your holiday."

"Thanks so much for that."

"But I was sorry, of course, to hear about your uncle, is it?"

"Yes, sort of an uncle."

Mr Hooper's attention had switched to his son. "You can leave the car there. I've arranged for it to be collected later. Now grab your things and follow me."

They went into the long low building where a bit of time was spent readying for departure. Mr Hooper went off to attend to some formalities, returning a short while later.

"Right, *twende*, let's go; we should make it well before dark."

Picking up their bags they walked out on to the tarmac apron where a variety of light aircraft were parked. A plane was coming in to land on the runway beyond. Charlotte was inwardly buzzing

212

with a real thrill of anticipation. Ben felt he had almost left the ground already.

"There," he said, pointing out a sleek red and white, single-engine plane, gleaming in the late afternoon sun, "that's us."

Reaching the plane the bags were carefully stowed in a locker in the rear fuselage. Ben helped Charlotte in to the small back seat.

"It's a bit cramped, but you'll be fine once you settle down; now strap in."

He climbed in to the left-hand front seat. His father was walking round the aircraft performing various checks. He then clambered in, sitting beside his son in the other front seat.

Ben turned round to face Charlotte. "All OK?"

"Good, thanks."

"Great, now I just want to tell you something about the route. We're going to head off towards the Ngong Hills, because I want to show them to you; then we'll fly over Karen, and I'll point out my school, before we start heading north. As we get nearer home we should have some good views of Mount Kenya."

Charlotte's mind was busily taking this all in. "The Ngong Hills are the ones you had a watercolour of, in your room in Churchill Hall."

"That's right, well-remembered; painted by my gran; and referred to in the opening sentence of Karen Blixen's book, *Out of Africa*."

"Yes, I read it, on your recommendation; beautiful writing I thought."

"Yup, written with great affection and understanding; happiness perhaps with an undercurrent, at times, of sadness; not surprising really considering what she went through. Anyway we'll be flying right over where she lived."

A benign smile on the face of Mr Hooper was beginning to be overtaken by signs of slight impatience. "If you've finished chatting, we should get going."

"Of course, Dad." Ben turned back to the controls and put on headphones. Mr Hooper did the same. Shortly after the engine started and the propeller swung into motion. They taxied to the end of the runway where they waited for another plane to land. When it had cleared they took up their position for take-off. Ben and his father were doing some final checks and Charlotte could just hear a muffled voice as Ben was talking to the control tower. The engine then roared and the plane jolted forward, picking up speed rapidly. Charlotte had never been in a small plane before and had never experienced such a sensation of speed over the ground. Pressed back into her seat, wide-eyed and thrilled she watched the ground fall away beneath them as they took to the air. Moments later, as they continued to gain height, Ben was pointing and Charlotte could see coming into view a range of four distinct hills. Her face up against the window, she remembered the opening lines of the book Ben had been so passionate about, which he had quoted to her, far away, on that dramatic day in Bristol: 'I had a farm in Africa, at the foot of the Ngong Hills.'

The plane began to turn, arcing away from the hills, and Ben was soon pointing again. Below Charlotte could see the tower in the heart of Ben's old school, surrounded by scattered buildings and numerous playing fields over a wide area. She nodded and smiled. He too smiled, but picking up on a look from his father he then turned all his attention to the important business of flying the plane.

As they headed further north, approaching the equator, there was an increasing sense in Charlotte of a dream-like quality to the late afternoon. Was this really happening? Almost unbelievable. Such anticipation, but also some confusion, apprehension even, but surely not fear. She wrestled somewhat with thoughts and emotions, but her spirits started to rise again, higher and higher, as the scene unfolded far below. The patchwork quilt of cultivation of the Kikuyu heartlands was beginning to fade away into the great expanse of the untamed African landscape.

LAIKIPIA

The Equator runs across these highlands... and the farm lay at an altitude of over six thousand feet. In the day time you felt that you had got high up, near to the sun, but the early mornings and evenings were limpid and restful, and the nights were cold.

The geographical position and the height of the land combined to create a landscape that had not its like in all the world. There was no fat on it and no luxuriance anywhere; it was Africa distilled up through six thousand feet, like the strong and refined essence of a continent. The colours were dry and burnt, like the colours in pottery... Upon the grass of the great plains the crooked bare old thorn-trees were scattered, and the grass was spiced like thyme and bog-myrtles; in some places the scent was so strong that it smarted in the nostrils...The views were immensely wide. Everything that you saw made for greatness and freedom, and unequalled nobility.

The chief feature of the landscape, and of your life in it, was the air... Up in this high air you breathed easily, drawing in a vital assurance and lightness of heart. In the highlands you woke up in the morning and thought: Here I am, where I ought to be.

Karen Blixen
Out of Africa

Saturday

It was dawn in Laikipia. Streaks of delicate, early morning light were beginning to illuminate another day on the great plateau, rising up some thousands of feet above sea-level, extending northwest of Mount Kenya into the vastness of over three thousand five hundred square miles. Occasional wafts of a soft breeze rippled over the semi-arid plains and acacia thickets, up across scattered hills and down through gorges. The coldness of the night began a steady retreat before the rising tide of warmth. There was some domestic stirring in the very few, isolated ranches and homesteads, but a far more extensive, wholly different stirring in the immense expanse stretching away to the north. Here was one of the greatest of all biodiversities of African wildlife.

Charlotte lay in bed, hands behind her head, propped up on two soft pillows, reflecting on the events of the previous evening. The plane had landed just before dusk. A short but bumpy drive in a Land Rover had brought them within sight of the buildings of the ranch as the equatorial night descended with the suddenness of the switching off of a light. Ben's mother couldn't have made her feel more welcome. Supper had followed drinks and then there had been coffee and more drinks, beside a log fire which was not at all what she had expected. Conversation had flowed back and forth, about her and about them, but most of all about this special place in which she found herself so unexpectedly. Sympathy was, of course, expressed about what had befallen Alice's husband, but there was clearly a determination to make the best of the situation, for Charlotte's sake. She sensed that there was a real enthusiasm for her visit; for the opportunity to show her and to share with her things they cared so much about. The coolness of the night air had done nothing to diminish the warm feeling she felt inside as she was then taken outside by Ben and shown across to the guest cottage, a little way from the main house. Told to lock herself in, she had also been given the assurance that there was a night watchman on duty, patrolling the grounds; at least that was what she had understood Ben's reference to an *askari* to mean. She hadn't been able to sleep at first, with so much going through her mind and hardly able to believe where she was. But fatigue had eventually taken over and her dreamlike state had gradually transformed into real dreams as she drifted off from consciousness, lulled by the chorus of sounds of the African night.

Her thoughts were interrupted by a sudden knocking on the door. Jumping out of bed and pulling on a dressing gown which had helpfully been provided for her, she opened the door a crack. There stood an African man, smiling shyly. He was holding a tray bearing a teapot, milk, sugar, cup and saucer.

"*Jambo, memsahib.*"

"Ah yes, *jambo*, thank you."

She ushered him in and he carefully put down the tray on a small table.

"Thank you," she said again.

"*Asante,*" he said with a note of encouragement.

"*Asante,*" she said slightly hesitantly.

"*Ndio, mzuri, mzuri sana,*" and he broke into a broad grin as he turned and left the room.

Short Swahili lesson over, she poured a cup of tea and pulled back the curtains. For a moment the view rendered her immobile. She was looking down a small ravine to a plain below, dotted with acacia trees, stretching as far as the eye could see to hills beyond and ever further to a distant horizon, still streaked with the last fading pink remnants of dawn. Taking it all in she became struck with the realisation that nothing she could see related to man, nothing was man-made. The landscape was quite simply devoid of human intrusion. She had never seen the like of it on such a scale. Regaining motion, and looking to one side, she noticed there was a French window leading out to a small patio. Letting herself out onto it she inhaled the still cool air, subtly laced with unfamiliar scents; a promise of new experiences. Settling herself into a rustic wooden chair she looked out over a balcony rail fashioned from a slim, curved branch of pale wood and began sipping her tea. Minutes passed, and more minutes, but for a while, for Charlotte, in the dawning of that new day, time stood still.

Then a dog barked and she became aware of the sound of voices, some way off behind her. It was time to move. Returning to the room she washed and dressed, putting on a light linen shirt and three-quarter-length trousers. Looking at her face in the mirror she decided that a little eye make-up was all that was required. She then brushed back her hair and glanced at her reflection, first left, then right. With a nod she felt ready to embrace the day.

Walking over to the main house she was able to see it properly, in daylight, for the first time. Before her was a rambling building, partly of stone, but mainly of wood, under a thatched roof. It was to an extent covered by flowering creepers and flanked by dark red bushes of bougainvillea. Openings between pillars along much of the front led onto a broad verandah with two central steps up to it. There stood Ben, surrounded by dogs.

Several of the dogs, some brown, some black and tan, swirled around Charlotte, tails wagging in friendly greeting.
"I didn't know you had so many dogs," she said, patting various bobbing heads.

"Ah well, these are the *shenzis*, the outdoor farm dogs."

Another dog was emerging, coming down the steps from the

verandah, a large, light brown dog with a black muzzle and distinctive ridge running down his back. He regarded Charlotte with mild curiosity as he sniffed the air.

"*Et tu Brute*," she smiled reflectively.

"You've remembered."

"It was a day to remember."

"Come in; breakfast is ready. You must be hungry. I certainly am."

She followed him up the steps, across the verandah, through the living room where they had sat chatting the previous evening, and into the dining room. Ben's mother was in there alone. She rose from her chair and, slightly unexpectedly, kissed Charlotte on the cheek.

"I hope you slept well."

"Yes, I did, thank you. I woke quite early, but it was no hardship. I so enjoyed the dawn and having my tea outside taking in the view; it's quite something."

At that moment the door from the kitchen opened and the man who had earlier brought Charlotte her tea emerged with a pot of coffee which he carefully put down on the table.

Charlotte smiled at him in recognition. "Talking of which, this is the man who brought me that tea. He also taught me a few words of Swahili, but I'm afraid I don't know his name."

Mrs Hooper looked slightly surprised, but Ben quickly responded. "This is Kimani, the houseboy."

Kimani nodded, but said nothing. As he retreated to the kitchen, Charlotte called out after him, "*Asante*".

"He's a good worker and he's been with us a long time," said Mrs Hooper firmly. "But—" and her voice took on a tone of patient explanation, "—we don't tend to chat to him, or the other servants for that matter, when they're serving."

"I see," said Charlotte. Her eyes had narrowed somewhat and Ben was watching her warily, wondering what might be coming next. "Why," she asked, "is he referred to as a 'boy', a houseboy? He's quite a mature man by the looks of him."

"It's just common parlance here," said Ben swiftly, pre-empting any response from his mother. "It dates back to colonial times."

Charlotte shot him a look and then turned towards his mother. "You mentioned other servants."

"Yes, indeed; apart from the farm workers, of course, there's the *mpishi*."

"Cook," interjected Ben.

"And a kitchen *toto*, as well as a woman who does washing and ironing and a couple of *shamba* boys."

"Quite a staff," murmured Charlotte.

"Pretty much what would be expected," said Mrs Hooper, just a faint note of irritation creeping in to her voice.

"And it provides much-needed employment," added Ben, he hoped sounding not too defensive.

"Now," said his mother, brightening again, "do help yourselves."

Ben ushered Charlotte towards the sideboard. There she made her selection from an array of fresh fruit, mango, pawpaw, pineapple and grapefruit, and Ben did the same, although in somewhat greater quantity. There followed freshly boiled eggs brought in by Kimani with a basket of warm toast.

"There is some marmalade," said Mrs Hooper to Charlotte. "But you might like to try some of our local jams and jellies." She indicated towards a collection of jars in the middle of the table.

"Oh yes, thank you; I would."

"They're made by Ben's granny, my mother; you'll meet her later. That's guava and the other one, there, is loquat."

"Interesting," said Charlotte, diplomatically, as she tasted one then the other, flavours new to her permeating her senses. "Actually, I particularly like this one."

"My favourite too," beamed Mrs Hooper. "That's the loquat jelly; I prefer its smoothness to the consistency of the guava."

Ben had visibly relaxed. They had moved on to safer ground. While the toast was being finished more coffee was poured. Kimani shuttled back and forth, beginning to clear away.

"Thank you, Mrs Hooper," said Charlotte. "That was a perfect breakfast."

"You're most welcome dear, and do call me Rose."

Nodding thanks, Charlotte then inclined her head towards Ben. "And what's your sister's name?"

"Carol. Unfortunately you're not going to get to meet her. As I think I've told you before, she's a teacher, in Nairobi. She does normally spend time here, during the school holidays, but she's away at the moment, visiting friends."

Ben's father had appeared in the room. He had breakfasted much earlier. "Good morning, good morning. How are we all?"

Following general confirmation that all was well, very well in fact, Mr Hooper turned to his son. "I'm sure you'll want to be showing Charlotte round, but before that I'd welcome a bit of help with some cattle, if that's OK?"

"Sure Dad, no problem," said Ben, while glancing at Charlotte.

"Of course," said Charlotte quickly. "I don't want to be in the way at all."

"There's no question of that," said Mr Hooper with a broad, reassuring smile. "You're most welcome here. There's plenty of time for everything; I only need Ben for an hour or so."

As they got up to go, someone else came into the room.

"Ah Gran, good timing," said Ben greeting her warmly, "just in time for me to introduce you to Charlotte."

Young and old stepped forward, regarding one another with close interest. Charlotte saw before her an elderly, but still very upright woman with grey hair tied back in a bun. She was wearing a simple, home-made cotton print dress. Bare arms and legs revealed that the sun had taken its toll, but the overall appearance was one of dignified elegance, faded somewhat, yet elegance nonetheless. But what Charlotte noticed most of all were the eyes: bright beady eyes; all-seeing eyes. Looking back at her the old woman began to smile, approvingly it seemed.

"So, you're Ben's girlfriend, I understand? Striking, I must say."

Sensing that Charlotte was uncertain how to respond, Ben came to the rescue.

"No Gran, she's not my girlfriend; she's a girl who's a friend."

"Is there a difference?" she asked, half amused, wheeling round towards her grandson.

"For sure."

"There wasn't in my day. Anyway," she added with a hint of mischief, "you make a fine couple."

Ben and Charlotte exchanged uncertain looks. Mrs Hooper was making as if she were busy tidying up. Mr Hooper smiling, possibly even smirking slightly, patted Ben on the shoulder. It was time to go.

Granny Sullivan, as she was widely known, took Charlotte by the hand. "I'd love to chat to you, my dear. Come and sit with me for a while on the verandah."

And so, that day on the high African plateau unfolded in layers of conversation, exploration and surprise. Granny Sullivan and Charlotte talked at length. There were things that they each wanted to know from the other, mutual interest, although at times tinged with a degree of wariness. Coffee was served by Kimani while Granny Sullivan was expounding on her early life on the Cherangani farm, pioneering times filled with days of both adventure and mishap, good times and bad, but never dull. Charlotte had many questions. Then Granny did too; she wanted to know more about Charlotte, of course, but particularly about Ben and what she knew of his year in England; not just what he had been doing; she was probing at a deeper level.

Ben, meanwhile, was busy with his father, out on the ranch in the rising heat and swirling dust of the late morning. Together with a number of the ranch workers they were rounding up cattle and driving them into an enclosure. The last of the animals safely in, he checked the time on his watch. Waved away with a smile by his father, he hurried back to the house. There he found Charlotte, still on the verandah, but by now alone, sitting quietly and reading.

"There you are; so Gran's gone."

"Yes, she said that she was going back to her place."

"OK, yeah, she has her own small house nearby. Dad built it for her and Grandpa when they sold their farm and moved here. How did you get on?"

"It was really interesting chatting to her; quite a life she's had; so different from anyone I've known before, I suppose."

"She's an amazing woman and was really important to me when I was growing up."

"Yes, well, I can believe it, and she told me some quite

interesting things about you."

"Sounds potentially embarrassing."

Charlotte raised her eyebrows and smiled, but said no more.

Ben decided that he should move the conversation away from himself and back to his grandmother. "As I think I've told you before, she has a really deep understanding of this country, you know, and of its people."

"Yes, I can see that, but…" Charlotte was frowning slightly, wanting to say something she regarded as important, but sensing the need to tread carefully; the last thing she wanted to do was to cause offence to people who were being so kind and hospitable to her.

"But what?" asked a puzzled looking Ben after a pause.

"It's the people, the African people I mean."

"She really cares about them, you know."

"Yes, yes, that comes across, but there's also a peculiar dichotomy here which I find difficult to understand; too complex perhaps."

"What on earth do you mean?"

"She regards Africans as a race apart."

"Many would agree with that, including Africans themselves."

"Yes, but it's not just them being a race apart." Charlotte swallowed hard. "She, and I'm sure she's not alone, many other of the colonialists, particularly, I imagine the old colonialists…" Charlotte was beginning to stammer, not sure exactly how to put it, or, indeed, whether to say anything further at all.

But it had gone too far to be left hanging in the air. "What is it you think about them?" prompted Ben. Still no immediate answer. "Come on, you can tell me," he insisted.

Summoning up her courage, and looking Ben in the eye, she

said quietly, but firmly, "They regard Africans as an inferior race."

Perhaps Ben knew Charlotte well enough, based upon past conversations, even debates, to know that something like this was coming. But it was still a shock for it to be spelt out, to hear the words. He shook his head, but said nothing. They sat there for a while, together but in silence.

Brutus lumbered into view and nudged first one, then the other in amiable greeting. Ben patted him on the head instinctively, but without really taking notice of him while he remained looking distracted. Charlotte then leant towards Ben and put one hand on his outstretched arm. "Sorry, I shouldn't have said that, whatever I may think, rightly or wrongly. It was unkind of me, particularly when you're being so kind to me."

Ben edged closer to Charlotte and took both her hands in his, shaking them slightly as he said, "It's OK, really it is; I've always respected you for speaking your mind." Recollections brought a smile to his face. "It's led to some pretty lively discussions, but it hasn't stopped us being friends, has it?"

There was look of relief on Charlotte's face, but no immediate answer. Perhaps she thought that none was required.

"It hasn't, has it?" pressed Ben with slight concern.

"No, no, of course not. I've come to regard you not just as a friend, but as a very special friend. I want you to know that."

Ben's immediate response was to squeeze Charlotte's hands more tightly, but before any further thoughts could enter his mind he heard his mother's voice calling out to them as she came out of the house on to the verandah.

"Lunch will be ready shortly."

Immediately Ben let go of Charlotte's hands. They sat back in their chairs and dusted themselves off emotionally.

"Great Mum, thanks," said Ben, adopting a studied air of nonchalance.

Charlotte added her thanks as Mrs Hooper turned and went back into the house.

A light lunch followed, the usual traditional Saturday lunch in the Hooper household: cold meats and salads, cheese and home-made pickles, freshly baked bread made by *mpishi*, still warm; simple, but good. Kimani came and went between the kitchen and the dining room. Charlotte noticed that he was wearing what she later discovered was called a *kanzu*, a long tunic, almost like a nightshirt, and on his head was perched a rather comical-looking red fez, Tommy Cooper style. Finding it somewhat curious she wondered why he was dressed like this, but thought it better, perhaps, not to ask; she was left with the assumption that it was just another example of lingering colonial tradition.

Afterwards was rest time. Ben suggested to Charlotte that a chair under a shady tree in the garden would a good place to be. He provided her with a book to read, *A Field Guide to the National Parks of East Africa*, by John G, Williams.

"You might find this provides some helpful information," he said.

"Oh really?"

"Yes, although there's no Laikipia national park, the Samburu and Isiolo game reserves lie just to the north of us. The section in the book on those reserves is well worth a read, particularly with regard to the animals found there, many of which are also found here. So you can swot up a bit before we go out later."

"Will do. I've heard you talk of Samburu, haven't I? I think you've mentioned, rather mysteriously, 'legacies of Samburu',

227

whatever they might be."

Ben was anxious to move the conversation on. "I'll also look out for you the *Field Guide to the Birds of East and Central Africa*, by the same man. He's a great expert. Through his children, whom I know from school, I've been lucky enough to meet him. The birdlife which he identifies and describes so well shouldn't be overlooked; it's amazing."

"It all sounds great. Did you say we're going out later?"

"Yup, late afternoon, after a cup of tea."

"To do what?"

"I'm taking you on a *sanduku* drive."

"Sorry, a what?"

Ben smiled at the look of amused puzzlement on Charlotte's face. "A surprise, you'll see soon enough." He had begun to enjoy surprising her and she didn't seem at all averse to it.

Charlotte had brought the field guides with her and she placed them within easy reach as she settled herself into the front seat of the Land Rover. Ben was busy loading something into the back. A moment later he was climbing into the driver's seat. Charlotte sensed happy anticipation, excitement even. Ben handed her a pair of binoculars.

"These will be useful. I shall rely upon you to be my look-out when I'm driving."

"What will we be seeing?"

"You never know for sure; that's a large part of the fun of it when you're out in the bush."

He started the engine and pulled out of the yard at the side of the house. They drove for a while before turning off onto a track. They were heading north, away from the main part of the ranch, into wild country. As they did so they began to see animals and yet more animals. Ben pointed out various different kinds of antelopes. Charlotte was surprised how many there were and she eagerly thumbed through relevant pages of the field guide, studying key features and learning names. Ben took great pleasure from her obvious enthusiasm and shared her delight when she spotted and correctly identified some Grant's gazelles.

"But what are those?" she asked suddenly. Putting the binoculars to her eyes she took a closer look. "Yes, giraffe, of course, but of a kind I've never seen before."

"Ah," said Ben, following her gaze; "*Giraffa reticulata*, special to this part of Kenya, reticulated giraffe."

"They look sort of reddish brown, with a network of white lines, almost like crazed china."

"Yes, good description; I like it. They're quite different from the common giraffe, which you might be familiar with; they have rather blotchy markings. There's a useful colour plate in the field guide where you can compare the two."

Charlotte flipped through the book to the relevant page. She was really getting into this.

A few minutes later Ben slowed the Land Rover down to a crawl and then stopped completely. Something had caught his keen eye.

"Let me have the binoculars for a moment." He scanned a thicket a little way off at the base of a small hill. "Yes, I thought so." He handed the binoculars back to Charlotte. "Have a look."

"Oh yes, I see now, a light grey, kind of antelope, I suppose, with white stripes along the body; and, gosh yes, large ears, twitching slightly and swivelling in our direction."

"You bet they are; he's listening carefully and watching us intently with those shiny, dark eyes. But have you any idea what he is?"

Charlotte shook her head and carried on looking through the binoculars. Ben removed the field guide from her lap and found a picture page showing several different types of antelope. As she lowered the binoculars from her eyes, he handed her the open book.

"Have a go at identification," he said with a smile.

She scanned the page, rather too quickly in her excitement. "Kudu," she pronounced rather breathlessly.

"Very good, but what sort?"

"What do you mean?"

"Greater or Lesser?"

"Greater."

"No, you're guessing now; take another look through the binoculars. It's too small for a start, but look particularly at the neck. Has it got a distinct fringe hanging down?"

"No, no, I can't see one, not at all."

"That's because it's a lesser kudu," said Ben quietly, trying to avoid sounding triumphant, or, more irritating still, a know-it-all.

In truth, Charlotte had been slightly irritated for a moment. But this had quickly passed, overtaken by a sense of wonderment. She continued to look through the binoculars for a while before turning towards Ben.

"There's so much to take in. I've never before experienced anything remotely like this, you know."

"I'm really chuffed that you're able to do so now, even for a short time. I promise you we're going to make the most of these few days."

Charlotte was studying Ben's face as he spoke, but then turned away, binoculars to her eyes, and made out as if she were studying more details of the kudu. But the animal had melted away into a thicket of acacia.

"Right," said Ben, starting up the engine, "time to press on and look for some big game."

They drove for quite some while before turning on to an even smaller, bumpier track leading down a slope to a long line of trees.

"Elephant country," said Ben.

Knowledge and instinct were rewarded not long after. There among the trees large shapes were moving, slowly, but deliberately. Charlotte sat forward, gripping the front of the seat, staring out intently.

"You did bring your camera?" asked Ben, without taking his eyes off where they were heading.

"Oh yes," said Charlotte, reaching for her bag, on the floor between her feet. "It's a bit basic, I'm afraid."

"I'll get you quite close; but not too close," he added, based on past experience.

They crept closer as the elephants began to emerge more from the trees. It was a good mixed group: a matriarch and other females, two quite small babies, and some male and female adolescents, including one rapidly developing young bull. Ben turned the vehicle sideways on to the animals, at what he judged to be a safe distance, and edged forward slightly. A short further turn would head them back up the track if it became necessary to make a quick retreat. Charlotte was unaware of the manoeuvring, still less the reason for it. Her whole attention was on the animals and doing her best to capture on film something at least of their magnificence.

"I worry about that fellow," said Ben after a while, pointing in the direction of the young bull.

"Why ever?" asked a surprised sounding Charlotte.

"Because he's going to turn into a fine tusker which will make him a prime candidate to be poached."

"Really," a shocked look on Charlotte's face. "How big a problem is poaching? I've heard you talk about it, of course, but round here?"

"Getting bigger all the time."

"Surely something is being done about it?"

"Not nearly enough. The more I think about it, and I think about it a lot, the more I reckon that we can't just leave it to the Government and the Game Department; we've also got to become involved."

"Who's we?"

"My family, and others like us, who are lucky enough, goddam privileged in fact, to live in special places like this. We need to move on from farming and ranching into conservation and encourage people, tourists I suppose, to come here and bring in much needed money to fund it. I've been talking to my dad about this and he's in touch with other like-minded people."

Charlotte was watching Ben closely and listening carefully. She detected signs of real fervour. "What about the local African people?" she pondered. "Do you think that they will support any such efforts?"

Ben smiled; typically astute Charlotte he thought. "Damn good question. Their participation may be the very crux of it. I reckon they really do need to be involved and, crucially, to benefit from it. That must be the way forward."

The elephants were moving further away. Ben checked his watch. It was time for them to move on too. He started the engine and they headed back up the track.

"That was quite something," said Charlotte with a contented sigh.

"We're not done yet," said Ben. He pointed across the plain to the rocky ridge of an escarpment. "That's where we're now making for."

"Oh, any particular reason?"

"Yup; I've had reports of a female rhino and her calf which have been seen in the vicinity. It would be great if we could find them."

Charlotte nodded enthusiastically and reached for the binoculars.

"Good," said Ben, noticing what she was doing. "Keep a careful lookout because I really have to concentrate on the track in places; there are some big boulders and deep potholes to be avoided."

They drove on for a while, ever closer to the escarpment. There were a few false alarms; Charlotte pointed excitedly into the near distance at what turned out, on closer inspection, to be rocks or shadows. Ben was quick to try to dispel any embarrassment on her part, assuring her that the difficulty of what she was doing should not be underestimated, even in the case of a large animal because of its ability to merge so completely into its natural landscape. Nevertheless she was beginning to give up hope as they reached the foot of the escarpment.

"Are we going up?" she asked, seeing the winding track ahead.

"Yes, indeed; there's a great view from there; a perfect place to watch the sunset and to enjoy the *sanduku*."

Charlotte opened her mouth to ask a further question, but then froze. The vehicle had begun to climb and the slight elevation gave her a view just beyond an acacia thicket a little way off to the left. She put the binoculars to her eyes.

"This time," she almost hissed rather than spoke, "yes, this time, I'm sure of it."

Ben pulled over on to some level ground at the side of the incline and followed Charlotte's gaze. He didn't need the binoculars. "Good girl, you're damn right this time; well spotted, well spotted indeed."

An adult rhino was emerging from the thicket, head up towards them, horn thrust forward, ears twitching, nostrils carefully scenting the air.

"Black Rhino," whispered Ben. "See that distinguishing feature of a prehensile upper lip?"

"He or she is looking straight at us," said Charlotte, still hissing slightly.

"Probably can't see us too well; hasn't got good eyesight, but can sense us all right. Look at those ears and nostrils working overtime."

"Do you think it's the rhino we've been looking for?"

"Well, I'm pretty sure it's a female. Can I just have the binnies for a mo?"

She handed him the binoculars and he studied the thicket carefully. "Yup, I think I can detect some movement, just off to the side of where she's standing. We should just wait quietly for a while."

Quiet patience led to a baby rhino's head coming into view, peeping cautiously out of the cover of the thicket. Then slowly it emerged before scurrying the remaining steps to be at its mother's side. What followed was one of those special moments in life, which occur just occasionally, but which are likely to be for ever remembered. The mother rhino, apparently satisfied that there was no imminent danger, lay down on her side to suckle her baby. Latched on, the little animal's budding horn fitted precisely in its mother's groin; designed by nature to perfection.

Silent minutes passed, punctuated only by the occasional grunt from the animals and the whispering of the grasses in little puffs of breeze. But Ben was conscious of passing time. "I hate to leave them, but if we don't get going now we're going to be up against the fading light." As Charlotte nodded Ben started the engine and slowly eased the vehicle back on to the track. As they wound their way up the escarpment more and more of the surrounding country came into view, seemingly limitless space stretching away in every direction. The ground began to level out and Ben pulled up beside a flat rocky outcrop.

"That's where we're going to be for our sundowner." He got out and stretched before walking round to the back of the Land Rover. As Charlotte joined him he opened the rear door and pointed to a sturdy wooden box.

"The *sanduku*," he announced with obvious pleasure.

"Ah," was all Charlotte could manage.

The box was now open and she could see bottles and a glass being carefully unwrapped from linen cloths. There was also an ice bucket visible at one end. Ben half turned towards her. "Gin and tonic?"

She nodded.

"Ice and lemon?"

Again she nodded before quickly adding, "Sorry, I'm at a bit of a loss for words; thank you, this is just quite frankly..."

"What?"

"Amazing."

Ben finished pouring and mixing. He handed her the glass and selected a bottle of Tusker for himself.

"Cheers," he said, "welcome to Laikipia."

"Thanks Ben, cheers; I can hardly believe I'm here; have to

pinch myself." Guiding her over to the flat rock, they sat down together on the edge, looking far out over the plains below to distant hills. The stone was still warm from the heat of the afternoon sun. But the tide of the day was beginning to recede, leaving cool air gently washing over and soothing the rugged landscape. Bright colours were ebbing away into subtle, softer shades. In the stillness there was only the occasional ripple of sound, puffs of breeze whispering in the acacia thickets and, far below, distant animal sounds, stirrings of creatures of the night. To the west the sky was becoming streaked with shades of pink, brilliantly illuminated against the darkening sky. Over to the south-east the outline of Mount Kenya was just discernible at times, partly concealed by thin wisps of cloud; shyly, mysteriously it came and went from view.

There was the slight rattle of ice as Charlotte took another sip from her glass. Ben followed her gaze towards the mountain. "Should get a better look at it tomorrow."

Charlotte did not answer directly. She simply said, softly, "What an amazing end to an amazing day."

Ben put down his bottle and gently rested his hand on Charlotte's shoulder. "I can't even begin to tell you how much I've enjoyed showing this place to you."

As he spoke, Charlotte shuffled closer to him, causing Ben to drape his outstretched arm round the back of her neck. There they sat, motionless for a while, in that wild, remote place, in the gathering and gently enveloping dusk.

Reluctantly Ben broke the spell. "We better get going, I'm afraid. The track down to the bottom of the escarpment can be rather tricky in the dark, but we can just about make it while there's still some light." He took a final swig from his bottle. Charlotte had a last sip from her glass before tipping away the rapidly diminishing cubes of ice. She stood up, brushing herself down. Ben was already up and repacking the *sanduku*. She handed him her glass which he carefully wrapped up before placing it into the box. All safely stowed, the rear door was shut and they took their seats. Ben started the engine and began threading the vehicle between still just visible rocks and clumps of bush, twisting and turning down the steep incline to the plain below gradually being swallowed up by the night.

Nothing much was said on the way back. But then nothing much really needed to be said.

Sunday

It was an early start. Kimani brought tea to Charlotte just before dawn. She drank it while getting dressed, pulling on some thicker trousers than her own borrowed, at Ben's suggestion, from Carol's wardrobe. A warm jersey was also required to ward off the high altitude early morning chill. Pulling back the curtains she could see the first streaks of light in a pale water colour wash sky beginning to illuminate the wide open landscape stretching to a far horizon. Gathering up her hat and dark glasses she headed out of the door with a keen sense of anticipation.

Ben met her at the front of the house and escorted her to the yard off to one side at the rear of the property. He gestured towards two horses, bays, ready saddled being held by a young African man. "Here are the girls, all set to go."

"So I see," said Charlotte, stroking each one on the muzzle in turn.

"You have ridden before?" asked Ben.

Charlotte shot him her well-known 'that's a silly question look'. "I've told you where I was brought up in the country; riding was almost compulsory there, from a young age."

"Of course," said Ben, somewhat ruefully.

Charlotte immediately gave him a playful shove. It was too good a day to be anything other than happy and relaxed.

Ben noticed that Charlotte appeared to be getting on particularly well with one of the horses. "That's Firefly," he said. "You ride her; she can be lively, but I know you'll be able to handle her well. And she's really smart; she always remembers all the potholes and anthills which need to be avoided." He thought about adding that she didn't panic if she saw a snake, but decided against it.

"Sounds like my kind of girl," said Charlotte, swinging herself into the saddle with effortless ease. Ben, looking on admiringly, didn't move for a moment.

She caught his gaze and smiled, eyebrows slight raised. "Well, are we ready?"

"Yes, yes, of course." He turned and mounted the other horse. "Right, let's go, follow me."

They set off down the track leading away from the ranch buildings. For a while Charlotte simply followed Ben. But gradually she drew her horse up closer to his until they were riding side by side. The quality of the early morning light and the cool, refreshing air had a comforting, intoxicating effect producing an irresistible feeling of well-being. In between pointing out particular features of the landscape, Ben absorbed the contentment of companionable silence. Glancing in Charlotte's direction from time to time, he noticed her tipping her head right back and shutting her eyes as she became immersed in the atmosphere of the day.

"Right," he said, reaching a particular point on the track. "Here's where we head off across the plain."

"Sounds exciting," said Charlotte, suddenly alert. "What can we expect? Wild animals presumably?"

"Yup, but we're not going to do anything too crazy, involving the Big Five for instance."

"Which animals make up the Big Five?"

"Lion and leopard, elephant, rhino and buffalo."

"Right," she said with a little disappointment, but rather more relief.

"But what we can do is get up close to the plains' game. You can't really do so in a vehicle, nor on foot, but on a horse you can get right in amongst them, be at one with them; it's an amazing experience which I particularly wanted to share with you."

Charlotte was immediately infected by the intensity of his enthusiasm and eagerly urged her horse forward as Ben set off. They didn't have to ride for long. Ben drew his horse to a halt, holding up one hand. Charlotte pulled up beside him.

"There, see," he said pointing to a group of animals a little way off, "Zebra."

Charlotte looked closely and began to focus on the detail. "They're not like the zebra I saw in the Nairobi National Park."

"No," said Ben smiling, "that's because they're not the common zebra; they're Grévy's zebra which are found particularly in this part of Kenya. Look carefully, as we get closer, and you'll see they have rather natty pinstripes which stop just before lovely creamy white bellies. And check out their large ears surrounded by a thick furry fringe. Now I'm not going to say any more. We must be completely quiet as we ride in amongst them."

They walked the horses forward steadily in unhurried silence, ever closer to the grazing animals. A few heads looked up in their direction, regarding them with mild curiosity before returning to their morning feed. And so domestic *equus* passed through and among wild *equus*, all together as one in an immensity of unrestricted wild space.

"That was quite something," whispered Charlotte as they drew away.

"I know; it's really special when you so completely blend into the natural environment. Now let's see what else we can find; some common zebra, perhaps, for you to make the comparison? Oh, and I'd really like you to get up close and personal with reticulated giraffe, like those we saw yesterday evening."

So, on they rode, across that great, high plain, dotted with flat-topped thorn trees and rocky outcrops. Scattered hills were dwarfed by the appearance on the distant horizon of Mount Kenya, shed of all clouds for an early morning display of magnificence. As well as more zebra, and the giraffe they sought, other animals were to be seen, including some of the smaller, shyer antelopes, duiker and dik-dik, not otherwise so easy to detect. And birds, birds everywhere, of a kind Charlotte had never seen before, on the ground, in the treetops, and soaring high overhead. The overriding sense was one of boundless freedom.

Gradually Charlotte became aware that they were looping round and heading back towards where they had set out. Ben pointed to a lone, distant tree. Beside it Charlotte could just make out a parked vehicle. A little beyond it a thin plume of smoke rose straight up through the still air.

"That's where we're making for. The ground's quite good here, so race you."

There was no need to wait for any response. Charlotte immediately kicked her horse into action and he had to ride hard in pursuit. Drawing alongside her they rode fast, close together until pulling up just short of the tree. There stood one of the farm workers who held the bridles of the panting horses as they dismounted. Charlotte was also breathing hard. She flung back her windswept hair, eyes shining.

"What have we here?" she asked, taking in the scene.

There, under the tree, stood Kimani, looking somewhat bashful, but as ever eager to please, gesturing towards a camp table and two canvas chairs.

"Breakfast is ready," said Ben, with obvious delight.

As they settled themselves into their chairs, Charlotte noticed that the horses had gone. Ben explained that they were always set free to find their way back to the stables, not far away. The smoke, seen earlier, was coming from a small charcoal brazier. Delicious smells were beginning to permeate the air.

"It's amazing what good food you can cook on a little *jiko* like that," remarked Ben. "You're hungry, I hope?"

"Certainly am."

Kimani was approaching the table with a tray bearing two glasses of orange juice, mugs, a thermos of coffee, milk and sugar. They were carefully laid out before he returned to fetch warm rolls, butter and home-made jams. The main event was to follow; plates of eggs, bacon, sausages, tomatoes and dark succulent mushrooms, the best Charlotte had ever tasted. They chatted, intermittently, between hungry mouthfuls. But for the most part they were content with just being there, together.

Looking across the plain, from under the shade of the tree, Charlotte noticed that Mount Kenya was still visible, though the morning was warming and fluffy clouds were beginning to bubble up in the shimmering air.

"Don't tell me you've climbed that as well?" she said, pointing.

"Not really."

"What do you mean, not really?"

"Well, I've been up to Point Lenana, over sixteen thousand feet. You can slog your way up there without any special skill. But the main peaks, Batian and Nelion, over seventeen thousand feet, they're a different proposition. Look, you can still just see them."

Charlotte looked hard at where he was pointing. She could make out sharp, jagged pinnacles of rock, streaked with snow and ice, towering high over the lower slopes of the mountain. "Yes, they look pretty formidable."

"Absolutely; you need proper mountaineering skills to get up there, and those I don't have."

"Presumably it is climbed though?"

"Yup, by those who know what they're doing, with the right equipment." He began to chuckle.

"What?" asked Charlotte, with a surprised, quizzical look.

"I'm reminded of *No Picnic on Mount Kenya*."

"Sorry; you'll have to enlighten me further."

"It's a book by an Italian, by the name of Benuzzi, if I remember correctly. During the Second World War he was a prisoner, a prisoner of war, in a prison camp somewhere near the foot of the mountain. And I think he had been a keen climber before the War, in the Alps or Dolomites presumably. Anyway, he looked out every day from the prison camp at this wonderful mountain and, increasingly, he longed to climb it. So, together with two fellow prisoners, who wanted to do the same thing, a plan was hatched to escape, with the sole purpose of climbing the mountain."

"Pretty unusual for an escape plan."

"Too right; anyway, they somehow managed to cobble together some improvised equipment and meagre rations, waited their chance and slipped out of the camp without being noticed."

"And did they make it up the mountain?"

"Not quite, unfortunately. They were out over two weeks and a couple of them reached sixteen and a half thousand feet up the north-west ridge. It was a remarkable achievement, considering that the conditions conspired against them and, of course, despite their best efforts, they just weren't properly equipped."

"Were they then captured?"

"Not exactly." Ben was chuckling again. "To the astonishment of the camp commandant they broke back into the camp. Initially they were sentenced to twenty-eight days in solitary confinement, but, on reflection, the commandant commuted it to only seven days in acknowledgment of what he referred to as their 'sporting effort'."

"What a wonderful story."

"Yup, it's well told in the book which was published after the War, first in Italian, but subsequently in English. You should look out for it some time."

Charlotte was looking thoughtful. "To me, what's so heart-warming about it is that, in a time of war, these men broke out not to escape to try to re-join the war, to kill people or anything like that, but to do something so, so, oh I don't know quite how to put it, so life-affirming I suppose."

Breakfast had finished and was being cleared away. "Right," said Ben, "time to go; I'll drive you back."

"What about Kimani and the other man?"

"They'll be fine. They'll finish clearing up here and then someone will drive out to collect them."

As Ben took his seat behind the wheel of the vehicle he caught Charlotte's eye. Thy exchanged glances and smiled. It had been a start to their day that had made spirits soar, as high as the great birds of prey they had seen earlier, effortlessly riding the thermals.

Charlotte sank back in her chair, absorbing the detail and atmosphere of the living room. Above the stone fireplace hung the massive horns of a bull buffalo. On one side of the chimney there were crossed spears on the wall and on the other a Maasai shield, below which was displayed a short sword in a blood-red scabbard (a Maasai *seme* she later discovered it to be). In front of the fireplace was a fire screen containing within its frame a beautiful Granny Sullivan embroidery of a male peacock fanning his tail feathers to full spectacular effect. There was an animal-skin rug on the floor and a few other, smaller animal skins draped over the backs of two sofas. But in amongst the Africana there were also fine Persian rugs, admittedly showing signs of wear, fading somewhat and with corners chewed by generations of dogs. In front of the sofas was a circular coffee table made from a large African drum. Scattered about on cabinets and occasional tables was a broad spectrum of ornamentation: African carvings of figures and animals, in amongst small pieces of English antique silver, Indian copper and brass jugs, ceramic bowls, ash trays, cowrie shells from beaches of the Indian ocean, photos old and new in a variety of frames. The eclectic nature of the room was reinforced by the pictures on the walls: more artwork by Granny Sullivan; watercolours by her of African landscapes, mountains and lakes, flame trees and jacarandas in full flower, great bushes of vibrant bougainvillea and tumbling cascades of golden shower; and there were photographs too of a variety of wild animals, including two particularly eye-catching black and white enlargements, one of a bull elephant face-on to the camera and the other of a female cheetah, sitting on an old anthill with her three young cubs surveying her territory of the great savannah; alongside which were scenes of old rural England, bucolic figures at harvest home and rustic cottages; and all under the watchful gaze of a man and a woman of the early nineteenth century, finely portrayed in their separate oil paintings, side by side on the wall as, presumably, they were in life; family portraits no doubt, a long way from home.

Granny Sullivan was still in the room where she had been all afternoon, dozing and reading intermittently. Charlotte glanced in her direction. Drooping eyelids had finally succumbed and the old lady was snoozing again. Mrs Hooper was supervising things in the kitchen in preparation for Sunday afternoon tea, a traditional family event. Having shown Charlotte round the ranch earlier, Ben and his father had gone off for something else which was apparently a Sunday afternoon tradition, a *pumzika*; and whatever that was Charlotte had yet to discover.

A little time passed quietly and then things started to happen. Mrs Hooper appeared from the direction of the kitchen carrying a large tray bearing cups and saucers, milk and sugar, and a particularly fine silver teapot; another transported heirloom. In her wake followed Kimani, stooping slightly, carefully pushing a heavily laden wooden trolley. Ben and his father were entering the room from the other direction, rubbing their eyes and stretching. Charlotte sat forward. Granny Sullivan shuddered awake, beady eyes instantly alert. Mrs Hooper started to pour tea through a silver strainer. The tray, Charlotte noticed, was covered with a beautifully worked, antique lace cloth. Kimani handed round bone china side-plates, linen napkins and small, slender knives. Returning to the trolley he picked up a large platter, neatly stacked with sandwiches, carefully cut into triangles, crusts removed. He then began to do the rounds.

"Some are plain cucumber and others are cucumber and marmite, Ben's favourite," announced Mrs Hooper, "so take your pick. There are also cheese and tomato, egg and cress and Shippam's salmon paste."

The sandwiches went round with happy chatter about this and that. Mrs Hooper wanted to know how things had gone on the morning ride. Ben was talking ranch matters with his father. Granny Sullivan mainly applied herself to the sandwiches before Charlotte brought up the subject of one of her paintings on the wall; a watercolour of a long, pink-fringed lake shore.

"Lake Nakuru, a soda lake," said the old lady, adding, between mouthfuls, "with countless flamingos; goodness knows how many; hundreds of thousands; into the millions at certain times; quite a sight to behold."

"Is that where the fish was caught?" asked Charlotte, pointing to a framed photo on a nearby side-table of a much younger Ben, proudly holding up a fish.

"No," said Ben, overhearing the question and being keen to join in the conversation. "That's a black bass I caught as a kid in Lake Naivasha, a freshwater lake to the south of Lake Nakuru; there's also another lake, Elementeita, in between the two."

There followed talk of the various Rift Valley lakes and happy reminiscences of family camping trips and exploration, picnics and bird-watching, boating and fishing; tales of hippo and crocodile and wild animals of the night snuffling and snorting round tents; carefree days. Mr Hooper produced a map to show Charlotte. Mrs Hooper dug out some other photos, including, to Ben's slight embarrassment, one of him as a young boy, barefoot and naked, staring out over a shimmering lake from under a thatch of platinum hair, proudly holding a makeshift spear.

Scones were now being offered round by Kimani with

creamy butter and a large jar of strawberry jam.

"These are Mum's contribution," said Mrs Hooper.

"Yes," interjected Granny Sullivan, leaning forward slightly. "Although I say so myself, my scones are generally regarded as the family best."

"The aunts may have something to say about that," said Ben, teasingly; before quickly adding, "but yours are delicious too."

Rapidly filling up as she was, there was no question of Charlotte not having a scone. She found, in fact, that she thoroughly enjoyed it and she complimented the old lady accordingly. Ben, still in tease mode, commented that she hadn't, of course, sampled the aunts' scones. His grandmother gave him a withering look. The scones were coming round again. But on this occasion Charlotte politely declined. Out of the corner of her eye she noticed Mrs Hooper cutting up a chocolate cake. This, no doubt, would have to be sampled too. When duly proffered, she begged a small slice only, though it was admittedly delicious, freshly made. Finishing at last and firmly pushing her plate to one side, another picture on the wall caught Charlotte's attention. Craning her head to one side, she took in the details of a long, rectangular black and white photograph. It pictured, in a formal group, a contingent of soldiers and other military personnel, all in uniform, mainly Africans, but with a few European and other races amongst them. They were ranged in front of the Albert Memorial, in London. The mount of the photograph had some writing above the picture and more writing with four small printed drawings below. Screwing up her eyes slightly, Charlotte could just make it all out. Above was written 'Victory March — London 8 June 1946'; below 'East African Victory Contingent'; the drawings depicted Trafalgar Square, Buckingham Palace, Marble Arch and the Houses of Parliament. What Charlotte was looking at so closely hadn't gone unnoticed. "Can you pick out Mum?" asked Ben.

"I'm not sure, let me look more closely," she said, getting up. "Yes, possibly, I think so, sitting in the front row." She turned towards Mrs Hooper. "So you were in the services during the War?"

"Yes, I was very young. I went straight from school into the 'Fannies' as they were known."

"The what, sorry?" It was a question asked with a hint of embarrassment. Out of the corner of her eye, Charlotte could detect that Ben and his father were smirking slightly. Granny Sullivan remained detached.

Mrs Hooper moved the conversation on, swiftly, with an explanation. "It was an abbreviation of a kind; let me think, what's the correct term?"

"Acronym?" prompted Ben.

"Yes, that's it; I was in the First Aid Nursing Yeomanry, otherwise known as the Princess Royal's Volunteer Corps."

"Part of the army, then?" queried Charlotte.

"No, not as such. It's actually an all-female charity which has provided nursing and intelligence services, in both world wars in point of fact."

"And you were chosen, as part of the contingent from the various services, to go to England for the Victory March?"

"Yes, it was a great honour, I suppose. One of my rare visits to England."

"A rare visit, indeed, for you my dear," added her husband. "But, of course, a one and only visit for most of the contingent, particularly the Africans."

"It must have been quite an experience, perhaps even something of a culture shock for the Africans," said Charlotte with slightly furrowed brow. "How much did they get to see?"

"All the main sights of London," replied Mrs Hooper, "those pictured below the photo and others, of course, including even the crown jewels. There were also some trips into the countryside."

"What did they make of it all I wonder; could you tell?"

"No, not always; sometimes they were a bit bemused, I think, rather nonplussed perhaps." She gave a little laugh. "I remember one of the KAR men in particular."

"King's African Rifles," interposed her husband.

"Yes, at the end of the trip, shortly before we shipped home, he was asked the question, I think by a reporter, what had impressed him most about England. The reporter was presumably expecting him to ooh and ah about the places he had been to, the things that he had been shown, the glories of England. But the man simply answered 'the number of butcher shops'; really rather amusing, and sweet I think."

Granny Sullivan had tuned back in to the conversation. "Typical African; no appreciation for civilised things."

Charlotte, looking shocked, opened her mouth to say something. But Ben was swift to intervene. "I think the man's reaction is entirely understandable, if you think about it. Why should he have any real appreciation of a culture of which he knew nothing? On the other hand, easy meat is something to be impressed by if you're an African, particularly a rural African; he would be thinking, you don't have to hunt it, catch it, rear it, but just walk round the corner for it in most places; now that is something to admire."

Granny Sullivan was looking mildly irritated, wondering whether to respond, but was saved by the bell, a small brass bell. Mrs Hooper was ringing for Kimani and he appeared in the room a moment later.

"*Maji moto.*"

"*Ndio memsahib.*

"Right," Mrs Hooper said, smiling, "I think it's time we had a fresh pot of tea."

Shortly after, more tea was poured as the conversation moved on to safer ground. When all had finished Kimani began to clear away and was followed out to the kitchen by Mrs Hooper. Granny Sullivan made her way back to her cottage, escorted by her son-in-law. Ben and Charlotte remained sitting for a time, Charlotte in contemplative mood.

"That was a wonderful tea," she said, after a while. "But I feel I haven't thanked your mum properly and I must do later."

"I'm sure she'd appreciate that, but it wasn't laid on specially; as I think I mentioned, this is our traditional Sunday afternoon tea."

"And that's what I find to be something of an enigma."

"Oh, why so?"

"Because it was so traditionally English, perhaps in a rather charmingly old-fashioned way, and yet, here we are, in the wilds of Africa, in a place that couldn't be more different from England."

Ben sought to make light of it. "Well, as you know, it seems in some ways, as they say, 'we're more English than the English'."

Charlotte remained in a rather more serious frame of mind. "Still?" she asked. She didn't expect an answer and none was received.

Later that evening they were all back in the living room. A log fire was burning in the grate, warding off the chill of the high altitude night. The great bull buffalo horns cast a long shadow over the animal skin rug on which Brutus was lying contentedly in front of the grate, warming his stomach. Mr Hooper had pulled his chair close up to the fire and was knocking out his pipe on the stone surround. Rose Hooper and her mother were sitting on one sofa; Ben and Charlotte on the other. There was the clink of ice in glasses and the rustling of the pages of a long out-of-date *Woman's Own* magazine being flicked through by Granny Sullivan. The strains of a Viennese waltz faded away as the record playing on the battery-operated gramophone in one corner of the room came to an end. Getting up from the sofa, Rose made her way over to select something else to put on. Moments later the music of *The King and I* was to be heard.

"My favourite musical," she sighed, sitting down again.

"Oh no, Mum, not this again," moaned Ben, although, in truth, he looked faintly amused rather than at all annoyed.

"You thoroughly enjoyed it when I took you to see it at The National Theatre in Nairobi years ago," she retorted.

"No, I didn't; I thought it was sloppy and I didn't want any of my schoolfriends to find out I'd been to see it."

His father was chortling. There was no move to change the record and so the music played on. Brutus remained deeply asleep with the odd rumbling at each end.

"He looks very relaxed," remarked Charlotte.

"A bit too relaxed, if you ask me," said Mr Hooper, pushing his chair further away from the slumbering dog, insulating himself in a puff of smoke from his pipe.

"I think he should go out," said Granny Sullivan.

"No Gran, he's fine really; I don't want him to go out unsupervised at this time of night because a leopard has been seen round about recently. I'll take him out later."

251

Granny Sullivan's mind had moved on. She was reaching for something on the side table which she had brought with her earlier, an old brown photograph album, its well-worn pages bound together by faded yellow cord ending in tassels secured by wooden beads. "Now, my dear," she said, turning towards Charlotte, "you've been kind enough to show interest in all the things I've been telling you about our early days here; so I thought, perhaps, you might like to see some snaps."

Ben was looking rather wary. "But, for heaven's sake," the old lady added quickly, "don't feel in any way obliged to do so; I won't mind in the least." She put one hand gently on the cover of the album and sighed. "It was all so long ago."

Charlotte had sat forward, hands clasping her knees, listening intently. "I really would like to see them." There was no question of her just being polite.

"Well, in that case, my dear, come and sit beside me here." She sounded so pleased. Rose moved up to make space and Charlotte came over, seating herself between the two women. Ben looked on, in contemplative mood. His father, sunk back amongst the cushions in his chair, had dozed off.

Granny Sullivan carefully placed the album on her lap and opened it at the first page, patting it slightly. The backs of her hands, Charlotte noticed, bore patterns formed by the tropical sun; they were hands with the hallmarks of a lifetime of hard work, capable, clever hands. Leaning towards her, to look more closely at the album, Charlotte detected a faint scent of lavender. She read the neat inscription at the top of the page: 'Trans Nzoia 1923'. Below were some photos of an old-fashioned car being towed up a river bank by a team of oxen.

"Our honeymoon," laughed Granny Sullivan. "We had been married the previous afternoon, in a mission church, and had then set off bound for a place where we were meant to be spending the night. But the car became stuck fast in the mud, crossing that river, and we had to foot slog it back to the mission just before it got dark."

"So, did you have to spend the night there?" asked Charlotte.

"Yes, there was no other option. The mission fathers put up camp beds for us in the school room." She laughed again. "Not exactly what I had envisaged for a first night of wedded bliss."

"And you managed to get going the next day?"

"Yes, Bert, my husband, managed to drum up a team of oxen from somewhere and, there you are, these are the pictures of us being pulled out."

One by one the pages of the album were turned revealing black and white photos, fading and beginning to yellow in places, windows into the past of a pioneering life and an unfolding family story. 'Cherangani, the house that Bert built' read one caption beneath a picture of a stone building with a corrugated iron roof, fronted by a thatched verandah. Beside it stood a tall, rangy, resourceful looking man, smiling beneath his pith helmet. There followed scenes of life on the farm, cattle being herded, rows of coffee and banana trees, chickens in the yard, dogs everywhere, the maize crop in good times, cobs piled high in the wire crib, by contrast bare maize storks in bad times, stripped by locusts. One picture which particularly caught the eye was of an ancient-looking, broken-down tractor being towed away by horses.

"Poor Bert," interjected Granny Sullivan. "It was his pride and joy. He bought it when we could least afford it, I might add. He couldn't resist tinkering around with old engines, but I had a feeling it was never going to work properly. The African labourers found it highly amusing of course; that this fancy

European machine proved so useless and ended up being pulled by horses, just like the good old plough."

Charlotte looked again at the picture. The tractor was being followed on foot by a dejected-looking Mr Sullivan. In his wake streamed a happy band of laughing *totos*, jumping for joy.

More pages were turned and more photos were looked at, many featuring the family itself; babies, christenings, little girls growing up, parties, family gatherings, assemblies of them in their Sunday best outside the mud and wattle church; the family at play, tennis on Christmas day, fishing in the reservoir, fancy dress, running races, happy smiling faces; and also, of course, the family at work, herding animals, beating out bushfires, harvesting maize, African labourers sweating and toiling with them or, when knowingly being photographed, standing proudly to attention for the camera.

Charlotte paused at a page of pictures of Rose, as a young girl, with a variety of animals. "Quite a collection; were these all your pets?"

"Yes," she said leaning in for a better look. "Well, sort of." She pointed to a picture of herself reaching up to a baby giraffe. "This came to us as an orphan. It's mother was shot by a neighbouring farmer, for trampling crops. The poor little thing fled in terror and ended up on our farm. Somehow we kept it alive. Mum was brilliant at experimenting with various milk concoctions and after a while it began to thrive."

Granny Sullivan was nodding in agreement. "It did well, but we couldn't keep it, of course, as it began to grow bigger."

Rose sighed. "I'd have loved to rehabilitate it into the wild; but that wasn't a real option either; it would never have survived."

"So what happened?" Charlotte asked.

"It was sent abroad to a zoo, I'm afraid."

Charlotte decided it was time to move on to the next photo. Under the caption 'Suzanne' could be seen Rose crouching down feeding a delicate little antelope with dark, dewy eyes, the kind of eyes that looked right into one's soul. "A baby buck of some kind?" she enquired.

"Yes, a duiker. She was found by some of the farmworkers. I don't know what happened to her mother, though I feared the worst. She was with us for some time, but when she was nearly fully grown she disappeared one day, hopefully back to the wild." Rose paused for a moment of reflection. "I loved her to bits and cried for nearly a week after she had gone."

"That's a young pig," said Charlotte, by way of a statement rather than a question, looking at another photo.

"Indeed," responded Granny Sullivan, "and what a trial she proved to be."

"Snow White, she was certainly quite a character." A flood of memories brought a smile to Rose's face. "I won her at a fair in Kitale was she was a tiny piglet. She was brought up as a pet and liked to mix with the dogs. She probably thought she was a dog."

"I think she did," interposed Granny Sullivan. "She took to chasing cars down the drive with the dogs; which was quite a shock for people visiting us for the first time."

"And I think the final straw, for you Mum, was when Snow White, as a nearly fully grown sow, insisted on trying to get on the sofa in the evenings."

It was a mental image which caused Charlotte's shoulders to heave with laughter. "What did you do?" she asked, turning to Granny Sullivan.

"Banished her to an outhouse for a time, but in the end, she had to go to market"

"So you don't know, I suppose, what eventually became of her?"

"Not exactly," said Rose. "But, put it this way, I didn't eat bacon sandwiches for some time after."

These were, of course, stories which Ben had heard before. But he was listening in nonetheless. "Find the picture of Jacko," he called across the room.

"There he is," said Rose, pointing to the adjoining page.

Charlotte looked to see a photo of a smallish monkey with a dark body but a white chest. Its long tail was draped over the back of a chair on which it was sitting. The eyes, set in a jet-black face, shone brightly, perhaps with a hint of defiance. "Did he live in the house?" she asked.

"For a time," replied Rose. "He particularly liked the bathroom for some reason; probably because of the warmth from the airing cupboard and he took to sleeping in there at night."

"But then he was banned," said Granny Sullivan firmly.

"And I've been told why," added Ben, with obvious amusement, but pausing for effect.

Rose was saying nothing and Granny Sullivan was raising her eyes to the ceiling. So Charlotte pressed Ben further. "OK, why?"

Ben was delighted to provide the answer. "Because he was found one morning, sitting on a shelf, peeing on Grandpa's hairbrush."

It was time to move on again. A few more pages were turned to reveal a picture of two disconsolate young girls in smart new school uniforms, complete with blazers and hats and rather uncomfortable-looking stiff leather shoes. Underneath was written 'Weymouth 1936'.

"My sister and I don't look too happy, I'm afraid," remarked Rose.

"No," responded her mother, "and you didn't last there too long either."

"Poor Mum; you and dad went to such trouble, and expense presumably, to give us an English education. But we were far too deeply rooted here."

The next pages featured happy homecoming pictures, the girls back on the farm. One was of particular interest to Charlotte. It showed the sisters with two boys, slightly older, wearing bush jackets and shorts, crumpled socks round their ankles. They were standing proudly in front of a wigwam they had constructed from tall stalks of maize.

"Our cousins," murmured Rose.

"The lost boys," said Charlotte quietly.

Granny Sullivan's head swivelled round. "How on earth do you know about them?"

"Ben's told me."

"Goodness, he seems to have gone into a lot of detail about the family."

Ben opened his mouth to say something. But Charlotte got in first. "He has often spoken to me about his family and also this country. It's clear that he is passionate about both."

There followed moments of almost complete silence in the room. Even Brutus and Mr Hooper had stopped snoring. The only sound was of a clock on the mantelpiece, quietly, but relentlessly, ticking away time. Charlotte became aware that Rose was fumbling for a hankie to dab moist eyes.

"I'm sorry," she said with a note of concern. "Is it upsetting you to look at these photos?"

"They always bring out mixed emotions in me," was the

reply. "I love looking at them in some ways; they bring back so many happy memories. But then I start thinking that those times are long past; there's so much I miss and I look long, and longingly, at people who mattered so much and are no longer with us. And I start to wonder about the future and worry, I suppose, about what it holds for us here in a time of such change and uncertainty."

Ben had been prompted to get to his feet. He came over and went down on one knee in front of his mother, clasping both her hands. "Mum," he said, "we can have a great future. It's up to us to make this happen. This is still a fantastic country," he added with rising intensity in his voice. "We're so fortunate to be here, to be a real part of it."

Granny Sullivan had been flipping through the pages and the years. There was just one more photo to look at, right at the end of the album. The picture showed an African man holding a toddler, clinging to him affectionately, one arm round his neck.

"Gosh," remarked Charlotte, "I can see that's you Ben; you still have the same hairstyle."

Ben picked up the album. "Okumu," he said quietly. "He looked after me a lot when I was a kid; taught me a lot too." Happy recollections made him smile. "I reckon I could talk Luo and Swahili before I properly learnt to speak English." He closed the album and handed it back to his grandmother saying, "that reminds me; I must go to see him some time." Granny Sullivan merely raised her eyebrows.

"Right," said Mr Hooper, rising from his chair, stretching and yawning. "Time for bed, I reckon. I'll walk you back," he added, looking at his mother-in-law who was also getting up.

"I'm going to turn in too," said Rose, with goodnight kisses first to Charlotte, then to Ben.

"I don't know about you," said Ben, looking hopefully at Charlotte, but I wouldn't mind staying up a bit longer."

"I'm up for that," was the unhesitating response.

"Well then, goodnight to you both," said Mr Hooper. "Just bear in mind that I'll be turning off the generator shortly; so light the camping Gaz lamps."

"Kimani has already lit one for you, Charlotte, in the guest cottage," added his wife.

"And I have my torch to escort her there," confirmed Ben.

Final goodnights having been said, Ben and Charlotte were left alone in the room. He walked over to the gramophone and put on a record. No music but a melodic voice began to filter into the room. Turning round to face her, he smiled, proffering a bottle of whisky in one hand and a bottle of armagnac in the other.

Monday

"You did see the leopard, didn't you?" asked Ben, helping himself to some more toast at the breakfast table.

"Yes, just a glimpse," responded Charlotte, sitting opposite him. "You handed me the binoculars in the nick of time before he came down the tree and vanished into the thicket beyond."

"Good, he was a little way off, but we were lucky to see him at all. Leopards are pretty elusive. They are to be found here and in a number of places in the country, but you'd be surprised how many people never get to see one."

"He was close enough for me, thank you, bearing in mind we were on foot."

And on foot, indeed, they had been. Ben had suggested an early morning walk, a particularly special time of day when it was cool and still, the clear air refreshing and invigorating. Rarely was the effort of dragging oneself from bed before sunrise more worthwhile. On foot, walking quietly, there was usually more to be seen. Unobtrusive and frequently unobserved, one could blend into and become part of the wild landscape and all within it. Charlotte had needed no persuading. She had just questioned why Ben had been carrying a rifle, but had been assured it was a precaution only and most unlikely to be needed. No big game had been come across, until the highlight of the leopard, but they had seen a variety of other animals and, in turn, had been observed by them with cautious curiosity, some retreating shyly into cover. And as they walked the joy of the fresh, new day had been celebrated by a chorus of birdsong.

Buttering his toast, Ben was pondering something. "Talking of Okumu yesterday evening brought to mind, as I mentioned, that I must go and see him some time. I gather he hasn't been very well." He looked across the table at Charlotte. "I've since wondered whether, perhaps, you'd like to come with me. It would help Dad if I could pick up something for him today in Nanyuki and Okumu lives just nearby. So, if you came too, you could see a bit of Nanyuki, and the surrounding country; and also meet Okumu."

There was a swift intervention from Granny Sullivan who had appeared in the room to speak to her daughter. "Nanyuki's hardly very exciting to drag Charlotte off to. There's not much to see there. And why on earth do you need to visit Okumu? He was only a servant after all."

"He was more than that," replied Ben firmly. "And is still more than that, to me at least."

Granny Sullivan was shaking her head. "I've never been friends, as such, with African servants, still less socialised with them. They're so different from us, on a completely different wavelength." She caught Ben's eye. "And, in my view, it just isn't necessary, or even appropriate."

By now Ben too was shaking his head and it was Charlotte's turn to intervene.

"Really, don't worry about me. Actually I would rather like to go to Nanyuki, to see somewhere else, and also to meet Okumu."

Ben shot her a grateful smile. Granny Sullivan raised her eyebrows and left the room, tut tutting to herself.

Mrs Hooper had been looking on, somewhat nervously, from her end of the table. She leant across and patted Charlotte on the arm. "It's kind of you to offer to go with Ben, but, really, you don't have to, if you'd rather do something else with your limited time here." She looked across to Ben. "You could go another day."

Mr Hooper had just come into the room and picked up on the conversation.

"That's right. Or I could perhaps go to Nanyuki myself, later today."

But Charlotte's mind was firmly made up, much to the pleasure of Ben. As coffee was poured, a plan was made for them to set off later that morning.

Granny Sullivan was right in a sense. On the face of it there wasn't much to see in Nanyuki. But Charlotte enjoyed being there nonetheless, seeing somewhere different and absorbing something of its atmosphere. It still had the feel of a frontier town, somewhere to stock up with supplies before heading off into the wilderness of the north, or where to stop and relax, perhaps, on the way back, to brush off the dust, drink cold beer and talk of adventures. There was also the charm of a country town, supplying the needs of farmers from around Mount Kenya and providing a market for an enticing array of fresh produce. It remained essentially colonial in character, but comfortably so, with something of a benign old-worldliness about the place.

Having picked up the required supplies Ben parked the Land Rover in the wide, tree-lined main street. He and Charlotte then set off for a walkabout. She was entranced by the sights, sounds and smells in some of the small shops, or *dukas* as Ben referred to them. Vibrant fabrics caught the eye, carvings of wild animals, bright beadwork, tools, lanterns, rope, sacks of dried foodstuffs, and a wide range of nearly everything else required for a rural life, stacked high in the smallest of spaces, often accompanied by occasional whiffs of kerosene, spices and a tantalising blend of the aromas of the town. Indian merchants and African traders engaged in cheerful banter and bargaining, Ben translating where necessary. Charlotte did succumb to a brightly coloured *kikoi*, much favoured wraparound wear Ben assured her, and a finely carved rhino, a choice he particularly approved of. For his part he insisted on buying her a bracelet of traditional Maasai beadwork, something to remind her of her visit, not that she felt she was ever likely to forget. On principle she shied away from having one of the traditional elephant-hair bracelets, of the kind Ben wore, so giving him cause for thought.

Feeling the need for coffee they made for the Sportsman's Arms on the north side of town. Time had stood still in this pub-cum-hotel, a bastion of the old colonial establishment. They then headed back the other way, at Ben's insistence, for him to take a particular photo of her with her camera, one for the record as he put it. She duly posed by a sign declaring itself to be on 'The Equator'.

"Legs apart," commanded Ben with a cheeky grin.

"I beg your pardon?"

"One foot in the northern hemisphere, the other in the southern."

"Oh, I see." She duly complied and the camera clicked.

"Charlotte astride the world," Ben proclaimed. "A picture for the archives, to show grandchildren one day."

"Maybe." A smile had crept across her face as a little jump brought her feet back together.

An African man sidled up to them, grinning under a rather rakish hat. He was holding a bucket of water in one hand and a matchstick in the other.

"Here we go," muttered Ben.

Charlotte looked puzzled, trying to make out what the man was saying in a mixture of broken English and Swahili.

"He wants to demonstrate something," explained Ben. "I think it's called the 'Coriolis' effect of the earth's rotation. The result is that in the northern hemisphere water drains through a plughole anticlockwise, whereas in the southern hemisphere it flows away clockwise."

"And he can show this here?" Charlotte was frowning, sounding doubtful.

"Just watch."

The man put down the bucket on the north side of the equator sign and dropped in the matchstick. With a flourish he removed a rudimentary plug and held up the bucket for the water to drain away. Sure enough, the matchstick began to swirl around in an anticlockwise direction as the water seeped out. He then walked a few paces to the southern side, refilled his bucket and repeated the process. Charlotte watched closely as the matchstick duly spiralled clockwise. The man looked triumphant, but Charlotte still wore a puzzled frown.

"I can't believe there's such a difference, just each side of the line."

"Nor should you," whispered Ben. "The effect is too small to be demonstrated anywhere near the equator; so a sleight of hand is required."

"Oh," she said beginning to smile. "Well, it's quite enterprising of him, and entertaining." Much to his delight she dug in her purse to find some shillings to place in his strategically placed bowl.

Ben looked at his watch. "Before we go to see Okumu I think we should have a bite to eat somewhere."

"Anywhere particular in mind?"

Ben was thinking something through. "Yes, actually, The Mount Kenya Safari Club. I'd like you to see it."

"Is that near here?"

"Not far, a few miles south-east of the town."

They were soon driving up to an imposing long, white two-storey building with various cottages and ancillary buildings set in over one hundred acres of beautifully landscaped gardens and grounds.

"Impressive," murmured Charlotte. "Did you say it's a club?"

"Sort of; it's a luxury country club-cum-hotel, specially designed for the rich and famous. I'll show you round."

Ben found a park in semi-shade and they walked up to the main building. There was a lot to admire; beautifully appointed rooms, comfortably and tastefully furnished with accompanying artefacts and pictures to be appreciated. A terrace led out to a swimming pool, shimmering blue and enticing. Beyond, peacocks were strutting proudly on manicured lawns against the backdrop of Mount Kenya.

"Stunning, I must say," commented Charlotte. "What's the

story here, how's this all come about?"

"It's quite an interesting history actually. I'll tell you about it while we have something to eat and drink."

They made their way back to the terrace and settled themselves at a table. A few guests were at adjoining tables, middle aged and prosperous looking; faint traces of conversation revealed mostly American accents. A largish woman whose bikini-wearing days should really have been behind her, but who was wearing a bikini nonetheless, was on a sunbed by the pool. Ben signalled to a smartly uniformed waiter and they ordered club sandwiches, a glass of white wine for Charlotte and a Tusker for Ben. Settling into his chair, Ben began to tell the story of the place.

"It was built originally, back in the thirties, as a private house, believe it or not, called *Mawingo*, a Swahili name meaning 'clouds', referring, I suppose, to the clouds which so often cloak the mountain."

"Crikey, quite some house; there must have been some money there."

"Oh yes; Rhoda and Gabriel Prudhomme certainly had the cash to pour in and complete the building in a year, I believe. She was a woman in her fifties who had been married to an American millionaire. Apparently she was stunningly attractive. Anyway, she had come to Kenya on holiday with friends where she met her toy boy, Gabriel."

"Sounds French."

"Spot on. He was tall, dark and handsome, actually I'm making that up; he probably was, but I don't really know. But he was certainly young and adventurous. He had his own plane and was a big game hunter. He took Rhoda and her friends on safari and there's no prizes for guessing where that led to."

"She ran off with him, presumably?"

"Yup, she left her husband and two grown-up daughters in the States and shacked up with Gabriel. When her divorce came through, she and Gabriel then got married, in Paris I was told. Afterwards they returned to Kenya and lived for a time in Njoro, becoming part of the Happy Valley set."

"I remember you talking about the Happy Valley set before; you seem to know an awful lot about them."

Ben grinned. "Yes, mainly from my dad. He's full of it; excites his imagination I think; probably wishes he'd been part of it."

Charlotte had a quizzical look. "And your mum?"

"No way; she'd have thoroughly disapproved. They're very different, you know, my parents." He paused, looking thoughtful, tempted to say more, but deciding against it, before Charlotte prompted him further.

"And then the Prudhommes moved here?"

"That's right. They fell in love with this beautiful site which was then virgin forest at the foot of the mountain. Eventually the owner, another American, was persuaded to sell to them, and building began."

"And were they happy ever after?"

"I'm afraid not. The Second World War came a year later. Rhoda went back to the States and Gabriel joined the Free French fighting in Algeria. They never got back together. The romance died and they ended up getting divorced."

"Quite a story. But what then happened with the house here?"

"There was a further drama there, which, again, I've been told about by my dad. Apparently, Rhoda had given *Mawingo* to Gabriel and so she lost out. Then Gabriel died, not long after the

War, and the house went to his family. But they never lived in it. Instead, it was sold and turned into what was referred to as an 'inn'."

"It's a lot more than that now," remarked Charlotte, taking in the surroundings.

"Certainly, that's because it was taken over by Hollywood stars."

"Really?"

"Absolutely. At the end of the fifties William Holden and some friends stayed here. They liked it so much that they and a few others subsequently clubbed together, bought it and transformed it into what you see today. Some further adjoining land was also acquired to make into a small, thousand-acre game reserve."

"So people can stay in the height of luxury and see animals on their doorstep."

"That's right; great in a way, if you can afford it." Ben paused. "But I also have something of a problem with it."

"Oh?"

"Well, my thinking is that this is all fine and dandy, for a few days perhaps; but if you want to go on *safari*, and have a real taste of things, this is not what the country's all about, lounging around in excessive luxury, with animals laid on for your convenience next door."

Charlotte was beginning to nod. "I take your point."

Ben was becoming increasingly fired up. "Christ yes," his voice was rising, "you've got to get out into the wilds, the real wilds, stay in a remote lodge, or, better still, under canvas—" he was very much warming to his theme, "—places where you can look up at a billion stars, listening to the sounds of the night; or shine a torch beyond a campfire and pick out green eyes watching and waiting."

"I see."

"Yeah, this is all beautiful, luxurious, but it's not the real thing; not what the country means to me."

"You get really quite passionate about this country of yours."

"Yes, sorry, speech over." He looked at his watch. It was time to move on, to a very different kind of place.

Okumu appeared to be waiting for them. He was sitting patiently on a wooden chair outside the open front door of his little house, looking expectant. He half rose from his chair and clasped Ben's extended hand in both his hands.

"*Amosi,*" they exchanged greetings.

"*Ber ahinya,*" they each replied.

Okumu looked questioningly at Charlotte and she heard Ben mention her name and launch into what she presumed to be some kind of explanation. She had begun to recognise the sound of Swahili, but the conversation was partly in another language which was totally unfamiliar to her. Ben was being addressed by the name "Omollo" which Charlotte picked up on. She looked at him with raised eyebrows, repeating the name.

"That's me," he nodded smiling.

Ben pulled up two other chairs and he and Charlotte sat down beside one another, facing Okumu. As Ben and Okumu resumed their conversation Charlotte began absorbing detail. Sitting before her was an elderly looking, rather frail man. The little hair he had was grey and there was a cloudiness in his eyes with something of a look of sensitivity. He was wearing a faded shirt and khaki trousers too long for him, partly concealing bare calloused feet. Yet, for all this, he retained an air of quiet dignity. There were sounds from within his house. But Charlotte couldn't see beyond the cloth which had been pinned up on the inside of the single window. Somewhere behind the house a cockerel crowed belatedly. Off to one side, by a stack of firewood, a mangy dog was dozing in the dust, reflecting the torpor of the afternoon.

In the ongoing conversation Charlotte picked up on some words, at least, of possible meaning to her: *hospitali* and *daktari* in particular were mentioned several times. Her educated guess was that Ben was worried about Okumu's health and was pressing him for information.

Breaking off at one point Okumu called out something over his shoulder. There was a muffled reply from inside the house. Shortly after a young woman appeared, adorned in a colourful headscarf, coyly avoiding eye contact. She was holding three tin mugs of steaming, achingly sweet, milky tea which were duly handed round.

"*Asante*," said Charlotte, pleased to be able to say something appropriate at least.

"*Mzur*i," was the response, and Charlotte knew what that meant too. But then language became more difficult. "Daughter?" she enquired looking at the young woman and then glancing in the direction of Okumu. Neither understood, but Ben, smiling, quickly explained.

"No, she's his young wife, Charity. He insisted on taking another wife a few years ago. His old wife is back where they're from, in Nyanza Province, with their grown-up children." Seeing Charlotte looking rather surprised he added, "It's the way of things."

Okumu was nodding vigorously, assuming that something was being said that he should be pleased about. Ben briefly explained to him that he had been talking about marriage. This promptly launched him in to a related topic of conversation. Having looked Charlotte up and down, approvingly it seemed, the old man asked a question of Ben. There was a hint of embarrassment in the response, although Ben was also smiling as he glanced in Charlotte's direction.

"What's being said?" she asked with a puzzled frown.

Ben hesitated for a moment. "He wanted to know if I'd been to see your father."

"My father?" There was a note of astonishment in her voice. "Whatever for?"

There was more hesitation and further embarrassment on the part of Ben. "To agree a bride price."

"Crikey." It was Charlotte's turn to feel embarrassed as she wrinkled up her brow, but curiosity led her to pursue the matter further. "So, tell me, what did you say in reply?"

"I told him there's another man, ahead of me, who will be making an offer, who has more to offer."

Okumu was saying something else to Ben.

"What?" asked Charlotte.

"He's saying I should still make an offer, a better offer."

The discussion continued for a while, but without further translation. Initial embarrassment had given way to a degree of amusement on the part of Charlotte. She was flattered even, but also rather unsettled. Minutes passed and she became aware that Charity had slipped back into the house. Looking around and about, her attention was then drawn to a cardboard box which she had noticed Ben earlier putting down unobtrusively beside the old man's chair. It was partly open and glancing in she could see rice, sugar, tea, some other packets and tins, batteries and, tucked down the side, an envelope; simple necessities of life, yet barely affordable for some.

As the afternoon faded Ben and Okumu began rambling happily down a winding track of nostalgia. Ben painted the scene for her, at intervals, but there was nothing she could really contribute. She was perfectly content to be looking on, a quiet observer. Amidst sighs and laughter there were precious shared recollections: of being stuck up the tall tree; swirling round and round on the swing made from the old tyre; the day when Okumu tried to remove a dangerous snake from under Mrs Hooper's dressing table stool, but ended up chopping the stool in half with his *panga*; Ben's birthday party, the time when Granny Sullivan had hidden round the garden for a treasure hunt little bags of home-made fudge, all promptly found and eaten by the dogs, leaving the children to discover later only shreds of chewed crepe paper; Okumu to the rescue, making better cuts and grazes; expertly removing *jiggers* from Ben's feet; and oh, how Okumu laughed when he made bows and arrows for his son and Ben, the hunters who then set off so bravely into the bush, but who returned a very short time later. There was "do you remember?" and "oh remember"; remember, remember; days of carefree innocence; days gone by.

They finished at last, eyes glistening. It was time to leave. As Ben got to his feet, the old man did too. For a moment they held one another in a silent embrace. Then Ben turned to go, Charlotte joining him having raised one hand towards Okumu in silent farewell. They headed off together without looking back.

"How old is Okumu?" asked Charlotte, shortly before they reached the car.

"Well, I call him *mzee* sometimes, as you probably noticed, but that's not considered rude; it's a term of respect."

"He's clearly getting on."

"Yeah, but he's probably not as old as you might think."

"Haven't you ever asked him his age?"

"There's no point, because he wouldn't know, at least not exactly."

"Why ever not?"

"For many Africans, like him, there was no actual record of their birth, no registration or anything like that."

"I see; but they must have some idea of how old they are."

"Oh yes, of course, by working backwards, or knowing that they were born at about the time of a particular flood or famine, or when the great plague of locusts came."

Charlotte pondered this for a moment. "However old he is, he looks rather frail to me."

"Yup," Ben nodded. "I suspect the problem is that he's really quite ill. He might even decide to die; to will himself, to die."

"Whatever do you mean?"

"It happens," was all Ben was prepared to say in response. He turned his head away abruptly, but not in time to avoid Charlotte noticing a single tear on one cheek.

As they set off on the drive back Charlotte had a further question. "Had you sent word to Okumu that you were coming to see him?"

"No, why?"

"Because he seemed to be expecting you."

"He probably was."

"How so?"

Ben grinned. "Difficult to explain; difficult for a *mzungu* to understand."

"Can't you try at least?"

"Well, I suppose, the best I can do is say that Africans often have a kind of instinct for things; perhaps they can even operate in some other dimension, unknown to us."

"Really?"

"Why not?" He laughed. "For all the talk of differences between them and us, in some ways they may even be superior."

"Interesting thought. I don't suppose your granny would agree."

"Almost certainly not."

They were quiet for a while, thinking things through. Ben then had something else to say on the subject. "Other differences are Africans' concepts of time and space, of distance even."

"Oh?"

"Yup, so, for instance, if, on your way somewhere, you ask an African how much further, the answer often is *mbali kidogo*, a little further, which can mean anything from a hundred yards to ten miles."

"So, not very helpful."

"Well here's the thing, to their mind, it is what it is, and you just have to go on further and further, and a bit further if necessary, until you get there; makes sense; you can't shorten the distance; there's no point fussing about it."

"Yes, that does make some kind of sense I suppose."

Ben's mind was whirring. "I can give you other examples. Once, when I was down in The Mara, I was waiting to meet an American who was flying in from somewhere. The plane landed on the airstrip and the American duly appeared. As he did so, it happened that a Maasai man was standing nearby watching things. For some reason, showing off presumably, the American asked the Maasai how long it took him to get there from the nearest town. Having been translated, the answer came back two days. 'Ah', said the American 'I've got here in just two hours'. The Maasai remained looking impassive, unimpressed even, while this was translated for him, but then replied with something that sounded like a question."

Charlotte was intrigued. "Does history relate what the question was?"

Ben guffawed. "He simply asked what the American was going to do with the other two days."

"The American must have been rather nonplussed."

"Yeah, well it's a wholly different perspective I suppose. I've been caught out by it too. I remember an occasion when I was in Tanzania. I'd been visiting friends and I had to get a bus back from a fairly remote place. There were a few Africans, also obviously waiting for the bus, and I asked one of them when the bus was due. He didn't understand the question."

"Why not?"

"Simply because there was no set time and no concept of a timetable. The bus would just come at some time and then people would get on; it might be only a matter of minutes, but it could also be several hours, or even longer. It was a completely relaxed atmosphere. A couple of men were crouched chatting under a tree. A companion had gone to sleep on the ground beside them. Another fellow, a little way off, had got a fire going and was roasting some *mealies* for himself and his young wife sitting nearby feeding her baby. An old *bibi* meanwhile was calmly trussing up some chickens she was taking to market. There was no fuss, no bother, no worry about the time. Whenever the bus came they would simply get on it and go on their way."

"There's something rather metaphysical about that," said Charlotte thinking it through. "And a refreshing change from the sort of stresses and strains we often put ourselves through, about things we can't change or have no control over."

"Indeed so."

Charlotte looked out of the window. It was getting dark as

the car was climbing up onto the plateau. "We must be nearly there," she said, stretching.

Ben grinned. "*Mbali kidogo.*"

The family were sitting round the table in the dining room, just finishing supper, when there was a commotion outside. Kimani then burst into the room with an urgent report from one of the night watchmen.

"*Simba, simba!*" and a further torrent of Swahili.

Ben quickly explained to a surprised-looking Charlotte that some lions had been spotted near one of the cattle enclosures.

"Right," said Mr Hooper, quickly getting up, "we must try to head them off."

"I'm with you," said Ben. He then glanced at Charlotte. "Would you like to come too? It might be quite exciting and you haven't seen lions here yet."

Mr Hooper was looking a bit uncertain about the idea, but Charlotte was already on her feet.

"Do by all means go, dear, if you want to; it'll be fine," said Rose Hooper encouragingly. "I'm quite happy to stay here on my own."

Moments later, outside in the yard, Ben jumped into the front seat of the Land Rover, next to his father who was at the wheel. Charlotte scrambled into the back. A night watchman with two farm workers were already in a truck, with the engine running, waiting for the off. The Land Rover moved forward with the truck following and they headed into the black void of the night.

Ben patted the rifle which he had picked up on the way out, at his father's request. "We shouldn't have to use this!" he shouted over the roar of the engine, turning back towards a wide-eyed Charlotte. "But, at the most, a couple of warning shots might be required." She nodded blankly.

It was not far to the area where the lions had been sighted.

"Turn on the spotlights," commanded Mr Hooper. Ben did so and the blaze of light from the roof of the vehicle immediately illuminated a wide arc of grassland interspersed with thickets of acacia. A few pairs of startled green eyes looked back at them, but not those of any lions. There was movement off to one side as a smallish creature with black and white stripes and a bushy tail scuttled away.

"That looked like a skunk," remarked Charlotte quietly, sensing the need to keep her voice down.

"Yes, quite similar," replied Ben. "It was actually a zorilla, a small carnivore, seldom seen because it's strictly nocturnal. So, there you are, you're getting to see stuff you wouldn't normally get a look at."

"I wish we could get a look at the lions," interposed Mr Hooper, rather testily.

"They might have moved on," volunteered Ben brightly.

"Maybe, but then the question is where to? I'd be much happier finding them and then making quite sure we usher them well away from here."

The vehicles had slowed right down and they crept forward, all eyes straining into the field of light. After a while it was felt that they had gone too far. So they turned and made their way slowly back, repeating the process several times.

"This is getting us nowhere," said Mr Hooper. "We're going to have to get right off the track and skirt around the bush."

"OK hang on," Ben called back to Charlotte. "This'll be a rough ride." So it proved to be. She gripped the seat tightly as the Land Rover bumped and lurched its way over ruts and rocks, tussocks and mounds, the lights of the following truck dancing along behind. Still nothing and doubts started to creep in.

"I bet the buggers are lying up somewhere, watching us," said Mr Hooper, frustration beginning to take hold."

"Quite likely," agreed his son. "So perhaps we need to get really close up to the thicker bush."

"Worth a try, I just hope we don't knacker the Landy." Charlotte silently hoped so too, pulse quickening at the thought of possibly being stranded in a broken-down vehicle. She quickly reminded herself that the truck was not far away.

The lights had picked out a particularly thick clump of bush.

"No way we can see through that," grunted Mr Hooper.

"No, but let's drive right round it," suggested Ben. "Might flush something out."

They did so, without result, but decided to go round just once more. There was suddenly a flashing of lights from the following truck which was slowing to a halt. Mr Hooper turned round the Land Rover and drove back, pulling up beside the truck. A conversation ensued from which it emerged that one of the men had seen movement on the edge of the thicket. All eyes scanned the place pointed out, but there was nothing now to be seen. Nevertheless, it was felt worth waiting a while. Some minutes passed, feeling much longer to those watching, but patience suddenly yielded its reward. There was a distinct stirring from deep within the bush and then the shape of something emerged at the far end, followed closely by another shape. The vehicles were quickly turned in that direction and the lights immediately picked out the retreating backs of two large tawny bodies, angrily flicking long tails with black tufts.

"Got you at last," hissed Mr Hooper.

Charlotte was craning forward for a better view.

"Two young males," Ben told her. At that moment one of

them stopped and raised his head, providing a clear view of his developing black mane. Looking back contemptuously at the vehicles, he half opened his mouth in a silent snarl.

"How's that for some teeth?" said Ben.

"Awesome," replied Charlotte. "And I'm just as impressed with the size of his paws."

Mr Hooper was conferring with the driver of the truck. The plan was to follow the lions, keep them moving in a direction away from the ranch. It was easier said than done. Several times the lions tried to turn some other way. Twice they disappeared for a time in thick bush. The men in the truck had knob-ended sticks, *rungus* as Charlotte heard them being referred to, which were used to good effect; banged against the doors of the truck the resultant din flushed the lions from cover and sent them on their way. The country began to open up a bit and the lions picked up speed. Not long after it was deemed that they were heading far enough away. Finding their way back to the track, the vehicles turned for home.

"Magnificent young fellows," mused Ben.

"Do you think they're part of a pride?" asked Charlotte.

"Probably been forced out of a pride; more likely."

"Yes," agreed Mr Hooper. "They're almost certainly brothers, not far from reaching full maturity. So it's time for them to go off and make their own way. They probably haven't developed their hunting skills very well yet; so I bet they're looking for an easy meal and one of our *ng'ombes* would fit the bill nicely."

"Eventually," added Ben, "if things work out for them, they will form their own pride, but they're likely to have to fight for it, by driving off an old male or seeing off rivals."

"Sure," his father shrugged. "It's the way of things out here,

278

the way of the wild."

They were soon back at the ranch. Ben was first out of the Land Rover and held open the rear door for Charlotte. "Well," he said, "that was one way to end a day, I suppose."

She thought about it for a moment as she was getting out. "You know," she replied, looking at him directly, "you people lead quite extraordinary lives."

Tuesday

Dawn was breaking and the high altitude landscape rose up to be embraced by the sun, starting the last full day of what had been an extraordinary few days for Charlotte in Laikipia. She had risen early, as soon as Kimani had brought in the tea. Now she was sitting in her favourite spot on the verandah, knees up under her chin, gazing down the gorge, past rocky outcrops and acacia thickets to the immense landscape beyond. But on this morning her eyes were unseeing as she wrestled with mixed thoughts and sought to reconcile her emotions. Brooding clouds bubbling up on the horizon matched her mood. But as the clear light of the morning crept over her, so her spirit began to lighten, imperceptibly at first, but irresistibly. The high air enveloped her, comforted her. Tilting her head back, she breathed deeply, eyes shut, hugging her knees ever closer.

Unmeasured time passed before she stirred and made her way back into her room, treading lightly. The fire for the water tank had been lit long enough and there was warm water for her to wash. She dressed in khaki shorts and a light-coloured cotton shirt. Checking her appearance in the mirror, she was rather pleased that the clothes set off to good effect, her smooth arms and legs which had become increasingly tanned. Her mind wandered as she reflected further on things, but then, becoming

279

focussed once more, she had a final look in the mirror and nodded in satisfaction before setting off to the main house.

Ben had been rather quiet at the breakfast table. But looking up from his plate he caught Charlotte's eye. "We must make the most of today," he said firmly.

She nodded, rather than answered, holding his look for a moment before glancing away. From the end of the table Granny Sullivan's beady eyes were upon them.

More toast and coffee were brought in by Kimani. Plates and cups were replenished amidst general chit-chat. Rose wanted to know what plans Charlotte had for the rest of the summer, when she returned home. Ben made a determined effort to avoid listening in, but talked instead to his father about farm matters, whilst surreptitiously slipping pieces of bacon rind to Brutus sitting expectantly beside him. As breakfast was coming to an end, Granny Sullivan pushed aside her plate. She had a question for Ben.

"So, what are you going to do today?"

"Oh, yes, well I thought I'd take Charlotte up north, look for some big game and, perhaps, if we're lucky find the rhino with the *toto* we saw a few days ago. I think Charlotte would like a second viewing, if possible."

Charlotte was nodding in agreement, but before she could say anything there was an intervention from Mr Hooper, directed to Ben. "Be careful; I heard on the radio this morning that a gang of poachers has been spotted in the area. Rangers from the Game Department have been sent to investigate."

"Crikey, OK," said Ben, frowning slightly, wondering what to do.

"Do go," added his father, "but, as I've said, be careful,

that's all; if you see the least sign of trouble, get the hell out of there at once."

Listening in, Charlotte's initial moment of concern had given way to her being intrigued. "I understand, from Ben, that poaching is a serious problem." There was a swift response from Mr Hooper; this was a subject upon which he held strong views.

"Becoming more and more serious. Elephant and rhino are under increasing threat; elephant, for their tusks of course, and rhino for their horn."

"But it sounds as if steps are being taken to tackle it," mused Charlotte. "I mean I heard you mention rangers going after the poachers."

"Yes, yes," Mr Hooper gave a deep sigh. "but it's never going to be a complete solution."

"No?"

"No, because it's not addressing the root of the problem."

"Which is?"

"The trade, particularly the international trade in these products."

Charlotte's brow furrowed. "But could that ever be stopped?"

Mr Hooper was leaning forward slightly, one fist clenched on the table. "I truly believe that this is what we must campaign for, a complete ban. It's the only hope for the future if we're going to save these great animals in the longer term." He paused before adding, "Which may not actually be that long."

Ben, too, was fully engaged on the subject. "Dad, I think I'm right in saying that you feel that the thinking is moving in this direction, the right direction, here at least."

"Hopefully, but not it seems in some other places."

Charlotte was looking puzzled. "But surely other countries,

other African countries which have these animals, would have the same concern and be of the same mind?"

Mr Hooper sighed again. "If only." He raised his eyes to the ceiling before looking back towards Charlotte and continuing with unmistakable intensity. "The thing of it is that some elements, in certain of the southern African countries in particular, want, for reasons of their own, to maintain what they believe will be a controlled trade, from so-called 'sustainable sources', so they say."

"What sort of sources could those be?" was the immediate query from Charlotte.

"Animals which have had to be culled, for some reason, or those which have been hunted under licence."

Charlotte was continuing to look puzzled, with an increasingly furrowed brow. "But I thought I'd been told that big game hunting had been banned."

Mr Hooper shook his head. "Not everywhere, I'm afraid; here, certainly, a few years back, and quite rightly so; but in some other countries it still goes on, driven by big money which, it is claimed, helps fund conservation, although I bet a lot of it just goes to line pockets."

Ever one to ask searching questions, Charlotte wanted to know more. "I've noticed, though, that you have guns here. Are they not for hunting?"

Ben was quick to interject. "No way."

"That's right," agreed his father. "I have shot and will continue to shoot animals occasionally on a 'needs must' basis, but never for sport. Killing animals for so-called pleasure, particularly magnificent big game animals, I find abhorrent."

"You do, though, have the buffalo horns and animal skins in the sitting room," observed Charlotte. Ben gave a wry smile; her sharp mind once again, he thought.

"Yes indeed," acknowledged Mr Hooper. "But they're relics of the old colonial days when hunting was commonplace." He glanced towards Granny Sullivan, who was showing signs of irritation, but which didn't stop him adding, "I like to think we're older and wiser now."

"But there's still big game hunting in some of these other countries you refer to?" mused Charlotte.

"Regrettably, and pretty awful it is too in many cases."

"Hell yes," agreed Ben. "I've heard that often it goes on in small enclosed reserves where the animals are readily available, with no possible escape."

Mr Hooper's jaw was clenched tightly and there was a muscle twitching in his cheek. He leant forward again, eyes flashing. "That's right; big, brave men from America, Europe and elsewhere travel there to hunt. The animals are fenced in, cornered and shot. There's no danger involved because there are professional hunters on hand who often have to intervene to kill off the animals when the visitors make a hash of it, as they often do."

"Wasn't there a case of some guy wanting to shoot an animal with his crossbow?" asked Ben.

"Quite right," agreed his father. "Not surprisingly he didn't make a clean kill, the animal was left in agony and one of the professionals had to put it out of its misery. I tell you what, I'd like to set that fellow running and shoot him up the arse with his own crossbow." His fist had come crashing down on the table. "Sorry," he said, regaining some control over his feelings. "But what the hell's the matter with these people? Where's the sport? It's just a form of brutal cruelty, reflecting the worst of mankind I'm afraid."

Ben decided that it was time to move the conversation more directly back to the issue of stopping poaching. "The theory, I think I'm right in saying, is that supplying ivory and horn from these supposedly legitimate sources for trading purposes will eliminate the need for poaching."

Again there was a quick response from Mr Hooper, eyes flashing once more and nostrils flaring. "Yes, and a deeply flawed theory it is too. It presupposes that demand will be met from the sustainable sources. But it won't be. The supply from such sources will serve to fuel the trade even further. It will be impossible to meet the demand wholly from such sources. So, guess what? No prizes for guessing the obvious. Poaching will continue, probably on an ever-increasing scale, to help meet the demand."

The room fell silent for some moments and no one even moved until Charlotte ventured to ask just one final question. "Do you think that people can be made to see the light on this?"

Mr Hooper spread out his hands wide. "We have to keep battling on, but we're up against powerful vested interests, short termism driven by greed. In the longer term I just hope that we can save these great animals. They'll probably last my lifetime, but I'm not so sure about Ben's, still less his children's. What a tragedy it would be if they were lost." He looked round the watching faces. "A tragedy for the world."

Ben leant across the table from where he was sitting and put one hand on his father's arm. "That's why, Dad, we must do everything we can, within our own means, to combat poaching and promote conservation. We've talked about this, endlessly. I believe that there are real opportunities for us to make a difference here in this special place. Conservation should become far more of a priority for us than cattle ranching."

Watching closely Charlotte could detect a real zeal in Ben. He continued to look intently at his father who was deep in thought.

"Right," said Rose brightly from the other end of the table, picking up her little brass bell, "if everyone's finished, I'll ring for Kimani to clear away."

The Land Rover bumped and jolted its way through deep, sand-filled ruts and over large stones, varying in size and shape, but of invariable and unforgiving hardness. Glancing in the wing mirror Charlotte could see only their following cloud of dust, catching up with them as they slowed to avoid yet another obstacle, infiltrating the vehicle and depositing fine layers on every available surface. She swished one hand in front of her face to clear the air and adjusted her sunglasses. Looking over towards Ben she could see that he was concentrating hard on the challenges of the track ahead, one hand firmly on the steering wheel, the other resting on the vibrating gear stick, ready for the frequently required changes. They were heading north, further and further into the wild, untamed regions of the plateau. Ben had said little, in between pointing out some game, and his quiet reflected the stillness of the early afternoon. Clouds were building and the sun came and went, revealing itself in intermittent flashes of promise tinged with threat in air which had become hot and heavy.

They had seen some of the big game they had set out to find. Down in a partly dried-up riverbed Charlotte had marvelled at the strength of an elephant tearing down a tree to make accessible tender leaves in its upper reaches. Shortly afterwards they had come across some buffalo in the middle distance. As they had watched, so in turn they had been regarded sternly by the dominant bull, eyes fixed, shiny black nostrils twitching and ears flapping impatiently beneath the massive boss of his horns. Ben had been prompted to tell her more about buffalo, about their keen senses, of sight, sound and smell, which made them particularly dangerous, especially to anyone out in the bush on foot. He had related how two people the family had known had been killed by buffalo. One had been unwise enough to venture into thick bush and long grass where he had stumbled across a herd lying low. The other had had the misfortune to be caught out in the open, an artist working on his painting of a bull at what he had thought was a safe distance. After a while the bull had tired of being looked at and had charged across the intervening space, rapidly overhauling the retreating artist. Put it this way, Ben had said grimly, "It was not a good way to die." Listening, Charlotte had felt glad to be in the safety of a vehicle with the engine running. As they had then pulled away, so too the buffalo had moved off with a contemptuous shake of a mighty head.

But now, in the oppressive stillness, there was nothing to be seen, nothing to be heard, and barely a ripple in the great sea of the grassland.

"There's something not right," said Ben instinctively, frowning as he brushed the latest coating of dust from the windscreen and peering, as he did so, through the intermittent shafts of sunlight slanting across the corrugations of the track. He pushed the binoculars across the seat towards Charlotte. "Keep a good look out," he implored her.

She was taken by surprise by his tone. "What for?"

"I'm not sure; something; anything."

She shook her head, but picking up the binoculars started to scan the surrounding landscape.

"Nothing," she reported after a while.

So they drove on, leaving the track from time to time, bumping and jolting round thickets and anthills, the vehicle frequently bucking like a horse. Charlotte found it impossible to keep the binoculars still enough to be of any real use, so she put them back down on the seat. Ben, sawing at the wheel, was looking this way and that, head inclined forward. And on they went, back on the track, and off again, on and on, ever further. Thoughts of possible futility were beginning to insinuate themselves into Charlotte's mind as they drove up onto a ridge and looked out over a broad expanse of grass and bush, shimmering in the warm stillness.

"Still nothing," she announced in a languid tone, beginning to tire from looking for she knew not what, "nothing but grass and bush, a few bigger thorn trees; oh, and to add to it all, a boulder," she added with a hint of sarcasm.

Ben jammed on the brakes, skidding the vehicle to an abrupt stop in a cloud of dust.

"Where?" he demanded to know.

"Where's what?" She looked puzzled, taken aback even by the sudden sense of urgency.

"Where's the boulder? I wouldn't expect to see any boulders here."

She pointed a way off diagonally to the left, just beyond a big old acacia tree, its branches heavy with the nests of weaver birds. There, just visible above the long grass, was a grey mound.

Ben snatched up the binoculars and clamped them to his eyes, leaning across Charlotte as he did so. "That's not a boulder," he said through gritted teeth. Slamming the binoculars down onto the seat with a force which startled Charlotte, he took hold of the steering wheel of the Land Rover, revved the engine and rapidly headed the vehicle off the track in the direction in which they had been looking. Charlotte hung on as hard as she could, one hand braced against the door, the other gripping the edge of the seat, as they reared up and crashed down again. Ben gripped the wheel ever more tightly in his determination to steer as straight a course as possible. As they reached the big tree, Ben swung to the left so that he had a better view of what they were looking at.

"Oh God, no, no," he cried out as they slithered to a halt. Wrenching open his door, he leapt out and ran through the scrubby grass. Charlotte followed, a few seconds behind.

"No," shouted Ben as he became aware of her coming up behind him. "You mustn't, you really mustn't, go back to the Land Rover, go back." Turning round he grabbed her by the shoulders, stopping her in her tracks. "No, no, back," he insisted, his whole body, rigid with tension, but his voice beginning to crack. "I don't want you to see this; you mustn't see it; you really mustn't." But Charlotte could see, had already seen, beyond Ben and the image seared into her consciousness, becoming indelibly printed in her mind.

The grey lump, seen from afar, was the broad rump of a rhino, its legs crumpled beneath it where the great animal had been brought crashing down. Stretching forward from the body in an agony of contortion the monumental head lay in a sticky pool of semi-dried blood, slashed and torn and hacked, a mass of gore where its mighty horn had been ripped away.

As quickly as he could Ben turned Charlotte round and steered her back to the Land Rover. He could sense a rigidity in her, but as for himself he was beginning to shake and, as he let go of her, so he let rip in a stream of words becoming a torrent, louder and louder, increasingly agonised.

"Bastards fucking bastards I tell you I don't know I just don't know any more Christ I despair I really do so much so much what the hell can be done what the bloody hell can be done oh I don't know it's so bloody awful so bloody depressing can't people see what's happening the destruction the damage it makes me hate them hate this place hate this whole bloody country I give up on it I just sodding give up but what am I saying because I love it too it's my country and it's so great and I feel part of it and at one with the people and it's given me so much and I care God I care so much too much can there be too much and yet so much pain too depressing pulling me apart but must hang on in there must keep going so much to fight for so much worthwhile so precious and no I do love the place of course I do I can't help it I just can't help it even if I didn't want to and perhaps I shouldn't but I still would love the fucking place what am I saying because there's no would about it I do don't I yes I do I do I do what do I do love the big bloody beautiful sodding place it's in me in me in my blood always will be so what am I saying I don't know what I'm saying or even thinking not thinking actually not properly I'm just talking, talking, talking, talking, crap, fucking crap, complete bollocks, oh God, oh God, bloody hell man, get a grip just get a grip for Christ's sake."

Ben was slumped forward with his hands resting on the bonnet of the Land Rover. Charlotte patted him gently on the back as the tirade faded away. For some moments he was still and silent. Then turning towards her he blurted out an apology suffused with embarrassment.

"I'm sorry, really sorry, I'm not making any sense; ridiculous, ridiculous; forget it please, forget it; sorry."

Charlotte clasped his face in her hands and forced him to look straight into her eyes. "Believe me," she said, "there's absolutely nothing for you to be sorry about. I understood exactly what you were saying." She paused. "Actually it was a real insight." Letting go of his face she dared quietly to ask a question which was troubling her greatly. "Do you think that's the mother, or perhaps I should say could it be the mother of the baby rhino, the one we saw the other day and which I understand from you is now thought to be in this area?"

Ben shook his head. "No, it's a bull, a magnificent young breeding-age bull, in his prime." He paused before adding bitterly, "Was in his prime; possibly the father of the *toto*."

As Charlotte was taking this in Ben's mind was racing on. "Yes, and by God the *toto* and mother are indeed meant to be around here somewhere. Hell I hope they're OK. The bull hasn't been dead long, by the look of him, which means the poachers can't be that far away."

Breaking away from Charlotte, Ben swung open the driver's door of the Land Rover. "Quick," he called out to her, "jump in; we must go on and there's no time to lose."

"But," said Charlotte, looking concerned, "your dad told you to…"

"I know, I know, but I'll never forgive myself if I don't do something which might make a difference, save the day even; so come on, please, hang on in here."

Charlotte nodded blankly, but was jolted into action and climbed into the vehicle beside Ben. They set off as fast as the conditions would allow. Not long after things were not looking good. A terrified baby rhino was spotted blundering through the bush; but there was no sign of the mother. They soon lost sight of the young animal, but pressed on grimly, relentlessly.

Ben was muttering through gritted teeth. "God, oh God, I hope not, no, no, please, please may we be in time, to do something, anything; bastards, bloody bastards." Charlotte remained quiet beside him, rigid and motionless. Then suddenly, almost simultaneously, their eyes became fixed on an unfolding scene a way off in the distance ahead. Half a dozen or so men were fanning out in the scrub towards an area of thicker bush. Ben hit the brakes and before the vehicle had even slithered to a stop was grabbing up the binoculars.

"What can you see?" Charlotte demanded to know with a tremor in her voice.

"Definitely poachers: a ragtag band, but armed all right, at least two AK-47s for fuck's sake." He pounded his hands up and down on the steering wheel. "Shit, shit, shit."

"Any dead animal to be seen?" was the next question Charlotte hardly dared to ask.

"No, at least I don't think so. But they're clearly on the trail of something."

"So they haven't got the mother rhino." It was a statement more of hope than a confident assertion of fact.

Ben shook his head. "Can't be sure; they may have bagged her somewhere else and now be on the trail of another victim."

Charlotte clutched Ben's bare arm and he could feel her nails digging in. "Hadn't we better go for help?" she asked with a rising sense of urgency overlaid with trepidation. "Remember what your dad said, for goodness sake."

"There's no time for that. The mother rhino may, for all we know, be in that bush. We must at least try to drive them off." Charlotte opened her mouth to say something, but, before another word could be uttered, Ben slammed the Land Rover into gear. They lurched forward in the direction of the poachers and as they did so Ben flicked on all the lights, including the spotlights mounted on the roof, at the same time as giving repeated blasts on the horn. The men ahead of them turned in their direction, but stood their ground rather than taking flight.

"Damn!" shouted out Ben, rapidly pulling up at what he judged to be just about a safe distance. To Charlotte's increasing concern, he leapt out, yanked open the rear door, snatched up a rifle and fired off a volley of shots in the air. There was a quick response from men fully assured that the odds were in their favour. Rapid fire was returned making Ben immediately and painfully aware of his serious miscalculation of range as bullets whined past. Throwing the rifle back into the vehicle, he scrambled in himself, shouting to Charlotte to get down on the floor. Fortunately the engine started first time, roaring as he over revved. He turned sharply to the left, shielding Charlotte as best he could. Two bullets thudded into the door just behind where he was sitting and a rear window then exploded into flying fragments of glass. Crouched over the wheel Ben kept his head down as low as possible, peering ahead as he struggled to maintain control as they crashed over rocks and scraped through thorn bushes. But then, just as suddenly as it had started, the firing unexpectedly stopped and an uncertain silence hung heavily in the air. Ben dared to look up out of his side window. "Thank God," he blurted out, "the cavalry is here." Some way off, diagonally, two vehicles were approaching fast in a billowing cloud of dust. "You can get up now," he said to Charlotte. Panting hard, his heart still racing, he wiped away the sweat beginning to trickle from his brow, stinging red-rimmed eyes. A drop of blood had begun to ooze from Charlotte's bitten bottom lip. She looked anxiously in the direction in which he was pointing. "Game Department rangers, in the nick of time." He gave a deep sigh and breathed long and hard as he regained control of both himself and the vehicle. "Right, we can leave it to them." They headed away on to a better defined track. The poachers, off in the opposite direction, were on the run.

Ben was mulling things over. "This business of rhino horn is such a problem because of the strong market for it in the Far East."

"I can see that," agreed Charlotte. "But it's used, isn't it, in Chinese traditional medicine?"

"That's right, I'm afraid."

"And it's been part of Chinese custom, culture even, for centuries; so that's the real difficulty."

"But it bloody well shouldn't be." There was a rising intensity in Ben's voice and he began gesticulating with one hand off the wheel. "It's bullshit that there's any medicinal value in rhino horn; it's just keratin, like nails and hair; and, anyway, just because something has gone on for centuries in the past doesn't mean that it should continue in the present day and age. Things change for God's sake. We've moved on in the world. We've better knowledge, we're better informed as to what should and shouldn't be done. Christians are no longer thrown to the lions and the Spanish Inquisition would no longer be regarded as appropriate."

Charlotte wasn't sure that Ben's last points were really apposite, but she certainly got his drift.

Ben, for his part, was still fired up and running with the points. "I can think, though, of some people I'd like to throw to lions. The people behind poaching would be a good start."

The sky itself had been angry too with lightning on the horizon striking with flashes of fury. Billowing clouds had turned purple and yellow, bruised and hurt. But a soothing calm began to return to the plateau as a brilliant shaft of sunlight penetrated the gloom, slanting across the track leading home to the ranch.

Ben gave Charlotte a rueful smile as he joined her on the verandah before supper. He threw himself down in a chair beside her. "I've just been given the bollocking of my life by my old man."

"Well, of course, you did go against him; disregarded what he had said."

"I know, I know." There was a brief silence and then Ben began grinning.

"You don't look too sorry."

"That's because such good news has come through on the radio." He reached out and put one hand on Charlotte's upper arm. "The rangers found the female rhino in the depths of that thick bush, alive, thank God, alive. I tell you, we distracted those poachers in the nick of time. We saved her; we bloody well saved her."

Charlotte, eyes wide, took in the news for a moment, "What about the baby?" she asked slightly breathlessly.

"Rounded up safely; mother and child have been reunited."

Ben stood up and walked to the edge of the verandah. He looked out over the garden into the far distance beyond, the events of the day racing through his mind. The setting sun was speeding up, as it always seemed to do, when it reached close to the horizon, anxious to put itself away after a long day. The rock face of the nearby ravine reflected diminishing shades of golden light, gradually losing out to the lengthening shadows. A brief shower of rain, a little earlier, had infused the air with the scents of grasses, wild herbs and acacia. All was now still and quiet, save only for the faint hum of insects, the chorus of the twilight.

"I don't want this day ever to end," said Ben softly.

Charlotte got up from her chair and walked over to him. Without saying anything, she put an arm round his shoulders. Turning to face her, he suddenly looked serious. "But I had no business putting your life in danger; I'm really sorry, I really am. When all's said and done, despite everything, it was bloody stupid."

"I've never felt more alive," she said simply, but firmly and directly, her eyes scanning Ben's face.

He reached out and gently wiped a little spot of dried blood from her bottom lip. As he did so he felt her lips part. Their heads inclined towards each other and their mouths shared sweet saltiness.

There was a stirring in the sitting room behind them, the sound of voices, the clink of ice in glasses. The sun was down. Breaking apart they smiled and headed in to join the enduring ritual of the evening.

After supper Ben and Charlotte lingered long in the sitting room, until they were alone, long after even the generator had gone off and the electric lights had faded away. They were reluctant to let go of the day. The camping Gaz lamps flickered and guttered and the remaining logs in the fire gradually subsided into glowing embers. Late, late Brutus began to stir. Stretching he stood up to be let out. It was time, at last.

Ben escorted Charlotte to her room by the light of a torch, as he had done on each of the nights she had been there. But on this occasion she walked into the room, leaving the door open behind her. Ben paused in the doorway, looking uncertain.

She turned back towards him. "Are you coming in?"

Much later, in the darkest, stillest time of the night, Ben gently slipped from Charlotte's entwined arms and melted away into the blackness.

DESTINY

Destiny is all, destiny is everything

Bernard Cornwell
The Last Kingdom

Charlotte checked that her seat belt was securely fastened as the air stewardess walked slowly down the aisle of the plane. Settling back in her seat she closed her eyes and the events of the last few days rolled through her mind, four extraordinary days, days that create deeply embedded memories. The plane was turning at the end of the runway. It stopped briefly and then the engines became louder and louder. The overhead lockers began to tremble as the aircraft surged forward and rapidly picked up speed. Charlotte just had a glimpse of the terminal building, flashing past as the ground began falling away beneath her. She pressed her face to the window, clinging for as long as possible to the receding views of the Kenyan landscape. Gaining height the plane started banking to the right, settling on a northerly course. She wondered whether they would be flying over Laikipia and began thinking of all the things that might be happening down in that great wilderness, where the mother rhino might be leading her calf, where Ben was, perhaps out in the bush. Was he, just maybe, looking up in the sky and thinking of her? She shut her eyes once more and allowed her mind to recall sights, sounds, smells, touches even, senses which lapped at her consciousness and washed over her in gentle waves. Higher and higher, through and above the clouds, there was nothing now to be seen when she opened her eyes and once more looked out of the window. She was being carried further and further away. Leaning forward, Charlotte reached down to her bag under the seat in front of her and took out an envelope containing a letter which Ben had asked her to read on the way home. She smiled as she saw written on it 'plane talk'. Before opening it she reflected on their parting early that morning. At first she had been deeply shocked when Ben had told her that he would not be returning to England; that he was dropping out of Bristol and giving up on becoming a lawyer. But then, as she began to think about it, and the more she did so, it became really less and less of a surprise. Also, she had to admit to herself, it made things easier for her, for her own future. She opened the envelope, smoothed out the two single sheets of paper, and began reading:

Dear Charlotte,

I'm so glad, so very glad, that you've been to Kenya and, particularly, to Laikipia. I can't tell you how much it meant to me to be with you for those few precious days and to show you the place which means so much to me. I regard it as a gift, an unexpected gift, but one that I know I shall always treasure. Hopefully your visit will help you understand the decision I've made. It was difficult for me, at first, but I kept coming back to the strong feeling, an instinct even, that this is where I should be, where I must be, where I'm deeply rooted, in a place I care so much about. In some way, which I can't really find the right words to explain, your visit heightened my feelings and helped me make my decision. It made me realise, ever more clearly I think, how much life here means to me and how important it is to try to safeguard the future. I've been having long discussions with Dad about shifting our focus to game conservation, maybe bringing in visitors to see, as you have done, what fantastic wild life there is here and how vital it is to protect it for ourselves and, of course, for future generations. This will help raise much needed funds and provide employment opportunities and other benefits for the local people; it will be essential to have their involvement and co-operation. We must try to save this environment and its magnificent animals, particularly the elephant, and especially the poor old rhino; this could be its last stand and, by God, I want to be part of the fight for its survival. This is so much more important to me than becoming a lawyer in London, or Nairobi even, or anywhere else for that matter.

So wish me well, as I do you, as we go our separate ways. I've found our times together so stimulating, challenging at times, but really special and totally unforgettable. Hopefully it has been something of the same for you; I dare to hope so anyway.

Ben

Charlotte re-read the letter and then stared blankly out of the window at the darkening sky above the clouds. Gradually sleep overcame her and her mind flitted between dreams and semi-conscious thoughts, it sometimes being difficult to distinguish between the two. Hours passed as the plane droned on heading ever northwards over the vast distances of Africa. By comparison it swallowed up the land over Europe. Dawn was breaking and Charlotte awoke with a jolt from her uncomfortable seated position. She turned her head from side to side to alleviate the stiffness in her neck. Realising that she was still clutching the letter, she read it once more before folding it back into the envelope. She then removed the Maasai beadwork bracelet from her wrist and placed it carefully with the envelope in the bottom of her bag. The plane was coming down through the clouds. The seat belt sign flashed on, seats were clicking into the upright position and the air stewardesses were once more patrolling the aisle. Shortly after there was a jolt. They were on the ground and Heathrow Airport became visible in the early grey light of an overcast morning.

An hour later, walking rather stiffly, bag over her shoulder and struggling a bit with her suitcase, Charlotte emerged into the teeming arrivals hall of the terminal building. She scanned the crowd and picked out some one waving in her direction. It was Lawrence, making his way towards her as quickly as the crush would allow. As he approached she put down the suitcase. His arms were extended and she fell into his embrace.

"Let me take your case," he said as they stepped apart.

"Thanks, I'll hold on to my bag." She looped it over her shoulder and tucked it firmly under her arm.

"I'm so glad to have you back. But goodness, what a time you've been having. Your godmother phoned through to your parents and told them what had happened. I gather that you then went off to stay with Ben; quite an unexpected turn of events."

She nodded silently.

"You must tell me all about it."

Not quite all, she thought. There was a pause.

"Is everything all right?" he asked, a note of slight anxiety creeping into his voice.

"Yes, I'm just tired; but everything's fine; just as it should be," she added, her voice trailing away slightly.

"That's good to hear. Well, let's get you home."

She suddenly remembered to ask an important question. "Have you got your results?"

"Yes."

"And?"

Without immediately answering, he simply smiled.

"Come on," she prompted, "don't keep me in suspense."

"A first; I bloody well did get a first."

She grabbed his arm and pulled him to a halt. He put down her case and she did the same with her bag before enveloping him in a hug. "I thought you would, but I'm so glad to hear that you've actually done it." She hugged him tighter still, saying "I'm so proud of you; I really am."

A little time later there was a lull in the conversation as Lawrence concentrated on threading the car through thick traffic. Charlotte gazed out of the window at the surrounding vehicles, the buildings they were creeping past and the crowds of people surging along the pavements. Over four thousand miles away Ben sat on the *sanduku* rock in the morning sun looking far out over a landscape untouched by man. Back on the road, the car turned on to the A4 and began to pick up speed as it headed away west. Destiny.

EPILOGUE

Thanks to the determination and ceaseless efforts of landowners and conservationists in Laikipia, steps have been taken, and continue to be taken, to try to save the magnificent rhino from extinction.

In the 1960s estimates are that there were as many as about 20,000 black rhinos in Kenya. But from 1970 through to the 1980s numbers declined so dramatically that the stage was reached when less than 300 remained. This was almost wholly due to indiscriminate poaching. The great risk was that those remaining were too few and too spread out to breed successfully. In response, the Government of Kenya has adopted strict protection measures for rhinos, implemented by the Kenya Wildlife Service. Crucially these measures have been taken in collaboration with the private sector to establish intensively protected and heavily guarded rhino sanctuaries on privately owned land. In Laikipia, in particular, owners have worked together on a co-operative basis to further the interests of conservation of rhinos on private land. They have coordinated anti-poaching efforts and provided biological management of the rhino population in order to achieve maximum conservation benefits.

The battle to save the rhino is ongoing because poaching has intensified in recent years. This is owing to the increase in global demand for rhino horn from Asia and the Middle East to supply the traditional Chinese medicine market (which still falsely considers rhino horn to have medicinal properties) and to make ornamental dagger handles. A kilo of rhino horn can fetch up to $60,000 on the black market. To combat poaching the private sanctuaries in Laikipia have introduced an increasing range of additional measures, including the employment of more security and monitoring personnel and the use of extra equipment, vehicles and aircraft. Funds have been raised to help meet the considerable costs involved which also include veterinary expenses for treating injuries after poaching attempts and dealing with orphans.

As a result of these efforts of the private landowners of Laikipia, and like-minded conservationists elsewhere, black rhino populations are slowly but surely increasing, in some places at least.

GLOSSARY

Swahili to English, unless otherwise stated.

alma mater — Latin, literally, nourishing mother, but in this sense, school, college or university

amosi? — Luo, I greet you, how are you? (informal)

asante, asante sana — thank you, thank you very much

askari — soldier, warrior

baadaye kidogo — a little later

ber ahinya — Luo, very well

bibi — lady, or grandmother

boma — kitchen Swahili/slang, enclosure, cattle enclosure

bundu — kitchen Swahili/slang, bush, jungle

Bunyani — Kenyan colonial slang (derogatory), Indian

bwana — sir

chai — tea

chakula — food

daktari — doctor

dhobi — kitchen Swahili/slang, washing, laundry

duka — shop

et tu Brute — Latin, and you Brutus, from *Julius Caesar* by William Shakespeare

equus — Latin, horse

hakuna matata — no trouble, no problem

harambee — Kenya's independence motto, let's pull together

hodi — hello

hospitali — hospital
jambo — kitchen Swahili, hello
jiggers — parasitic burrowing insects, common in Africa
jiko — stove
Kaffir — Kenyan colonial slang (derogatory), African, black person
kahawa — coffee
kanzu — long coat or tunic
kiboko — whip, or stick for beating
kifaru — rhino
kikoi — Kenyan colonial slang, wrap around cloth garment
kipande — kitchen Swahili, identity card, pass, permit
Kuke — Kenyan colonial slang (derogatory), Kikuyu
maji, maji moto — water, hot water
mawingo — clouds
mbali kidogo — a little further
mbili — two
mbwa — dog
mealie — kitchen Swahili, Kenyan slang, corn on the cob
memsahib — kitchen Swahili, married woman, lady of the house
mgonjwa — unhealthy, ill
miraa — a plant chewed as a stimulant
mpishi — cook
mzee — old man
mzungu — white man
mzuri, mzuri sana — good, very good
ndege — bird
ndio — yes
ng'ombe — cow
panga — kitchen Swahili, machete
posho — kitchen Swahili, ground maize meal

pumzika — rest
rafiki — friend
rungu — club (as a weapon)
safari — trip, journey
sanduku — box
seme — Maasai short sword, dagger
shamba — farmland, agricultural plot
shenzi — coarse, rough
Shifta — Somali bandits
simba — lion
Swala Twiga — Gerunuk, Giraffe Gazelle
tackies — Kenya slang, gym shoes
toto — baby, young child
Tusker — Kenyan lager beer
twende — let's go
uhuru — freedom

MAPS

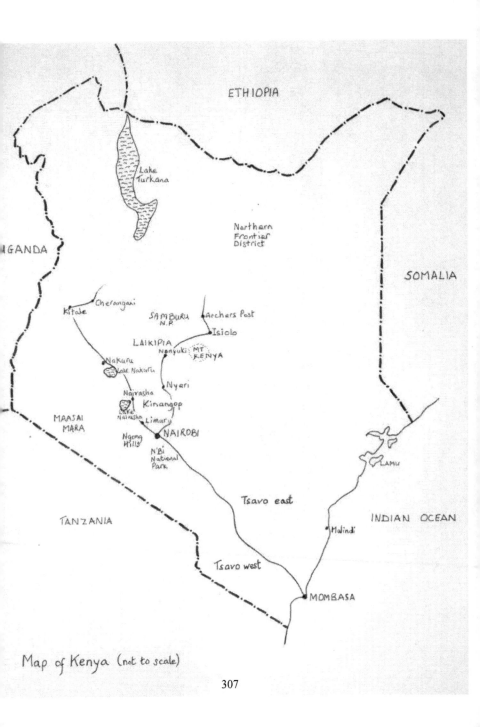

Map of Kenya (not to scale)

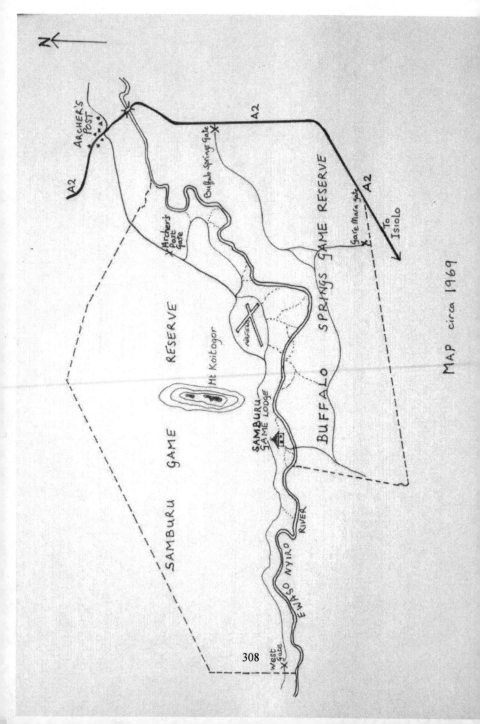

MAP circa 1969

N

ARCHER'S POST

A2

A2

Buffalo Spring Gate

Archer's Post Gate

BUFFALO SPRINGS GAME RESERVE

Gate Main gate

To Isiolo

A2

SAMBURU GAME RESERVE

Mt Koitogor

Nairobi

SAMBURU GAME LODGE

EWASO NYIRO RIVER

West Gate

308